Praise for Alisa Kwitney and *Cadaver & Queen*

"Fiendishly clever and gorgeously romantic. Alisa Kwitney spins an electrifying tale of beautiful monsters and mad scientists that will keep your nerves tingling and your heart racing long into the night."
—Carol Goodman, *New York Times* bestselling author
of *The Metropolitans*

"This is not a parody of Mary Shelley's classic but a clever new take on its elements in a mystery, complete with Victorian writing flourishes and the mild titillation expected from a romance novel."
—*Kirkus Reviews*

"A dark, thrilling and ingenious riff on the *Frankenstein* legend."
—M. R. Carey, author of *The Girl with All the Gifts*

"A page-turner from start to finish, fans of Marissa Meyer, Gail Carriger, and Cassandra Clare will find much to love. Highly recommended."
—*School Library Journal*

"Alisa Kwitney's bold reimagining of *Frankenstein* with Lizzie at its center is gripping, fierce and timely. Strikingly written and impeccably conjured, the monsters here are all too human."
—Gwenda Bond, author of the Lois Lane series

"A page-turning fantasy/romance that brings some joy and monster-righteousness to the traditional *Frankenstein* story, while adding its own unique wrinkles to the plot."
—*Locus* magazine

"The tension is high, the pacing is fast, the plot twists and turns in unexpected ways, the Victorian social and political scene is deftly sketched and the characters are vivid and satisfyingly complex. It swept me right away."
—Delia Sherman, author of *The Great Detective*

Books by Alisa Kwitney

Cadaver & Queen
Corpse & Crown

ALISA KWITNEY

CORPSE & CROWN

ink
yard
press

ISBN-13: 978-1-335-54222-9

33614082070987

Corpse & Crown

InkyardPress.com

Printed in U.S.A.

For my daughter, Elinor, born with a scientist's mind and an artist's eye.

1

AS THE HACKNEY COACH APPROACHED BUCKING-
ham Palace, a full moon broke through the dense fog overhead, casting an eerie, greenish glow onto the royal residence.
The horses, traveling fast over rain-slick cobblestones, nearly
lost their footing as they cornered sharply, passing the stately
east wing before slowing down and pulling into a smaller servants' entrance.

Inside the coach, Agatha DeLacey felt a sudden pang of doubt:
What if I forgot something? Opening her medical bag, she took
a quick inventory. Stethoscope. Thermometer. Carbolic acid.
A fresh bottle of ichor, along with a glass syringe and needles.
All there. Taking a deep breath, Aggie snapped the satchel shut.

Seated across from her, Ursula Shiercliffe, the Royal Victoria
Hospital's formidable head of nursing, gave her a sharp look.
"Everything in order, probationer?"

Feigning a confidence she did not feel, Aggie met the older
woman's cool gray eyes. "Yes, Matron."

"Then let us have no more displays of nerves," said Professor Moulsdale, accidentally elbowing Shiercliffe in the ribs as he adjusted his cravat. "You may be a mere nursing student, but tonight you represent our school, and I expect you to comport yourself with complete professionalism." Moulsdale patted his neat salt-and-pepper Vandyke beard and then ran his hand down the front of his bulging waistcoat, elbowing Shiercliffe yet again.

Shiercliffe thinned her lips and shifted as far from him as she could in the confines of the cramped coach, but said nothing. She did not defer to many people, but Moulsdale was the head of medicine at London's prestigious Academy of Bio-Mechanical Science and Engineering, as well as Queen Victoria's personal physician. He was not the sort of man one wanted to offend, and he was easily offended.

Aggie felt a squeeze on her arm. Elizabeth Lavenza, her friend and roommate, was struggling not to laugh. Not wanting to encourage her, Aggie gave a little shake of her head and looked out the window. Lizzie tended to be a rule breaker by nature—as the school's only female medical student and one of the few Americans enrolled, she had to be—but Aggie couldn't afford to take any chances. Lizzie had been chosen for this assignment because of her specialized skills, but Aggie was just in the right place at the right time. She could not afford to fail.

A moment later, the horses stumbled to a stop and the carriage door was opened by a young footman. Placing a step stool in front of the door, he stood ready to assist the first traveler to disembark.

Shiercliffe rested her hand on the footman's elbow as if liveried servants performed this service for her every day, but then, she was not the sort to show weakness, even under duress. Aggie and Lizzie were young and agile enough to clamber out on their own, but Professor Moulsdale, who suffered from gout, required the footman's hand to help lever himself down the steps to the ground.

"Right, then," said Moulsdale, "better get a move on. We don't want to keep Her Majesty waiting."

"If you are ready," said the footman, "you may follow me inside now."

Moulsdale went first, leaning heavily on his walking stick, with Shiercliffe right behind him. Aggie reached up to make sure her cap was still properly pinned in place before following them. She had been fast asleep when Shiercliffe had woken her up and told her to pack for a house call, and now she felt that strange mixture of alertness and disorientation that always seems to come with traveling late at night.

Walking beside Aggie, Lizzie stumbled over a loose stone.

"Put on your spectacles so you can see where you're going," whispered Aggie.

"No need, I'm fine," replied Lizzie.

There was a scrape of gravel as Shiercliffe turned to give both girls a reproving look. "I don't think I need to remind either of you, but a very great deal depends on what happens tonight. If things do not go well, Miss Lavenza, you may find yourself on a ship heading back to the former Colonies. And as for you, Miss DeLacey..."

Shiercliffe did not need to spell it out. Aggie would be heading back to her mother's cheerless house in Yorkshire. Drawing her cloak more tightly around her, she followed the matron through the servants' entrance and into the palace.

Queen Victoria's private chambers were dominated by a silk-draped canopy bed, several gilt-framed portraits of the late Prince Albert and the overpowering scent of dog. A fire blazed in the marble hearth, making the room feel like an oven. Already, a trickle of sweat had worked its way down the back of Aggie's neck and past her shoulder blades. The over-heated room was only partially to blame for her unease. The other cause was lying in bed, propped up by half a dozen lace-trimmed pillows, wearing a mobcap over her gray hair and an expression of stone-faced blankness. Difficult to fathom that this was the most powerful woman in the world—the Queen of England.

The elderly Queen did not acknowledge Moulsdale as he checked her heartbeat with the stethoscope. Staring out into the middle distance, she did not even blink when Moulsdale waved his hand in front of her eyes.

"Hmm," said Moulsdale, turning to the man sitting in an armchair on the other side of the queen's bed. "How long has she been like this, Lord Salisbury?"

"Since the morning, I'm afraid. She was like this when her lady of the bedchamber came in with her tea." Like Mouls-dale, Lord Salisbury was tall and stout and had trouble with his legs, but while Moulsdale was a bull terrier of a man, bright eyed and tenacious, the prime minister seemed more like a morose basset hound. "I was afraid of this from the be-ginning, you know."

Moulsdale replaced the stethoscope in the leather satchel. "My lord, pray do not jump to some dire conclusion."

Salisbury shook his head. "Do not attempt to mollycoddle me! I am not some society lady you can bamboozle."

Moulsdale's face registered a momentary flicker of irrita-tion, quickly concealed by a salesman's glib smile. "You are perturbed by Her Majesty's ailment," he said, pulling a bottle of bright green ichor from the medical bag. "Entirely understandable, but also unwarranted."

Shiercliffe, who was attaching a needle to the syringe, gave Moulsdale a look that contradicted his assertion, but Salisbury did not appear to take any notice. "I should never have listened to your outrageous proposal," he said, his gaze fixed on the queen's frozen countenance. "Better we should have let nature take its course last year than to—" He broke off, glancing at Lizzie and Aggie, who were both standing off to one side, trying to stay out of the way.

"Don't worry, my friend—it's perfectly fine to speak freely in front of these young ladies," Moulsdale assured the other man. Taking the syringe from Shiercliffe, he turned to Aggie and said, "Go on now, girl. You know what to do."

Aggie rolled up the queen's sleeve, baring one plump and flaccid arm before cleansing the area with a cotton swab dabbed in carbolic acid. As Moulsdale approached with the syringe, the queen showed no sign that she noticed or cared what was being done to her.

"Still and all," said Salisbury, "I see no sense in carelessly revealing our secrets to just anyone."

"I am hardly careless," said Moulsdale, injecting the syringe of ichor into the queen's arm without checking for air bubbles. "Miss Lavenza is one of our top medical students and has been sworn to secrecy. As for the redhead, she's a scholarship girl and dependent on the school's largesse, so we can trust her to be discreet." Moulsdale handed Aggie the used needle and syringe.

Ears burning with embarrassment, she unscrewed the needle and placed it in a small steel case for disinfection. *Buck up,* she told herself. *It's not like he's saying anything you don't know.* Still, it stung to hear the unvarnished truth stated so bluntly.

"Is this meant to reassure me as to the soundness of your judgment?" Salisbury sounded disgusted. "You've brought a charity case and a bluestocking to attend the queen. Not exactly a masterstroke."

"I must admit, I was dubious myself at first," said Moulsdale. "But it's a new century, and we must all keep pace with the times. Besides, Miss Lavenza is the daughter of the late Robert Lavenza, and something of an engineering prodigy herself."

Salisbury looked almost comically astonished. "Please do not tell me that you actually intend to let this chit of a girl treat the queen!"

"She may look like a chit," began Moulsdale, but Salisbury cut him off.

"Where is the professor who performed the initial procedure on Her Majesty?"

"Deceased in the fire that burned down our Yorkshire location, I regret to say. But Miss Lavenza is entirely capable of assisting me in setting Her Majesty to rights," Moulsdale added.

Lizzie placed her attaché case on an antique rosewood side table and opened it, revealing a small electrical device bristling with various leads and attachments. "I know I may seem young and inexperienced, but I am very well trained in the use of this equipment," she assured the prime minister.

Shiercliffe nodded at Aggie. "Go ahead and prepare Her Majesty for the procedure."

Aggie set to unfastening the row of tiny pearl buttons at the queen's throat, revealing two shiny metal electrodes. Even though Lizzie had told her what to expect, she still felt a ripple of discomfort. Here was undeniable evidence that the Queen of England was a Bio-Mechanical—an automated and reanimated cadaver.

Bio-Mechanicals were not meant to be capable of independent thought or emotion, and most of them could not speak intelligibly. Still, they did usually blink their eyes and move about, while the queen appeared to be frozen in place.

Why on earth had Moulsdale transformed Queen Victoria in the first place? Had it been a case of medical men wanting to use every possible intervention to preserve an important patient's life—even if the patient was now an empty shell of her former self? If so, Aggie thought that Moulsdale was misguided. The Prince of Wales was alive to step up to the throne should nature take its course, so why keep his mother, the queen, on this side of the ground?

Not your place to question the plan, Aggie reminded herself. *You're just here to do what you're told without making any mistakes.*

"Now," said Lizzie, approaching the queen with a glowing violet wand, "the application of ultraviolet light should help activate the newly transfused ichor, and then I'll follow up with a series of electromagnetic pulses that will invigorate Her Majesty. She'll be up and about again in no time."

"No! No more contraptions and no more empty promises," said Salisbury, addressing Moulsdale. "When I agreed to let you perform your black arts on Her Majesty last year, you assured me that the queen would be rejuvenated. Instead, all she did was shamble about whilst babbling absurdities—and now she can't do even that. She's a corpse walker who can't even walk!"

"I assure you," said Moulsdale, "there is no necromancy involved in what we do."

"Call it what you like," said Salisbury. "It's unnatural to bring corpses back from the dead, and I regret the day I let you talk me into it." Looking down at his feet, he bleakly contemplated his swollen ankles. "I suppose there's nothing for it now. We shall have to announce the sad news of Her Majesty's demise."

"My lord," said Shiercliffe, speaking up for the first time. "Her Majesty is most definitely alive."

"She is a soulless machine," said Salisbury, "given a semblance of life by your infernal medicines and devices. And it is my fault that she has come to this sad end." Rising painfully to his feet, the elderly prime minister looked down at his Queen. "May God forgive me, but I thought I was doing the right thing. When Her Majesty died last January, I panicked, thinking there would be nothing to deter the kaiser from challenging Great Britain's power. Now I see I was wrong to try to change the course of fate."

Turning off the power to the violet wand, Lizzie leaned over to whisper in Aggie's ear. "So Germany's kaiser is afraid of Queen Victoria?"

Americans. "Not afraid of—fond of. Kaiser Willy is the queen's first and favorite grandson," she whispered back. It was also common knowledge that the kaiser disliked his cousin Bertie—the next in line to the British throne. According to the newspapers, the kaiser's lingering affection for his British granny was the only thing keeping the impulsive, insecure head of the German empire from plunging the two nations into war. So this was the reason for keeping Queen Victoria alive—to keep the kaiser from declaring war on Great Britain.

The more sensational papers ran stories of undercover German agents and suspicious boats running military exercises along deserted shorelines. Of course, the tabloids also ran headlines about amorous octopus attacks and flesh-eating Bio-Mechanicals roaming the streets, so one could hardly believe everything they printed.

"My dear man," said Moulsdale, "trying to prevent a war is not cowardice. And there is no need to change our course."

As Moulsdale and Salisbury argued, Aggie became aware of a faint, scrabbling sound coming from the wardrobe. She had been hearing it on and off for the past few minutes, she realized. Could the royal bedchamber be infested by a mouse?

Then it hit her: the overwhelming odor of dog. Walking over to the wardrobe, she opened the door, revealing an anxious white Pomeranian.

Shiercliffe drew herself up as if confronted by a rat. "What on earth is that?"

"That's the queen's lapdog, Turi," said Salisbury, as Turi jumped onto a footstool and then up onto the queen's bed, where she yapped anxiously at her mistress.

"Someone get it off!" exclaimed Shiercliffe, who was clearly not a dog lover.

Before anyone could move, Queen Victoria startled them all by blinking and then breaking into a smile. "Absentia transformative?" she asked the little dog.

Turi barked again, then scampered back down to the wardrobe.

Kneeling down, Aggie saw that the dog had made itself a nest of silky garments. On closer look, she saw tiny white bodies nestled inside the silk. "Why, she's had puppies!"

The Queen nodded, looking quite pleased with this development. "Is the invention of the mother necessary?"

"You see?" Moulsdale tucked his thumbs into his waistcoat

as if he were personally responsible for the queen's recovery. "Her Majesty was just worried about her dog."

"She's back to abnormal, I suppose," said Salisbury, lumbering over to the chair he had vacated. "But that's hardly good enough. The kaiser has announced his intention to visit his granny this spring, and a date has been set for mid-May. What are we going to do if she malfunctions while he is talking to her? He's not a fool."

"Leave it to me," said Moulsdale. "That gives us three months. I'll make certain that Her Majesty is in tip-top shape by then. The kaiser will never suspect a thing."

"How can you be so certain?" Salisbury sank into his chair as if returning from an arduous journey. "Even if you repair the queen in time, what about the rest of it? Wilhelm is obsessed with Bio-Mechanicals. According to the latest military intelligence, his program is more advanced than ours."

"Utter rubbish," said Moulsdale, visibly bristling. "We have made recent advancements, and our new Dreadnaught model is state-of-the-art military technology."

"Excellent news," said Salisbury, in a tone that implied that he did not believe a word of it. "When can I see this marvel of engineering?"

Moulsdale did not blink. "Once the testing is complete. I always defer to the engineering and surgical departments as to the official rollout of new technology."

"Incendiary wench!" The Queen, propped up in her four-poster bed like a little doll, raised one plump, heavily beringed hand and pointed at Aggie. "Reconnoiter me with the nascent citizenry."

Salisbury frowned. "What is she on about?"

Shiercliffe approached the ancient monarch with a thermometer. "Feverish, I suspect."

"No, no, no," said the queen, becoming agitated as she flinched away from Shiercliffe's thermometer. "Full court dress! Present the debutantes!"

"I think she just wants to see one of the puppies," said Aggie. Lifting a sturdy little female, she brought it over to the queen. "Look how sweet it is," she said, stroking the puff of white fur above the gleaming, dark button eyes. "Did you know she was expecting?"

"More things than meet the eye in your philosophy," said Queen Victoria, looking at Aggie in a way that left her uncertain if this was a response to her question or merely the random association of a fractured mind.

It was only later that another possibility occurred to her: the queen might have been confiding something about herself.

2

IT WAS ONLY A FEW MINUTES PAST NINE IN THE morning, and already the Royal Victoria Hospital's receiving room was packed. On the front row of wooden benches, an elderly man leaned on his cane for support as he coughed prodigiously into a filthy handkerchief, while the workman sitting beside him scowled his disapproval. An old woman in a black kerchief was shielding her eyes from the weak winter sunlight streaming in the tall windows, while the heavily made-up girl at her side had fallen asleep, worn coat falling open to reveal a stained silk evening gown far too thin for the blustery winds outside. A young mother held her flushed toddler on her lap, telling him something as he watched her face with rapt attention, while the woman on her left sat clutching her purse over her belly, apparently oblivious to the two small children who tugged at her sleeves and then raced around her, screaming and laughing.

Still exhausted from last night's unexpected visit to the palace, Aggie approached the elderly man. "Name and nature of complaint, sir?"

The old man opened his mouth and then promptly resumed his phlegmy coughing, his thin frame shaking with the effort.

"Ah, terrific. I can tell you what the old geezer's got," said the scowling workman, leaning away from his seatmate. "Consumption. And with my luck, I'm going to bloody have it, too. Why'd I even come to this death shop?"

"So you could complain to someone new, I expect," said Aggie. "But I can't listen to your list of grievances till I attend to this gentleman, so you might as well let me get on with it."

The workman shrugged, clearly more amused than affronted. "Right, then, least that's some kind of answer."

She turned to the old man again, who appeared to have recovered his breath. "Now, sir," she began, but before she could finish, he was off again, making what sounded like a concerted effort to expel a lung.

"Here, take this," she said, pulling a freshly laundered white linen handkerchief from her apron pocket. His attempt to thank her turned into a great crescendo of a hacking retch, which ended when he disgorged a wad of something bloody into the white fabric. "Ta," he said, folding the fabric over and offering it to her.

"No, no, you keep it," she said, then belatedly wondered if she was going to get in trouble if she did not turn the used handkerchief into laundry by the end of the day. Sometimes she felt as though she were impersonating a nurse rather than studying to become one. "Now, sir, if you can just tell me your full name and what brings you into the Royal Victoria today?"

"Well," said the old man, "it's a bit embarrassing, but I 'aven't moved me bowels in a week."

Aggie looked at him in surprise. "But your cough..."

"Agh," said the man with a dismissive wave, "I've 'ad that for years."

Suddenly, the clanging of a cowbell cut through the cacophony of muted conversations, hacking coughs and high-pitched squeals.

"All right, everyone, listen up," said a booming voice from the back of the room. "We have sixteen burn victims coming in from an explosion at the match factory. They should be arriving in the next five to ten minutes and will need to be taken immediately into the operating theater."

There was a ripple of sound as patients and staff reacted, but the head of medicine clapped his hands. "Enough chatter! Time is of the essence!" He rang the cowbell again, and the room exploded into action.

Two nursing sisters grabbed the handles on a large metal washbasin and carried it out between them, while the attending doctor lifted an IV stand and barked an order for someone to find more. As other doctors and nurses raced to get to the operating theater, Aggie realized she was going to be on her own in the receiving room, with roughly thirty sick or injured patients in various stages of distress.

There was a piercing shriek—one of the children, thank God, and not a new catastrophe.

"Johnny bit me," wailed the little girl, tugging at her mother's sleeve. Aggie was about to turn back to the possible case of consumption when she realized that the child's mother was not responding to her girl's tugs. The head of nursing often complained about the dubious parenting skills of some patients: *Those people*, she would say, *are scarcely better than animals.* Yet even the worst parent would hardly ignore a screaming child who was hauling on her sleeve.

Something was very wrong.

Aggie leaned over the gaunt, dark-haired woman slumped against the bench. Underneath the brim of her black straw hat, her eyes were shut.

"Hello, ma'am? Are you all right?"

"Oi," said the workman, "I'm meant to be next!"

Aggie ignored him. "Ma'am? Can you hear me?"

The woman's eyes fluttered open. "I'm having some pain," she said softly. Her face was chalk white, but her lips were surprisingly dark. At first, Aggie thought it might be a cosmetic, but then she looked more closely. Blue lips—not a good sign.

Aggie took the woman's ungloved hand in hers. Cold. "Are you bleeding, ma'am?"

The woman took a moment to answer. "Yes," she said, as if confessing a shameful secret. "I wouldn't have bothered coming in, but it's been going on for a while."

Possible hemorrhage, then. Aggie suspected she already knew the answer to the next question, but she asked it anyway. "Are you expecting a child?"

The woman met Aggie's eyes directly. "Not anymore," she said flatly.

That was not the answer she'd been expecting. "Wait here," she told the children, "quietly now. Your mother is sick, and she needs you to behave yourselves." The siblings watched her leave, wide-eyed. Even if their mother survived this, they would remember this day as the end of a certain kind of innocence. From this moment on, these children would know that death can come suddenly and unexpectedly, on a perfectly ordinary morning, and snatch away the ones you love the most.

But death would not claim the children's mother that morning—at least, not if Aggie could help it. All she had to do was convince Dr. Moulsdale that the woman needed to be seen right away. The head of medicine was standing at the back of the room, speaking with Victor Frankenstein, the school's top surgical student and Lizzie's fiancé. Tall, dark-haired and athletic, Victor looked every inch a well-born gentleman, but his high, starched collar and specially designed left glove hid the fact that he was also a Bio-Mechanical. His enhanced left hand gave him remarkable strength, and Victor would have been the perfect prototype of a superior soldier to show the kaiser—except that his reinstatement as a student was the price of Lizzie's silence about the queen.

"Of course, my boy, of course," Moulsdale was saying to Victor, "the first goal is to save these men." He pointed to a parade of stretchers being carried in by men with ash-covered faces. Some of the bodies on the stretchers were ominously still. In a lower voice, he added, "But it is equally vital that any unfortunate victims who cannot be saved be procured for our Bio-Mechanical program."

"I understand, Professor," Victor replied. "But we haven't been able to locate two of the families, and the other two have wives who want to bury their men." Now he nodded to a couple of sobbing women huddled together near the door.

"I see, I see." Moulsdale stroked his neat, pointed salt-and-pepper beard. "You haven't released the bodies to them, have you?"

"Not yet, sir."

"Very good. Here's what you do, then—tell the wives you

need to perform an autopsy, for legal reasons, then send the bodies down to the morgue."

Victor looked as though he were about to object, but Aggie reminded herself that the needs of the living outweighed those of the dead. Summoning her nerve, she stepped forward. "Begging your pardon, Professor Moulsdale, but I have a bit of a problem."

Mousldale scowled at her. "It had better be urgent."

Victor, who knew her well enough to know she didn't usually ask for help, looked concerned. "What's wrong, Aggie?"

"That woman over there—front row, straw hat—I think she's hemorrhaging. I don't suppose you could take a look?"

Moulsdale glanced at his pocket watch. "Mr. Frankenstein needs to go back to the operating theater to handle the transfer of the bodies, and I need to check on the other victims. Where is the nurse who is supposed to be in charge?"

"Tending the burn victims," said Aggie.

"Well, then, go speak to the staff nurse."

"I'm afraid she's gone, as well."

"Botheration." Clearly, one poor woman bleeding to death could not compete with the possibility of fresh cadavers for the Bio-Mechanical program. "Well, make her comfortable and I shall send someone back here as soon as I can," Moulsdale said.

Here was the problem when death held as much appeal as life to a doctor—cures and healing procedures became weighed against other outcomes.

On the other side of the room, the woman had slumped lower in her chair. Her two children were trying to shake her.

"Forgive me, Professor," said Aggie, "but soon may be too late. My mother's a midwife, and I've seen these symptoms

before. I think she's having complications from a miscarriage."
She did not mention the other possibility, but it was there in
the air between them: a back alley, dirty equipment, possible
internal puncture and sepsis. Yet another reason a woman
needed to safeguard her heart. Nothing but trouble came
from being too close to a man, even a good one.

Moulsdale, clearly unmoved, was already heading toward
the door. "I'm sure one of the other doctors or nurses will
be back presently."

"But, Doctor, she needs help now. If you'd just—" Too
late, she realized her mistake.

He spun to face her, nostrils flaring. "Enough! Need I remind you that you are here to learn, not to teach? Make the
woman comfortable and do nothing until someone qualified returns." Turning to Victor, he said, "Now, come with
me and fill me in on the condition of the surviving victims."

Victor gave Aggie an apologetic look over his shoulder before walking away.

Damn it. Aggie forced herself not to think about possible
repercussions. Right now, she had other priorities. When she
got back to the woman in the black straw hat, she found her
breathing was more labored than before. Her children were
no longer racing around or arguing, but were staring at Aggie
as if she were truly in charge and about to do something to
save their mother.

"All right," she said, looking over the other occupants of
the bench. "You, there." She gave the sleeping dollymop in
the silk dress a little shake.

The girl yawned. "What's happening? Is it my turn to be
seen?"

"This woman is going to bleed to death if we can't help

her now." Aggie turned to the surly workman and pointed to a small examining room that opened off the main hall. "I need to carry her over there. Can you lift her with us? If your condition won't allow it, just tell me."

"Bloody ridiculous way to run a hospital," said the workman, getting to his feet and lifting the unconscious woman into his arms. "Where d'you want her, then?"

Aggie led the way, then helped position the now-unconscious woman on a cot. She thanked the man and then went to work without allowing herself the luxury of self-doubt or hesitation.

Twenty minutes later, Aggie had done what she could. She had used a vinegar solution to clean and disinfect internally and had used catgut ligatures to sew up the torn tissues visible to the eye. She would have given anything for some tincture of agrimony or yarrow to make a compress, but she had no idea where the doctors kept their compounding medicines. At least the bleeding appeared to have stopped, but there was no way to be certain that she hadn't missed some internal injury.

At least now she's got a chance. Aggie was just washing the blood off her hands in a basin by the patient's cot when she heard a familiar, disapproving voice behind her.

"What on earth do you think you are doing, probationer?"

3

AGGIE DRIED HER HANDS ON A TOWEL AND took a moment to collect herself before turning to face the head of nursing. "I can explain, Matron."

"Don't bother." In her expertly tailored black silk dress, Ursula Shiercliffe looked more like the queen of witches than the head of nursing, but Hecate was probably more forgiving of her apprentices. "I would have thought that after last night you would realize that we have a unique responsibility—and a vital duty to perform for our nation. Yet Professor Moulsdale tells me that you were challenging his decisions."

"I didn't mean to be impertinent, Matron. It's just—the patient was hemorrhaging and the other doctors and nurses were all in the operating theater." With a quick sidelong glance at the woman's children, who were sitting quietly in the corner, she added softly, "I had to do something, or the poor woman might have bled out right there in the receiving room."

Shiercliffe looked slightly mollified. "I understand that you care about the patients who walk in, DeLacey. But you must remember—even though we have moved into the Royal Victoria, we are still Great Britain's only Academy of Bio-Mechanical Science and Engineering, and our priorities have not changed. We help patients because it is right, but that is not our primary mission."

The school's primary mission, which had been drummed into all the nursing and medical students, was the research and development of a Bio-Mechanical army that would protect the nation's borders without sacrificing its young and able-bodied men. It was important work, to be sure, and a welcome escape from working as her mother's unpaid apprentice, but there were times when Aggie had a nagging sense of wrongness. No doubt this was a vestige of her working class upbringing—in her village, folks were superstitious and more likely to trust a local midwife or apothecary than they were to put their faith in some sawbones from the city.

Still, Aggie couldn't accept that she had done wrong in treating a patient when the only other option would have been allowing her to die.

"I take your point, Matron, but we're still a hospital, aren't we? And it's different here in London. I see more critical cases in a day here than I did in a month back in Henley."

"Yes, and the only reason you are seeing them is because the Crown has given us the funding to operate here. The Royal Victoria was on the verge of closing its doors for good before we arrived. Think how many of these poor people would die if our Bio-Mechanical program fails and the government no longer supplies the hospital with the money it needs to operate."

Aggie bit back the urge to retort that a hospital that merely appeared open to patients might be worse than one that was clearly closed. *You're not going to win her over,* she told herself. *Let it go.* "I see your point," she said out loud. "I am sorry, Matron."

"I'm glad you're seeing reason." She looked at the woman and sighed. "I suppose we can make room for her in Waterloo Ward."

"Oi," came a small, defiant voice from the back of the room. It was the young boy, fists bunched at his sides. "What you going to do with our ma?" Behind him, his little sister burst into tears.

"Oh, botheration," said Shiercliffe. "What are those children doing there?" She pointed at the boy and girl crouched silently in the corner.

"They came with their mother."

"Of course." The matron sighed. "You would think that people would consider their finances before breeding like rabbits. Well. They cannot remain in the hospital unattended." She looked at the boy. "I don't suppose there's anyone at home who is free to come fetch you? Your father, a relative, a neighbor?"

"Free to come fetch us," said the boy, rolling the words out as if they were novel concepts. "No problem. I'll just call for the family carriage to come pick us up, shall I? Or maybe the butler's free."

"Don't be cheeky with me, boy." Shiercliffe looked at Aggie as though she was responsible for the children's lack of extended family. "You'll have to summon someone from the workhouse to take charge of them while their mother recuperates."

"Is that really necessary?" The workhouse was a grim place for a child, and they would separate the brother from his sister.

A line appeared between Shiercliffe's brows. "What are you suggesting? That we let them wander around the various wards unsupervised?"

Now I've gone too far. "I'm sorry if it sounded as though I were questioning your judgment."

Shiercliffe softened. "You're a clever girl, Aggie, and good-hearted. And I can see why you sympathize with these poor tykes. But a girl in your position cannot afford to care too much. Leave charity for the rich and the powerful—they can afford it."

Aggie bit the inside of her cheek. "Yes, Matron." She hated to admit it, but Shiercliffe had a point. If she were to be kicked out of nursing school, she would have a stark choice—return to Henley and see if her mother would take her back, or survive on the streets as best as she could.

"Now, go to the laundry and put on a fresh apron. You look like a butcher's wife." She glanced at the woman on the cot. "I'll get one of the ward nurses to see to this woman… and her children."

"Thank you, Matron." Aggie bobbed a curtsy and risked a quick smile for the children. "You two mustn't worry," she said softly, kneeling down so she could look them in the eyes. "We'll be taking the very best care of your mum here. Promise."

The girl put her thumb in her mouth, but the boy regarded Aggie warily. "How do we know you're not going to turn our ma into one of your monsters?"

Aggie glanced up at Shiercliffe. "Is that what folks are saying?"

The boy nodded. "They say you're making your own army of monsters to rule the East End."

That was fast. The former Ingold Academy of Bio-Mechanical Medicine and Engineering had only moved into the Royal Victoria Hospital a month earlier. Still, Aggie was all too familiar with the way locals could resent an incursion of outsiders—especially ones involved in mysterious scientific studies that involved dead bodies. She had grown up in Henley, right in the shadow of the infamous medical school. Every autumn she would hear the noisy wheels of two-horse growlers clattering over the cobblestones past her home, transporting new students and their luggage from the train station in York to the mysterious school at the top of the hill.

Her younger brothers and their friends liked to chase the carriages, scooping up handfuls of manure from the street and hurling them at the coach's windows, shouting, "Vivisectionists! Butchers!"

Ingold was the only institution in Great Britain where students could learn the cutting-edge techniques of reanimating cadavers to produce Bio-Mechanicals, and the villagers embroidered the meager facts they knew with rumors and wild surmises, then repeated the tales around their hearths on long winter nights until the lies were clearer and sharper than truths. *I saw it with my own eyes, someone would claim—dead-eyed men, shambling along the side of the road, trying to return to lives they could not recall.*

My uncle managed to sneak into the laboratory, someone else might chime in, *and he watched an amputated hand curling and uncurling its fingers, till it inched wormlike across the table toward a scalpel.*

In the end, the locals' distrust and superstition had turned them into a mob that burned the school down last December. Aggie knew that if they didn't convince the East Enders that their new neighbors intended to help, not harm, this school could meet the same fate as the last one. Of course, the school's reputation would have benefitted from a bit more attention to women like this one, who could be saved, and a bit less focus on the acquisition of fresh corpses for the Bio-Mechanical program.

"What's your name?" she asked the boy.

The answer came grudgingly. "Timothy."

"Well, Timothy, it's not true. We're just like any hospital—we treat the sick and try our best to make them better. But some of our doctors also do research for the queen."

"Making monsters."

"Making Bio-Mechanicals, so if the kaiser ever tries to invade us, it won't be our young men getting shot and killed. So, now, what would we want your mum for?"

Timothy looked uncertain. "Dunno," he said. "Mums go missing on the street at night, though. They say the body snatchers aren't fussed what they take."

Aggie put her hand on the boy's thin shoulder. "Those are just awful rumors. I promise you, we're not going to do anything bad to your mum. We're going to help her."

His eyes searched her face. "You swear?"

"On my life. May I be struck blind if I'm lying."

Timothy contemplated this, then spat in his palm and held it out.

Hoping Shiercliffe would understand, Aggie spat in her own palm and then clasped the boy's hand in hers. She could see the relief that he could not quite hide—a spitshake was not quite a blood vow, but for people like Timothy and herself, it carried more weight than fancy words and signatures.

Shiercliffe cleared her throat. "That's quite enough of that,

DeLacey. Now go and wash your hands and find a fresh apron."

"Yes, Matron." She got to her feet and was heading out the door when Shiercliffe's voice stopped her again.

"You're a capable girl, Aggie, with more common sense than most. If you don't give in to these sentimental impulses, you might just have the makings of a decent nurse."

From Shiercliffe, this amounted to effusive praise. Aggie curtsied, then headed for the stairs, still assimilating the fact that the head of nursing hadn't gone sour on her, after all. The relief of it spread through her like a balm. Without the older woman's support, Aggie knew she wouldn't last long here. Her own mother had said as much.

"London, is it? You're just asking for trouble. Aren't nurses supposed to keep their legs crossed? We'll see how long that lasts. I reckon you'll be ruined by one of them young doctors and selling yourself on the streets within a year."

Her mother had been cutting an onion when Aggie walked out the door of her childhood home, and had refused to acknowledge her goodbye.

Aggie did not regret her decision. Sometimes, it was more important to have the hope that things would improve than to have the security of knowing that things would not get worse.

Of course, the flip side of taking a risk was that there was also a chance that things could deteriorate, and instead of gaining something new, you would lose what little you had.

4

A CLOUD DRIFTED OVER THE MOON, CASTING
the graveyard in shadow. The Artful Dodger didn't worry—
his eyes adjusted quickly to the shift in light, and he'd always
had a talent for finding his way through the dark. Maybe it
was in his blood—as a boy, his mother had taught him that
the Jewish calendar followed the moon, but he could no longer remember the names of the Hebrew months or the prayers
that attended them.

Ah, well. It wasn't as though prayers had helped his mother
much.

Stepping over a rotting tree stump, he spotted a bright
splash of orange—a small cluster of edible winter mushrooms.
At least, he was fairly certain they were edible. February was
too late in the season for deadly funeral bells, which looked
similar and also grew on deadwood, but still, he wouldn't be
the first to mistake a foe for a friend.

Well, nothing was certain in life, and he wasn't one to pass
up a free meal. Crouching, he picked as many as he could

cram into his handkerchief. He hadn't been thrilled about meeting Bill Sikes after dark in the thieves' cemetery, but he knew how to forage in nature as well as in rich men's pockets.

Faygie liked to claim that the thieves' cemetery boasted the finest pickings in London—the best dandelions for wine, the perfect nettles for tea, blackberries so sweet and tart the queen herself couldn't ask for better—but this was nothing but a humbug. Dodger had foraged in old churchyards from Mile End to Highgate, and the outcast dead didn't make better fertilizer than respectable citizens. Strip away the layers of silk and bombazine, and you couldn't tell a debutante from a bangtail.

Tying up his handkerchief corners to secure the mushrooms, he saw that he was standing at the foot of a fresh grave. Someone had taken the time to plant a wooden grave marker at the head, and to carve the words Beloved Letitia and the dates bookending the girl's brief life: June 1886–February 1903.

Seventeen—same age as me, more or less. He wasn't entirely sure of the year of his birth, but unlike Bill, he looked young for his age. Bill had attained both the size and scruff of a hardened criminal, while Dodger was lean enough to slip into small spaces and smooth faced enough to pass for innocent— so long as no one looked too deeply into his eyes. Thievery, like acting, was a profession that required the ability to lie with real conviction, and he was an excellent thief.

Dodger froze as something frantic rustled in the brambles. Whatever was on the other side of the thorny bush scampered off, low to the ground, and he let out his breath. Probably a fox. Where the hell were Bill and Nancy, anyway? These days, it wasn't exactly safe to go traipsing about graveyards on your lonesome.

Last month, the tabloids had broken the news that the Royal Victoria Hospital was now under new and shady management, followed by a series of increasingly histrionic headlines: "Corpse-Walker Docs Set Up Shop!" "Good Morgue-ing: Hospital Offers Deals on Fresh Bodies!" "'I Woke Up Screaming': Local Man Mistaken For Dead, Wakes Moments Before Ghoulish Doc Turns Him Into Bio-Mechanical!" The stories were accompanied by lurid illustrations, often of beautiful young women in clinging nightclothes being menaced by living corpses.

Rags like the *Illustrated Police News* were notorious for printing rubbish, but there was at least a grain of truth in these recent reports. The Royal Victoria was actively advertising for corpses, to be used "in service to the Crown." The advert promised as much as two pounds for a fresh body taken in the prime of life, with a ten shilling bonus if the body was no more than two days old.

A bloke could get quite creative over the prospect of two pounds, ten shillings.

A gust of cold wind rattled the branches of a yew tree, and Dodger shivered and blew on the bare tips of his fingers, exposed by his half gloves. Bloody Bill and his penchant for meeting in graveyards. Bill said he preferred to do business transactions away from prying eyes, and that in the graveyard they could look over what each of them had stolen that day and figure out what it was worth without worrying about being double-crossed by some other gang. Fair enough, but Bill never showed up on time, and Dodger would have preferred to take his chances somewhere where he could order a pint and a meat pie.

Something rustled in the bushes, and Dodger froze. A moment later, there was a scurry of something small—doubtless the mouse that the fox had been hunting. Sod it—his nerves couldn't stand much more of this.

He pulled a silver fob watch out of his waistcoat pocket to check the time: just after nine. Bill could have till half past, and not a moment more. Suddenly, there was a shift in the air, subtle but unmistakable for anyone who lived by his nerves. Without turning around, he said, "Hurry up and surprise me already."

Nancy stepped out of the shadows, smiling and shaking her head. "You must have the ears of a bat."

The watch was back in his pocket as he turned to greet her. "My love for you is such that I am exquisitely attuned to the merest hint of your presence."

"You saying I smell?"

Dodger smiled back at her. "Only of violets." The truth was violet water could only partially mask the scent of healthy girl, especially when she only had one dress. Not that he minded. He liked how Nancy smelled. "Where's Bill?"

She shrugged.

"Nance, you didn't come here on your own?"

She gave him a level look. "I came here the same way you did. What's your point? That I'm too helpless to fend for myself?" With a flick of her wrists, Nancy revealed two little switchblades.

"You're a dab hand with the blades, Nance, but face facts—neither of us can stroll around the way Bill does. He's got the size and the mug to scare away trouble—and he's got his dog, besides."

She retracted the blades and stashed them back under her sleeves. "Feeling jealous?"

That stung, but not as badly as it once had. "Don't worry, luv," he said, picking a berry from his hat and offering it to her. "I've learned my lesson. You're Bill's girl."

"I'm my own girl," said Nancy, and it would have been convincing if he hadn't watched her moon over Bill for the past three years. "Aw, damn. Would you look at that." She was kneeling down in front of the fresh grave.

"Did you know her?"

"Yeah, from the workhouse. Her bed was a few feet away from mine. We lost touch, though—haven't seen her in a year or so."

The back of Dodger's neck prickled with unease a moment before they heard the sound of footsteps. Nancy stood up, her face all lit up at the prospect of seeing Bill, but Dodger gripped her arm and pulled her back into the shadow of the yew tree.

Oliver Twist stepped into view, a shovel resting on his shoulder, and Dodger sighed. Just when he thought the evening couldn't get worse. He stepped out of the shadows, making Twist jump. "Hullo, Twist."

Twist straightened his jacket and tipped the brim of his top hat. Like Dodger, he affected a gentleman's dress. "Dodger. Wasn't expecting to see you here." Spotting Nancy, he added, "And the lovely Miss Grimwood. Don't tell me you're both working the resurrection game?"

"We're not grave robbers," said Nancy, planting her hands on her hips. "And even if we were, we wouldn't go digging up some poor girl what never caught a break in her life."

"Aw, c'mon, Nance," said Twist, leaning on the shovels. "Don't be so harsh. It's not like Lettie's going to care one way or another."

"It's not right," insisted Nancy. "She had enough of men bothering her when she was alive. Now she's dead, she deserves a bit of peace."

"Now that she's dead," said Twist, "she has it. If you believe in souls, then hers is off in a better place. What does it matter if I make a few bob from her fleshly container?"

"Leave off," said Dodger. "There must be some other grave you can desecrate. And don't the hospital want blokes for their experiments?"

Twist shrugged. "If the goods are fresh enough, they'll buy them piecemeal."

Dodger didn't bother to hide his disgust. "Christ, what happened to you? She was Nancy's friend. You remember friendship, don't you?"

Twist looked stung, then gave a bitter smile. "Better than you, I expect."

Twist and Dodger had been best mates, back when they were kids. Looking at Twist now, with lank, greasy strands of hair falling over his hollowed-out face, Dodger could barely recognize him. Yet a few years ago, Twist had been fair-haired and fine-featured, with a look of stoic melancholy that made passersby open their hearts and their purses. They had made quite the team, back in the day. While Twist stood on a street corner, looking like a forlorn angel and speaking to punters in a perfect imitation of a posh accent, Dodger would pick their pockets. Then puberty arrived, reshuffling the deck and changing the game. Dodger gained a little muscle but continued to look much as he had always done. Oliver, on the other hand, was transformed from appealing orphan to sullen, gangling, pimple-faced gawk.

When his abandoned orphan story no longer elicited any sympathy, Twist began to suffer from a host of imaginary ailments. One week, he was medicating a dry cough with Bayer's heroin syrup. Next time you saw him, he was drinking so much Stickney and Poor's paregoric that he saw ghosts in every doorway. Twist was at his most dangerous, though, when he was on Maltine's coca lozenges. You never knew what Twist was liable to do when he'd been sucking lozenges. He started believing his own stories—his mother had been a gentleman's daughter, every friend he'd ever known had either tricked him or abused him. Sometimes Dodger was the exception, but other times he was the worst betrayer of all.

Dodger wondered what nostrums Twist was taking today.

"Tell you what," said Twist. "How about I give you a cut? Seeing as how you and Lettie were friends and all." He gave the word friend a sarcastic emphasis.

Nancy made a disgusted face. "What's wrong with you? Don't you have any morals at all?"

"You're one to talk," said Twist. "I'd rather get my hands dirty on the dead then let the living touch me however they please."

Nancy spat on the ground. "Who d'you think you're fooling? Everyone knows you'll do anything for anyone when the need is on you."

For a moment, Dodger feared she had gone too far. A muscle twitched on the side of Twist's jaw, and Dodger tensed, ready to jump in if he needed to, but not wanting to move too soon and provoke an attack.

To his relief, Twist just gave a brittle laugh. "Have it your way, Nance. But one day, you're going to change your mind. Some punter's going to be pawing at you in the back of the pub, and you'll say, 'Know what? Twist had the right idea, after all.'" He tipped his hat to her. "When you come to your senses, I won't even ask for an apology. We are old friends, after all. And old friends have to look out for one another."

She flipped him the bird as Twist moved down the path away from them, out of sight.

"Nance? You all right?"

She didn't turn around. "Yeah, course I am. It's just— He's going to come back here, isn't he? The moment we're gone, he'll dig Lettie up and sell her for parts. And even if he don't—someone else will." Her shoulders began to shake.

Dodger hesitated a moment, then, very slowly, reached out and put his arms around her, holding her loosely so she could break away if this wasn't what she wanted. She put her head down on his shoulder, and he tried not to think about how she was letting him hold her, because that was wrong and selfish and he ought not be savoring this.

Then he looked up and saw that he and Nancy were no longer alone. "Hello, Bill," he said, as Nancy wrenched herself out of his arms.

Bill heaved the heavy sack off his shoulders and onto the ground, his pale blue eyes flicking back and forth between them. "What's all this, then?"

Dodger stiffened. Bill's voice was quiet, his expression neutral, but that didn't mean he wouldn't erupt into violence. Whether or not Bill wanted her for himself, he was not fond of others messing with Nancy. Bullseye, Bill's dog, gave a low whine and thumped her tail twice on the ground.

"Don't fret your eyelids," said Dodger as Nancy stepped

away from him. "Nancy was just feeling a bit low about her friend there." He indicated the grave.

"Twist was here," added Nancy. "After some fresh bodies to dig up. He was going to pull poor Lettie out of the ground and sell her to them witch doctors." Her face crumpled.

Bill hesitated, then opened his arms to her. She collapsed against him, and his eyes met Dodger's over her back for a moment. Dodger turned away, trying to hide his disapproval. Nancy and Bill's on-again, off-again romance was as predictable as sunrise. They would be all over each other tonight, and Nancy would be walking on air for the next day. Then, by the end of the week, she would crash down again when she realized that nothing had really changed between her and Bill.

Dodger grabbed his handkerchief full of mushrooms and slipped out the cemetery gate. He could hand over the day's takings and get his cut another time. He knew what it was like to lose a friend—and to know that it could just as easily have been you. They might never know what had killed Lettie—an infection, an accident, a violent customer. It didn't really matter. Life was dangerous in the East End.

Let Nancy find whatever comfort she could in Bill's embrace. Dodger would head over to the crowds at Covent Garden and take some foolish risks until he felt like himself again.

5

PULLING OPEN THE DOOR TO THE LAUNDRY, Aggie was blasted by a gust of humid air and hot linen. A young woman with a shiny red burn mark on her cheek was stirring a steaming vat of sheets. "Come to see Jenny?"

Aggie and the young laundress had become friendly over the past few weeks. After nearly a month of listening to middle class girls complaining about how exhausted they were from making a few beds, it was a relief to spend a few minutes with a girl who hadn't grown up with a maid and a cook.

"I'd love to see Jen," Aggie said now, "but the truth is, I've been told off for wearing a stained apron."

Clara wiped the sweat from her brow with the back of her arm. "There's none ready, but I can iron you a fresh pinny when I'm done here. Jenny's out back, if you want to see her."

"I'll be in your debt."

"And don't you forget it," said Clara as Aggie walked toward the back of the room.

A middle-aged woman with frizzy hair cursed as she attempted to feed the clean, wet cottons and linens through a mangle. "Hold up with the crank, Irma, something's caught and it's going to rip!" There were so many ways for a working woman to get burned and bruised and broken in the course of a day. Whenever some man started talking about how women were the weaker sex, Aggie thought about all the women she knew who worked in factories until the moment they went into labor.

Letting herself out the back door, Aggie paused, grateful for the rush of cool air. The sky was gray and overcast, threatening rain, and a very slender young woman was reeling in the laundry line, plucking clothespins out of sheets and uniforms and dumping them into a basket.

Aggie watched, feeling a bit guilty. Back home, she had dreaded Mondays because of the washing. No torture in hell could be as bad as having to do laundry, day in and day out. "Hello, Jenny. How are you?"

The young laundress turned. Small and thin, Jenny had dark shadows under her eyes and looked far too young and delicate to be doing a grown woman's work. "Keeping out of trouble, more or less. How 'bout you? Anyone get the vapors after changing a bedpan?"

"Not today."

Jen shook her head. "It might be worth coming down with some ailment, just to have some society girl carry out my waste water." Jenny mimed carrying a full chamber pot as far from her nose as was possible, and Aggie laughed.

"You think you're joking, but that's how some of them do it."

Jen plucked off two more clothespins and pulled a pillow-case from the line. "Suppose we have to admire them rich girls, actually trying to do something useful. Say, Ags…that herbal tea you brewed up for me last month. You haven't got any more you could make up for us?"

Aggie's stomach sank, but she kept her expression and voice as neutral as she could. If she sounded too sympathetic, Jenny would just see it as pity. "Sorry, Jenny, I don't. But if it was going to bring on your courses, it would've worked by now."

Jenny nodded, but Aggie was pretty sure she hadn't really heard her. Even though there was nothing she could do or say, Aggie felt as though she were abandoning the other girl.

It's not my fault, she reminded herself. Jenny was too far along for pennyroyal—or lurk-in-the-ditch, as they called it back home. The herb tasted like spearmint's poison sister and could keep insects away from your kitchen. A tiny amount could bring on your courses and give you the chance to go to London even after you'd done a really stupid thing with a boy because he made you feel good and you'd let yourself forget how dangerous pleasure could be.

Aggie had learned her lesson after losing her good sense in Byram's arms last semester. Never again would she let some boy get close enough to make her lose all common sense.

Jenny took a sheet down from the clothesline. "There's a doctor what says he can help me, only he charges an arm and a leg." She gave a wan imitation of a smile. "I suppose I shouldn't say that, seeing as how some doctors 'round here would want to be paid in arms and legs."

Aggie took one end of the sheet and helped Jenny fold it. "Is this a real doctor? Because a lot of them just say they are."

Jenny shrugged. "How would I know? He wears a white coat. Anyways, it's just a thought." She pulled a clothespin off a pillowcase and slipped it into the cloth bag tucked into her apron.

"Don't put your trust in white coats."

"Maybe you're right. One of the other girls says all I need to do is drink a few tablespoons of turpentine."

Aggie shook her head. "That might work. It might also kill you." She thought of the woman in the receiving room, quietly bleeding while her children raced around her.

"It might be worth it. My dad's gone, so everyone's depending on me. What are we supposed to do with a baby?" Jenny reached for another clothespin. "Never mind. Not your problem."

A drop of rain fell on Aggie's forehead, quickly followed by another. It wasn't her problem, but it could have been. Most of the other probationer nurses hadn't even kissed a boy, and none of them had allowed someone to put his hands all over them. They had never counted down the days till their monthly with trepidation.

"I'm sorry, Jenny."

"Yeah, we're all sorry." Jenny folded the pillowcase and placed it on the top of the pile of clean laundry in the basket. "Come on, grab a handle and let's get inside before it rains."

It was after nine when Aggie fetched her cape from the nurses' changing room and walked out into the gray London evening. The other probationer nurses had already left, but she had stayed late to spend a few minutes visiting Justine Makepiece's room. Aggie considered Justine a friend rather than a patient, and if she hadn't been so tired, she would have remained longer. As it happened, Aggie didn't make it two steps down the corridor when she was roped into helping the ward nurses bathe a recalcitrant patient. The patient, a stout dockworker, had arrived in a state of acute inebriation. Soused as a herring, he refused to be bathed and prepped for surgery on his gangrenous left leg.

"Heartless drabs," he shouted, insisting that the nurses were attempting to rob him of his clothes. Aggie, who was used to dealing with unruly drunks, had managed to persuade the fellow that he was actually in a very nice fancy house and that a bath was required before any other services could be procured. By the time he was clean, he had sobered up enough to remember that he was going to have to choose between his leg and his life. Miserable and contrite, he had settled down for the night with profuse apologies to Aggie and the other nurses, and she had left without letting him know that she had sore ribs from hauling him in and out of the tub.

Tying her bonnet around her chin, she thanked the night porter as he unlocked the hospital gates to let her out.

"You be careful out there," said the man, who had wire-rimmed glasses, a walrus moustache and wore his navy-and-red uniform as though he were a high-ranking officer. "Not the best time for a nice girl to be out walking unescorted."

"I'll be all right," she assured him. "It's not far, and I'm not exactly defenseless." She pointed to the umbrella she carried. "In the right hands, this can be a deadly weapon." She also had a scalpel in her pocket, but didn't feel the need to mention that.

"If you say so, miss. But bad things happen 'round here. They say the cobblestones like their portion of blood on the regular."

She laughed. "They'll have to look elsewhere, then. I grew

up in the north on tales of boggarts and redcaps and Lob Lie-by-the-fire, and old wives' tales don't bother me."

"There's other sorts of bloodthirsty wights that roam these streets. If you'd care to wait a bit, I would be only too happy to escort you home."

I just bet you would, you dirty old man. "Thank you," she said, "but I need to be getting back before I collapse."

"As you like." There was a rattle and clank as the porter locked the gate behind her and she set off, careful not to slip on the rain-slick cobblestones. From the outside, the Royal Victoria was a blunt, blocky, three-story building built like a fortress by a robber baron in the previous century. Supposedly, the knight had been some sort of bluebeard, disposing of wives when they became inconvenient and sealing their bones into various spare rooms. But then, the East End was filled with bloodcurdling stories. If all of them were true, there would hardly be a person left alive below Whitechapel Road.

There was a creak of hinges, and Aggie turned to see a side door opening onto an alley filled with rubbish. A white-coated figure stepped out, and Aggie caught a glimpse of a familiar pale face with protruding eyes and a receding ginger hairline. Henry Clerval. She knew the moment he spotted her, because he instantly ducked back inside.

What was Henry Clerval doing here? Whatever it was, he clearly didn't care for witnesses observing his comings and goings. Shivering in the light mist, Aggie drew her cloak more closely around her as she rounded the corner onto Philpott Street. The scuffling sound of footsteps behind her made her stomach clench, and she glanced nervously over her shoulder: two fog-shrouded figures were following her.

"Hey, Aggie! Wait up!"

A moment later, Nicholas Byram and William Frankenstein were standing beside her. Illuminated by the wavering yellow glow of a streetlamp, Aggie's erstwhile beau and Victor's younger brother looked like an allegorical painting: darkly handsome demon flanked by fair-haired, boyish angel. *Pity I always fall for the devils.* Waiting until they caught up, she said, "You two are out late."

"Some idiot plucked out his stitches," said Byram. "Said they were itching." By unspoken agreement, they all resumed walking at the same time, moving carefully over the patches where no gaslight illuminated the slick, uneven paving stones.

"Why did you have to stay?" She directed the question to Will, but Byram replied.

"According to Professor Grimbald, it was all our fault for not thinking to put a salve on the wound to reduce the itching."

"But it turned out for the best," said Will. "The porter told us that if we hurried, we could escort the pretty redheaded nurse."

"He's a worrier, that one. But I'm a big girl, thoroughly capable of solitary walking." She kept her eyes on Will and away from Byram's handsome, sulky face. It had been over eight weeks since they had last been alone together, and she wished she were less aware of that fact. It certainly didn't seem to bother him.

"You're not in Henley anymore," said Will. "I know you never used to think twice about walking home after dark, but this is the East End."

"It's only two blocks. How much harm am I likely to run into in two blocks?"

"Ah," said Byram, "but that's two blocks of notorious rookeries, where gangs of thieves roam like feral dogs and gin-soaked gentlemen consider any female abroad after dark fair game for their pleasure."

"Speaking of feral dogs, I thought I saw Henry Clerval lurking in a doorway. He hasn't come back to school, has he?"

"Not that I know of," said Will. "And I think my brother would have said something if his old friend suddenly re-appeared." Will gave the words *old friend* a full injection of irony. His brother's oldest friend had let his competitive spirit get the better of him and had decided that the best way to get out from under Victor's shadow was to murder him and make it look like an accident.

Luckily, he had not succeeded.

"Isn't Henry dead?" Byram's heel made a scuffing sound on the pavement, a sign he was tired. "I always assumed Victor got his revenge on the tiresome googly-eyed git."

"Very funny," said Will.

"I wasn't joking. The world is better off without homicidal gingers running around offing people."

"Oi," said Aggie. "Watch the ginger comments."

"Your hair is auburn," said Will.

"You haven't seen me in summer."

Byram quirked an eyebrow. "Don't tell me you turn orange in the warmer months. Well, I suppose I can just avoid you from May until October."

My hair color didn't seem to bother you when you were kissing my face off last December, she thought sourly. Not wanting Byram to pick up on her annoyance, she quickened her pace and asked Will a question about chemistry, which was not the best subject for either of them. Unlike Will, she refused to slow her pace to accommodate Byram's bum foot, but he was managing to keep up. Well, of course he was—Byram's pride would allow nothing less.

When she caught sight of her building, she said, "Thanks for walking me."

"Of course," said Byram. "You never know when some ruthless maniac might jump out of the shadows."

She shot him a sideways glance. "And you would put your life on the line to protect me?"

"Not my life, but I would certainly do my best to alert the constables in as expedient a manner as possible."

What was Byram playing at? Months of silence, and now this demented attempt at flirtation—or whatever it was. "Be still, my foolish heart." They had reached the row of small terraced buildings where she and the other Ingold students had their rooms.

"All joking aside, it really isn't safe to walk on your own," said Byram. "According to Wiggins, two bangtails were found with their skirts pulled up and their legs missing."

Aggie took this in. "Wiggins?"

"The night porter. He was on duty when the constables found them."

"Byram," said Will, in a chiding tone. "She doesn't need the lurid details."

Byram ignored him. "One also lost an arm."

Will looked pained. "Byram."

"A very tidy amputation, according to the badges. There's a thought the culprit was a medical student, or a doctor."

Irritated by his attempts at shocking her, Aggie found herself saying, "Or a garden variety pervert." She had spoken without thinking, but something in her tone had struck a chord; Byram's bad foot shot out from under him, and then, with a sharp huff of air, he was lying on the slick cobblestones as Will gave a shout of alarm.

"Byram! Are you all right?"

"Perfectly fine. Leave me alone, damn it. I can get up on my own." He met Aggie's eyes, and she was surprised to see a flash of real anger.

"I'm sorry," she said, wishing that she had never agreed to let them walk her back.

"Not your fault, unless you painted these cobblestones with grease," he said easily as he got to his feet and brushed off his trousers.

Will held out an arm. "Is your foot—?"

"I said I was fine. I do not require an examination. Unless, of course, Aggie wants to undress me and check all my vital signs?"

The nerve of him, flirting with her again, as though last semester's interlude in the tunnels had never happened. "You had your chance with me," she reminded him. "As I recall, you chased me like a dog running after a carriage—and then seemed at a complete loss when you actually caught me."

Byram looked discomfited and Will made a choking sound.

"Sorry," said Will. "Forgot how to swallow."

"Aggie," said Byram, "about last year… I enjoyed spending time with you, but if you thought that meant something more—"

"Then I'm five kinds of foolish," Aggie said, relieved to see that they had reached her boardinghouse, which meant an end to this exquisitely awkward conversation. "Don't worry, luv, I've got your number. You'll never give your heart to any girl."

For some reason, this made Byram look even more uncomfortable. "If I could choose to give my heart," he said with uncharacteristic seriousness, "I would give it to you, Ags." Then he turned abruptly and began heading back toward the hospital. Will shot her a quick look of apology before hurrying off to accompany his friend.

Well, that had been a masterpiece of awfulness, and now the pain in her ribs was a steady, throbbing ache. At this moment in time, a visit from some new Jack the Ripper might actually have been a blessing. At least, if something truly horrible happened to her, she wouldn't have to face Byram tomorrow.

Reaching into her apron pocket, she felt around for her skeleton key and fumbled it into the lock. An hour ago, she had been hungry, but now all she wanted was to lie down in bed and close her eyes for an hour or twelve. She opened the main door to the lobby and then walked as slowly as an old woman up the stairs to her room. The door opened with a creak, and there was a sharp squeak, a scuffle and then the muffled sound of laughter. The room was dark, but she could see furtive movements in the shadows.

Stifling a curse, Aggie rested her forehead against the door for a moment. "Sorry, Lizzie, but you'll have to relocate your anatomy lesson."

6

THERE WERE WHISPERS IN THE DARK, THE RUS-
tle of clothing and bedsheets, and then Lizzie adjusted the gas
lamp on the wall. It cast the room in soft golden light, revealing two identical brass beds, two white-painted pine dressers
and two small oval-backed chairs. The differences between
the two living spaces lay in the decoration: Aggie's side of
the room boasted a white crocheted bedspread, a lace doily
on her dresser and a decoupage knickknack box with shel-
lacked images of various artists' models admiring themselves
in mirrors while they used Pear's soap or Dr. Benton's den-
tifrice. After a day of cleaning up bedpans and mopping up
blood spatters, she liked a bit of order and prettiness about her,
and since she couldn't afford art, she selected the adverts that
used the new European style, art nouveau, with its curved
lines and jewel-like colors that made women look as mysterious as stained glass windows.

On Lizzie's side of the room, by contrast, there was an
untidy jumble of textbooks, papers, wool stockings, hairpins

and microscope lenses, and a chipped china cup overflowing with loose coins. In lieu of a bedspread, her bed was covered with a gray wool blanket purloined from the hospital—and by a strapping, six-foot-one male.

"Sorry to disturb you," said Aggie, putting her umbrella in the stand and untying her bonnet strings.

Lizzie pinned up a piece of unruly chestnut hair, which promptly fell back down again. "Haven't you ever heard of knocking?"

"Maybe you should've hung something on the doorknob, so I knew we had a male visitor. That's what the working girls do."

"Victor just stopped over for a few minutes on the way back to his room." Lizzie's cheeks were scarlet; Lizzie blushed more like a redhead than Aggie did. "And we weren't doing what you seem to think we were doing."

Aggie hung her cape on a hook. "You mean hugging the bear? Playing bread and butter? Making faces?"

"You're disgusting. What does that last one even mean?"

"Elizabeth was giving me a treatment," said Victor, sounding thoroughly offended. "With the magnetometer."

"Fine, have it your way." In all fairness, though, the wand-like device her roommate had invented to realign the body's electromagnetic fields was sitting on its cradle, and she didn't look as though she'd been tumbled—her wild mane of hair with its distinctive streak of white was more or less contained at the top of her head, all the tiny pearl buttons of her shirt-waist were still fastened, and her long skirt relatively un-wrinkled. As the school's only female medical student, Lizzie did not have to wear the standard uniform of lavender dress, long white apron and white cap. Her shirtwaist blouse and skirt were impossibly smart, made of much better fabric than Aggie could ever afford and expertly tailored.

It was Victor who looked thoroughly disreputable. He was wearing neither jacket nor waistcoat, and his shirt was gaping at the neck, revealing a generous amount of masculine skin and the gleam of the brass plate fused to the flesh over his heart and the two electrodes at his neck that marked him as a Bio-Mechanical.

"Far be it from me to give you a lecture on how to behave, Lizzie," said Aggie as Victor searched for some missing article of clothing, "but you might want to treat Victor in one of the wards next time."

"I did suggest that," said Victor, pulling his sleeve down over his left arm, which was grafted from another body and reinforced with brass implants.

"The wards are too public," said Lizzie. "We might as well just announce that Victor's a Bio-Mechanical." Lizzie pulled a cuff link out from beneath her pillow and handed it to him. "Here. We could come right out and explain that you weren't away for a year in a spa town in Germany, you were skulking about belowstairs and communicating in grunts. Of course, as a Bio-Mechanical, you would be a possession of the school with no legal rights, but hey, at least there would be no more secrets to keep."

Victor had been the school's star pupil, back in its old location in Yorkshire, until he had discovered a stunning secret about the old Queen—which had led to his waking up to find himself completely paralyzed and staring up at the ceiling of an operating theater. Believing him dead, Grimbald, the school's head of surgery, had turned his former protégé into a Bio-Mechanical. It had taken the faculty some convincing to accept that Victor was not just a mindless "corpse walker," but in the end, Lizzie had convinced them to allow him back into the school. It was probably petty to think it, but Aggie was certain that a less well-born and well-connected student might not have been as welcome. There were always exceptions made for those with money and connections that were not available to the likes of Aggie.

"You don't need to worry so much," said Victor, searching under the bed. "Ah, there it is." He draped his crumpled cravat around his neck. "Grimbald's in my corner now."

"You didn't hear Moulsdale last night," said Lizzie, placing the etheric magnetometer back in its case and closing the lid. "He promised the prime minister a Bio-Mechanical as advanced as the one the kaiser has supposedly got. That's a hell of a rabbit to pull out of his hat in less than three months."

"I have to admit, that worried me, too," said Aggie.

Victor pulled his cravat into an even knot, then pulled it apart again. "Grimbald has a theory that the critical factor is the freshness of the body, but the unvarnished truth is, I was still alive when they transformed me. Accidentally, of course. I can't see Grimbald agreeing to intentionally turn a living man into a monster." Victor made another unsuccessful attempt to tie his cravat correctly. "Blast."

"Here," said Lizzie, stepping in to help. "Let me do it."

"Sorry. When I'm tired, my left arm still operates a bit independently of my right." Most Bio-Mechanicals had no personality or memories intact from their former lives. Victor had two sets of memories, and two distinct personalities: his own and those of Jack, the original owner of the left hand and arm which had been grafted onto Victor's body. Jack's memories, though, usually took a back seat.

"There," said Lizzie, finishing the knot and giving her fiancé's cravat an approving look. "That should do."

Victor smiled down at her. "What would I do without you?"

Ugh. Aggie unscrewed her flask and took a quick swallow of her mother's sloe gin. There was nothing lonelier than standing in the force field of a couple's mutual attraction. The same force that drew them together pushed others away, and it was difficult not to feel as though they were the romantic leads in some dramatic play while she was cast into a background supporting role—the comic relief, or a sympathetic ear so the heroine could talk about her conflicted emotions and difficult choices, or a convenient plot device.

Best to aim for comic relief, then. Aggie took another swig of gin as Victor and Lizzie continued to argue about how monstrous he was or wasn't in soft, intense voices. "All right, I'm calling time. Say good-night so I can get ready for bed." Aggie replaced her flask in its hiding place. She hoped she sounded wry and halfway compassionate, when what she was really feeling was sorry for herself. The gin was burning a lovely path of numbness into her belly, but it was no substitute for having someone to hold her close and stroke her hair. *You know where that leads*, she reminded herself. That didn't stop her from wanting it, though.

"Sorry, Aggie," said Victor. "We didn't mean to make you uncomfortable."

"Then scoot so I can take off my damn corset."

Victor gave Lizzie a last, lingering look before opening the door a crack, glancing down the hall and then slipping out as Lizzie shut the door behind him. Turning to Aggie, she said, "You all right?"

"Just tired and cranky." Tired of keeping her own urges in check and cranky that Lizzie wouldn't do the same, at least in their shared quarters. Suddenly she remembered something. "I can't believe I forgot to mention it while Victor was here. I saw Henry Clerval when I was walking back."

"Are you sure?" Lizzie walked over to the window frame and tried to lift it.

"Pretty sure. I thought he was expelled last year."

"Actually, I think he took a leave of absence. I'll need to speak to Moulsdale about this. There's no way we're going to put up with allowing Victor's would-be murderer back in the hospital." Lizzie strained to lift the window again, but the wood was swollen from the radiator's heat.

"Here, you're going to break it. Let me do it." Aggie jiggled the frame and it gave way with a shower of small paint chips, letting in a gust of night air. She stood there for a moment, looking out at the other houses on the street. Jenny was out there in one of those buildings or one just like it. Poor girl.

"Okay, so what's really wrong?" Lizzie sat down beside her. "Spill."

Aggie waited until she had pulled her dress over her head before speaking. "My ribs hurt. Difficult patient."

"Do you want something for the pain? Willow bark tea?"

"That's all right. Just need to sleep." The gin had done its work, and Aggie felt as though she were a spring finally beginning to uncoil. Unhooking her front-lacing corset, Aggie breathed a sigh of relief as her tummy expanded to its natural shape. Whatever fashion genius had decided that all women needed to have breasts like swans and waists like weasels deserved a special place in hell. "Can you turn out the light?"

"Hang on, I just need to get my nightdress on and brush my hair."

Aggie closed her eyes and tried to sink into sleep, but vexing thoughts kept bobbing to the surface, keeping her awake. After a moment, she said, "Lizzie—there are other things that can happen, if you keep meeting Victor alone in the room."

"We're not stupid, Ags."

"Everyone's stupid when they're in love. I just... I don't want you throwing your career away."

"I don't intend to. Look, I'm a medical student, remember? I know about biology. And I'm not going to—what was it you said? Make faces. At least, not without taking some precautions."

Aggie laughed, trying to conceal her surprise. "Well, well, well. So you're taking precautions?"

Lizzie's blush was so fierce her face was glowing. "I said I would. If I needed to."

"Condoms? Vinegar-soaked sponges? Imagining Shiercliffe's face at the critical moment? Some methods are more effective than others, you know."

Lizzie dimmed the lamp. "I thought you wanted to sleep. So sleep."

The truth was, for all her bawdy talk, Aggie had never actually discussed birth control with anyone. She knew about condoms and sponges from eavesdropping on her mother, who used to advise married women desperate not to get pregnant again. It would never have occurred to Aggie's mother to tell an unmarried girl how to avoid getting pregnant.

As she drifted off, she thought hazily about what it might be like to touch a boy who didn't lose interest the moment the touching was over.

"Aggie. Aggie. Aggie."

She opened her eyes with a start to see one of the laundresses leaning over her, her face pinched with worry. There was a shiny burn mark on the girl's cheek, and Aggie struggled to recall her name. Clara. "Is it morning?" Her mouth felt dry.

"No. It's Jenny." For a moment, this response made no sense, but then Aggie realized what Clara meant, even as she said the words: "She's been hurt."

7

THERE WAS A TRICK TO STAYING OUT OF TROU-
ble when you were passing through a troubled place, especially in the small hours of the morning, when the streets were
still shrouded in shadows and fog. Walk with a purpose, but
not too brisk or it would look like someone was chasing you.
Stay alert, but don't tense your shoulders. Don't smile when
there's nothing to smile at but don't scowl, either. Above all,
don't second-guess yourself and look back the way you came.
Do that, and you wouldn't see what was coming at you until
it was too late.

The buxom redhead was doing just fine, watching her step
in the muddy, cobbled street, remembering to glance up in
time to avoid the costermonger's rattling pushcart—no jel-
lied eel for her today, ta very much, she's got places to be. She
carried her carpetbag like she had some muscle under that
black wool cape, but her small, beribboned hat was a good
twenty years out of date. From the hang of the cape, she also
had a hidden pocket on the left side—probably sewed her

valuables in, because London, the East End, hotbed of vice, can't be too careful.

Dodger put his boot up on a low wall so he could buff it with the sleeve of his jacket, watching out of the corner of his eye to see if Red would trip over the street urchins playing marbles on the stoop of the narrow wooden building, their hands and feet wrapped in rags to keep out the chill of the winter night. Most of London's children would be abed at 3:00 a.m., but these lot were waifs and strays, and no one told them what to do.

Red navigated the guttersnipes like a pro, flicking her skirts out of the way of a bright blue toe-breaker that went wide. Dodger nodded at the kinchin as he followed the redhead's progress down the lane. Interesting—she didn't bat an eye at the rancid wagtail leaning against a streetlamp, her haggard face ghastly under the flickering gaslight as she muttered sibyllic curses under her breath. Red might be lost, but she didn't look lost, and that was half the battle won right there.

The old bawd grinned at him as he passed, revealing the gaps between her rotting teeth. "Is it work or play you're after with yon glimmery wench?"

"Work, as always, Mother Fusty Luggs."

"Ooh, but can I watch?" She made an obscene gesture with her hands.

"Not tonight."

"Single-o, eh? Suit yourself." She cackled and blew him a kiss, and Dodger tugged at the brim of his top hat. He had to hand it to Faygie—her own mother might not have seen through her old tart's disguise. It was an ingenious way for a young girl to keep herself safe from gropers and lechers and snatchers. A young woman, walking on her own, could attract all kinds of predators.

Like this one. He was keeping his distance, waiting for the best moment to approach, when she went and broke the rules. She hesitated a step, seemed uncertain. She looked back, revealing her uncertainty.

You didn't want to do that in the rookeries. Of course, Dodger thought, watching as she hesitated, looking back was a mistake in other places, too. Look what it had done to Lot's wife—pillar of salt. Look what it had done to Orpheus—lost his girl, then got him torn to bits by a bunch of frenzied virgins.

Hang on, Red was on the move again, shaking off the lethargy of confusion and setting off like she knew where she was going.

Where was she off to, with such determination? To visit her lover? Pay for the upkeep of a bastard child? Perhaps she was off to pawn some bauble or to purchase an hour's oblivion.

She was mid-stride when Mad Stan jumped out at her from behind a wooden crate, grinning like a hideous jack-in-the-box. "Oh, the devil, the devil, the devil's dam," he sang tunelessly. She reared back; Mad Stan hadn't bathed or changed his clothes in years, and the smell of piss and gin he gave off could make your eyes water.

She ducked her head down and tried to walk past him, but Mad Stan moved to block her way, waving his arms as if trying to conjure something. "Scarlet woman, dance with me?"

"I'll kick you in the goolies, that's what I'll do. Let me pass."

Clearly, this was no lavender-water miss. Back in whatever county she came from, she probably sent fellows packing, tails between their legs. Too bad her savvy wouldn't help her much here.

"Give us a kiss first." Mad Stan bobbed and bowed in front of her like a drunken courtier, and now the street urchins had caught the scent of prey. Scooping up their marbles, they scrambled around her. "Are you lost, miss?"

"Spare us a tuppence!"

"Whatcher got in that big leather bag?"

"I haven't eaten in days, miss."

"D'ye need a place to kip the night?"

Dodger hung back, wondering how she'd handle the children; you could tell a lot about a person by how they treated stray dogs and street urchins.

"No, thank you," she said, firmly but not unkindly, in a teacherly sort of voice. She didn't show by so much as a flicker of an eyelash that they were blocking her way, but Dodger would have wagered supper that she was perfectly well aware of it. "I'm looking for Miller's Court. In Spitalfields. I don't suppose one of you could direct me there?"

"But of course, miss," said the oldest boy, who looked about eight but was probably closer to twelve. "For a shilling."

"Do I look like the kind of person who has a shilling to spare?"

The boy was unfazed. "You look like the kind of person who don't want to be wandering around these streets all night. And that's the worst street in London, that is."

Red hesitated, and the boy pressed his advantage. "Of course," he said with a smile, "we can make another kind of arrangement, if you can't afford the dosh." More like thirteen then; East End children grew up fast, if at all.

"What's that? I think your mother's calling you," she said,

shouldering past the boy, who nodded to one of the smaller children, who darted in front of her. Time to make his move, thought Dodger, before she was tripped and sent sprawling while the gang made off with her belongings.

She was *his* mark.

"Evenin', miss," he said, slipping through the knot of children and giving the leader a level look: *back off, this one's mine.* "I couldn't help but hear you might be in need of some assistance."

The children sidled off, throwing a few choice comments over their shoulders to save face. Dodger ignored them as the redhead sized him up.

"And who are you meant to be then?" Her accent was working class, from the north.

"The Artful Dodger, successful man of business, at your service." He held out his arms, displaying his tailcoat, the fine embroidery on his waistcoat and the silver watch fob.

Her eyes swept over him. "Sorry, luv," she said as she started to walk away. "I'm not buying whatever you're selling, and I'm not giving away anything you might want."

He fell into step beside her. "Perhaps I'm just a Good Samaritan wanting to help a maiden in distress."

She gave him a sidelong look. "Do I look distressed?"

"You look delectable, but these streets are a right maze if you don't know them."

She made an exasperated noise. "I can figure it out on my own." Looking at the alley, she hesitated, then chose to keep walking straight ahead, avoiding Mad Stan.

Dodger ambled along beside her, thumbs in his waistcoat pocket, trying to look as innocuous as he could. "Independent. I like that. Good thing you're not in a hurry, though."

Ah, that brought her up short. "Here," she said, holding a coin out in her gloved hand. "I'll give you sixpence for taking me there. And leaving directly after."

Oh, this was almost too easy. Anyone who showed sixpence had something better stashed away. Closing his hand around hers, he said, "Keep your coin, lovely. You can pay me when you're safe back home, if you like."

She faced him, and he knew he had won. She trusted him—a little, at least. "We need to get there the quickest way possible. Can you do that?"

"Just follow me." Dodger led her back through the alley, but this time, he whistled the first few bars of "Greensleeves," and Stan knew to keep himself to himself. She was a quick walker, the heels of her shoes ringing out on the cobblestones, and he could feel the tension in her. "What's your name, lovely? Or should I just keep calling you that?"

"Agatha DeLacey."

He glanced over his shoulder. "You don't look like an Agatha. Bet your friends call you Aggie."

She gave him a look that was not without humor. "But you and I," she said pointedly, "are not friends."

"Acquaintances, then," he said as they walked side by side. "Hang on," he said, grabbing her elbow and nudging her aside. "Puddle."

She gave him a wary look. "Is it much farther?"

"Almost there." Without breaking stride, he lifted her purse from inside her cloak, transferred it to his other hand and stashed it in his jacket pocket. "And what brings you out so late tonight? Secret meeting of the saucy redheads' society?"

She yanked her elbow away. "Touch me again and you'll have a black eye."

"Just trying to be a gentleman." No bracelets, but she was guarding the bag she was carrying closely, so it must have something valuable in it. He just needed to find a suitable counterweight, so she wouldn't notice when he had lifted it. "Oh, wait, I've got it. Attending a séance so you can handle a dispute over your grandmother's will."

"Will you just stop? A young girl might be dying right now. Could you please just shut up and take me where I'm going?"

He was quiet after that.

"This here's Dorset Street," said the young man with the unlikely name. It was a dark street of tall buildings, with huddled shapes clustered in doorways. At the sound of their footsteps, a feral cat that had been eating refuse froze, then bolted. "Miller's Court is just through this alley." Dodger, as he styled himself, seemed subdued as he led her through the narrow passageway. "What number?"

"Fifteen. Do you see a number?" It was difficult to tell with only the dim light from the building's windows to go by, but she thought the painted house number had peeled off or was now covered dirt.

"This is fifteen." He indicated a dilapidated building with smudged windows.

She hesitated. "How can you be sure?"

He shrugged. "Crossingham's common lodging house? Everyone knows it." Something in his tone made her think that Crossingham's reputation was not a good one, but that was hardly a surprise. She had already guessed that Jenny's family was poor, even by East End standards. Aggie reached into her pocket for her change purse and then frowned.

"That's embarrassing," she said, patting her cloak pockets.

"I was going to pay you for your trouble, but I don't seem to have my change purse with me. I was sure I brought it."

"No hard feelings," said Dodger. "Look, I'll even see you into the building."

Seventy years earlier, the lodging house might have been home to a decent family. Now it sheltered a constantly shifting cast of indigent strangers, and the entranceway stank of cabbage and piss. There was no light on in the landing and a bundle of rags in the corner shifted, revealing itself to be alive and the source of at least one of the odors.

Aggie stood at the bottom of the rickety stairs and peered up. "Jenny?" She paused, then called again. "Jen?"

Dodger came up behind her, which was a surprise. She wouldn't have thought he'd stick around. "You don't know which floor your friend lives on?"

She shook her head. "I just have the address. The girl who gave it to me had to get home to her kids."

"All right, then." Dodger knocked on the first door.

"What the hell do you want?" The man opening the door a crack looked as though he had just been disturbed in the midst of some unspeakable act. His eyes were red, and there was a glisten of grease on his lips and mouth.

"We're looking for—" Dodger began, but was cut short by a wrenching moan from upstairs.

"Jenny!" Aggie darted around him and raced up the rickety stairs, her boots pounding the old wood.

A woman with long gray hair opened her door halfway. "If it's the noise you're complaining about, you can go stuff it."

"No, no, I'm Agatha DeLacey—Aggie. I'm a nursing student at the hospital."

The woman chewed on the inside of her cheeks a moment.

"Oh, yeah—I know your name." She opened her door wider. "Come in, then."

The flat was as tiny and bleak as a prison cell, with soot-streaked walls from the coal-burning stove and no decoration except the wrapping from a package of Bird's Crystal Jelly Powder, hung on the wall like a picture.

"How long since she was attacked?" Aggie removed her cloak and hat and rested them on the back of a chair. The flat didn't have much in the way of furniture. Three children were curled up on a pile of blankets in the corner, asleep, and the family's only table was covered with loose pink and purple cloth petals, bits of wire and a small pot of glue. There was precious little money in making artificial flowers to adorn ladies' hats, and these children probably helped their parents from early in the morning until it was bedtime.

"Attacked?" Jenny's mother frowned. "Who told you she was attacked?"

"Jenny's friend Clara." Except now that she thought about it, maybe Clara had said something else, and Aggie had assumed she'd been attacked.

"Huh." Jenny's mother went over to one of her sleeping children and plucked a wire stem out of his hands. "Well, Jenny wasn't attacked. She went to see a doctor about a complaint she was having." She placed the wire stem on the table.

Aggie flashed on what Jenny had said to her, earlier that same day: *There's a doctor what says he can help me, only he charges an arm and a leg.*

"What happened with the doctor?"

"Ask her yourself." Jenny's mother indicated the other end of the flat, where a privacy screen had been pulled up, partly concealing the bed and its occupant. "No anesthetic, and he left her to walk home on her own, still bleeding." The woman gave Dodger a dark look. "That's what comes from trusting men." It reminded Aggie of what she had told Jenny: *Don't put your trust in white coats.*

"Maybe I should wait downstairs," said Dodger, his elfin face looking a bit pale.

"Wait!" Aggie hated to show weakness, but she had to admit that she was likely to get lost trying to find the way back on her own. "Can you wait to walk me back?"

"I didn't say I was going to leave," he said, holding his hat in his hands. "I'll wait for you below. I just can't bear the smell of blood."

She gave him a searching look. "All right." She fought the urge to tell him how grateful she was. Either he would be there when she was done, and she would tell him then, or he wouldn't.

Aggie asked for a pitcher of water and a basin to wash her hands, then walked over to the back of the flat. She pulled aside the privacy screen and then replaced it so she and her patient were shielded from view.

"Hello, Jenny," she said, sitting down on a stool beside the bed. "How are you feeling?"

"Like death, twice warmed over." Jenny's face was chalky, and there was a dark stain on the gray woolen blanket covering her. "Guess you're going to say I told you so."

"Of course not. But I do need to examine you."

Jenny turned her head away, as if she could separate herself from the rest of her body. "I don't care what you do."

Aggie gently pulled the blanket up. "Can you tell me anything about the procedure?"

"I would think you could use your imagination."

Aggie rubbed her hands together to warm them. "Can you tell me anything about the doctor or his practice? Was he from the Royal Victoria?" On closer examination, there was some bleeding, but that was to be expected.

"Not there," said Jenny, her voice tight with pain. "At the other place you was. Ingold."

Aggie frowned. "What was his name?"

Jenny closed her eyes. "Don't remember."

"What did he look like?"

"His hair was ginger—what was left of it. Googly-eyed bugger, but he spoke all posh."

That sounded like Henry Clerval. Like Victor, Henry had been a third-year student when he had left school, but unlike Victor, Henry's ambitions had outstretched his abilities. She wondered if he had been stealing supplies when she spotted him leaving the hospital earlier.

"I knew it was a mistake the minute I walked into his office," said Jenny. "He had these jars filled with hearts and livers and such, and an amputated arm swimming in some sort of chemical bath. Thought he was going to chop me up for parts."

That was certainly a peculiar choice in medical office decoration, but perhaps Clerval thought it made him stand out from the other quacks. "All right," she said, pulling down Jenny's skirt. "I think the bleeding is going to stop and you're going to be just fine, but as a precaution, I'll leave you with some styptic powder to encourage blood clotting."

A little while later, Aggie stepped out from behind the screen. Jenny's mother was sitting nearby, slumped over in a chair. "I've done everything I could," she said. "If you don't mind, I need to wash my hands again." There was no response. "Ma'am?" It took her a moment to realize that the older woman's chin was resting on her chest. She had fallen asleep.

"She was nipping at the gin to steady her nerves," said Dodger, startling Aggie as he unfolded himself from the floor where he had been sitting. "Not that I blame her. She left out the pitcher and basin, though, and a sliver of soap." He walked over to the table and picked up the pitcher of water. "Here. Put your hands out."

"Thanks," she said as he poured water over her hands. She lathered her hands with the soap and then held them out to be rinsed. "Thought you were going to wait downstairs."

He shrugged, handing her a towel. "Sometimes I surprise myself." He glanced over at the decorative screen shielding Jenny and the bed. "She going to be all right?"

"It's difficult to say. I hope so." In cases like these, death didn't always arrive in a dramatic torrent of blood. Sometimes, it sneaked catlike into the room and toyed with the patient, seizing them and releasing them again and again before finally taking the killing bite.

Don't think like that. Jenny will be fine.

Dodger held out her gloves and cloak. "You ready to head back now?"

She was too tired to guess why he was being so kind to her, or figure out what he expected in return. "Dear God, yes," she said. If there was a price to be paid, she'd deal with that later.

8

THE GLEAM OF A STREET VENDOR'S LANTERN
shone through the darkness. Aggie wasn't sure what he was selling, but the rich, nutty smell of roasting beans was wonderful.

A small crowd of customers was standing around, sipping
from chipped mugs and nibbling thin slices of bread spread
with butter. Two plump women wearing thin, shiny gowns
and rouged cheeks were chatting with each other, while two
younger girls sat nearby, pale and thin from factory work. A
drover on his way to the meat market leaned on his cow as
he chewed on a piece of bread.

"I'm surprised so many people are still awake," Aggie said.
It was a little after five in the morning.

"Some are still awake," agreed Dodger. "Others are just
getting started."

She paused as she watched the vendor put a mug under the
brass tap of a large tin pot and hand it to a man with a wheel-
barrow full of turnips and parsnips.

"That's not tea," she said.

"Nah, it's coffee. Want a cup?" Dodger reached into his pocket and gave the coffee seller a penny. After glancing at a young boy standing in his bare feet beside him, Dodger tossed the seller a second penny. He handed the boy a cup of coffee and a buttered slice of bread first, and then handed the next one to Aggie. He brought her over to a low bench that had just been vacated by two other customers and watched as she tasted coffee for the first time.

"What do you think?"

She took a second sip. It was stronger than tea, and she thought she might have wanted a bit more milk and sugar in it, but after taking a bite of the buttered bread, she decided it was fine as it was. "I like it."

"Brings you back to life, doesn't it?"

She took another sip and felt more wide awake. "That it does." It was odd, sitting next to this strange boy in a strange city, surrounded by other night owls. She watched the two soiled doves as they laughed and gossiped, then caught the drover letting his cow lick the butter from his hands. When she turned around, she caught Dodger watching her.

"All done?"

"Yes, thank you."

He took their cups back to the vendor and then walked beside her away from the light and the people, his hand hovering near her elbow but not quite touching. She stumbled, and that was the excuse he had been looking for. His hand closed over her elbow, making her feel warm. She stopped in her tracks.

"Why are you doing this?"

"Holding your arm?"

"No." She gave an impatient shake of her head. "All of this.

Taking me there, buying me coffee, bringing me home—what are you expecting in return?"

"Nothing."

"So you were just helping me out of the goodness of your heart?" She snorted. "Pull the other one."

"Maybe at first I wasn't thinking of helping you," he admitted. "But I'm not looking for anything now."

She turned to face him, withdrawing her arm from his hand. "Come on. You're a thief. You don't just help people." Suddenly, she realized something. "You pinched my change purse earlier tonight, didn't you?" She held out her hand. "Give it back."

His dark eyes held hers without a trace of embarrassment. "Check your cape pocket, Aggie. I already did."

She patted her pocket—it was there.

"Count it, if you like," said Dodger. "It's all there."

"Don't think I won't." Glaring at him, she opened the purse and counted each coin. He'd been telling the truth, though—he had left it all, down to the last thrup'ny bit. "What's your game, then? And don't hand me some rubbish line about love at first sight."

"Don't you believe in such a thing?"

Aggie stashed the purse back in her pocket. "Even if I did, it's not for the likes of girls like me. Or boys like you, for that matter." She knew she couldn't be looking particularly pretty at the moment, but she was well aware of her appearance even at her best: solid. Buxom. Strong. Not the kind of girl who got escorted and protected and cosseted. As for Dodger, he was a flash man, fond of quick wins and hasty escapes.

He shook his head, bemused. "So sure you know what I'm like?"

"So sure I know what men are like."

His laugh was a mixture of ruefulness and admiration. "Good Lord," he said. "You're more jaded than I am."

Maybe it was the whole unsettling drama of the night, or the unexpected impulse she felt to step into Dodger's arms and rest her head on his shoulder. Whatever the cause, anger flared in her, making her reckless and bold. "Give it a rest. What is it you're after, if it's not money? This?" Her gloved hands grabbed at his lapels as she tugged him closer and kissed him hard on the mouth.

It was a quick, blunt mockery of a kiss, intended to take this impudent lad down a notch. She drew back, folding her arms in front of her. "Or were you hoping for more than just one chaste kiss? A little tongue, perhaps? Or perhaps a five-minute alleyway romance?"

She expected some equally brazen rejoinder, or perhaps a passionate denial—*no, no, such base thoughts never crossed me mind*. Instead, he reached up and touched her cheek with such tenderness that she forgot to move away. "I didn't hope for anything. That was my first kiss, by the by."

"Now, that's a load of bull."

"On me life. Strike me down if I'm lying."

She gave a huff of exasperation. He was confabulating, of course he was, but there was a tiny sliver of doubt in her, and just in case he was telling the truth, she leaned forward and closed the distance between them again. A first kiss shouldn't be done in anger, after all. She pressed her mouth to his and then paused, their lips barely touching, breathing each other in and out. "There," she said softly. "That's better."

Then, for no good reason, she found herself closing that miniscule distance and kissing him again.

It was very different from kissing Byram—different from kissing any boy she had ever kissed before. He seemed to have no plan, no agenda, no final destination in mind. She was almost exactly his height, and everything lined up with startling, riveting exactness—chest to chest, belly to belly, hips to hips. They kissed some more, and then he buried his nose in her hair, breathing in the scent of her neck, nuzzling the curl of her ear. He pressed kisses into her skin, then cupped her jaw in his hand and kissed her again before leaning his forehead into hers.

"We should probably get you back."

"Yes," she said, flustered. "Sorry. I shouldn't have done that." Yet she knew, given the chance, she would probably wind up doing it again. She knew how to protect herself against most boys' stratagems, but this streetwise romantic was something unexpected.

He grinned at her. "Sorry won't do it," he said. "You compromised me."

She looked pointedly around them at the empty alley. "No witnesses."

"I was saving my first kiss for my one true love."

She snorted. "True love, me unbustled arse." Not that he meant a word of it.

He took her hand and raised it to his lips, his eyes sparkling with mischief. "I'll kiss that, too, if you like."

"Come on," she said, cuffing him lightly on the shoulder. "Let's get walking before you start composing a sonnet to my charms."

"Too late," he said, falling into step beside her. "I'm utterly besotted with you now."

"Not my fault if you're that easy."

"Blaming the victim? Typical."

She laughed at his affronted tone, and the spark between them flared back to life. "What do you want, Dodger?" This time, she did not ask it as a challenge, and this time, he didn't pause to consider the answer.

"I don't know. Maybe…just to get to know you better?"

"Sorry, luv," she said with a pang of regret, "but that's one thing I can't afford."

9

WILLIAM FRANKENSTEIN KNEW HE WAS IN TROU-
ble. He was fine as long as he remained stationary, propped up
by the polished mahogany bar, but when he moved his head
too quickly, the entire lavishly decorated room seemed to ro-
tate on its axis. He wished he could sit down, but that was
impossible. The Crown might be one of London's most luxu-
riously appointed gin palaces, filled with marble accents, gilt-
embossed wallpaper and an elaborately framed mirror over
the bar to reflect the profusion of flickering glass sconces, but
it catered to the poor, and the one luxury it did not offer was
a seat. The advert over the bar showed His Royal Highness
Prince Albert in full Highland tartan, saluting a bottle of The
Celebrated Balmoral Mixture, but even this elixir only cost a
penny a glass.

Unlike the public houses that offered cheap cuts of meat and
oysters, gin palaces served no food and offered no seats, and
most of the day laborers and washerwomen standing around
Will were drinking their dinner while growing steadily more

belligerent. On Will's left, a red-nosed man kept thumping his copy of *The Police Illustrated News*.

"It's happening, I tell you," he told his companion, a blowsy woman in a battered hat decorated with one cloth daisy. "The kaiser's secret corpse walker army is preparing to invade our shores!"

"You can't believe all the rubbish you read in that rag," said the woman. "Last week they was reporting that some amorous octopus attacked a bunch of girls on Brighton beach."

"Oh, yeah?" The man peered at her suspiciously over his glass of gin. "And how do I know you ain't one of them German spies?"

Will turned carefully to check on Byram, who was on his right, chatting up a curvy blonde in a faded red dress. "You're awful," she said to Byram in a tone that implied quite the opposite.

"Hullo, Will," said Byram, his arm draped over the bar so that it almost touched his companion's shoulder. "Meet Nancy."

Nancy's eyes gleamed with mischief. "A good friend, from what I hear," she said, offering her hand. He could feel the warmth of her skin through her lace half gloves. What exactly had Byram been telling her? Not the truth, but perhaps some hint of it, tucked in between the old stories about childhood friendship and boarding school hijinks. Nancy looked too young and fresh-faced to be a dollymop, but there was no mistaking her easy smiles. "Seems you two have gotten up to all sorts," she added. Dear Lord, she couldn't mean— Byram wouldn't tell her about *that*, would he?

"I've been telling Nancy all about the travails of being a second-semester medical student," said Byram, as if reading

Will's mind. "And that little prank we played with the skeleton in Grimbald's anatomy class."

"Oh, right. Of course." Will gave a weak laugh.

"You two certainly know how to have a good time," said Nancy, draining her glass. "I like a good time, myself."

I'll just bet you do, thought Will, and then realized what she was saying. "Byram, Old Man, it's getting a bit late. Perhaps we should be getting back to our room?"

"It's not even midnight yet," said Byram, regarding Will out of half-closed eyes before turning back to the pretty tart. "Oh, look, your glass is empty, Nancy. Can't have that. What are you drinking? Cream of the Valley? Dew of Ben Nevis? Mother's ruin?"

"Order me a gin shrub, darling, and I'll be eternally in your debt."

"Will you now?" Still gazing at Nancy, Byram said, "And what about you, Will? What d'ye fancy?" For a moment, Will found himself staring at his friend, struck anew by how handsome and un-British he seemed. With his thick, darkly waving hair and dark eyes, he could have been an Italian princeling or a Romany musician. Then Will became aware of Nancy, observing him as he watched Byram with amusement. *She's got your number*, he thought.

"Beg your pardon," he said, "but I have to go see a man about a dog." He nodded abruptly to Nancy, then accidentally kicked Byram's walking stick, which had been leaning against the side of the bar. It fell to the floor with a clatter, but Will didn't dare bend to pick it up. "Sorry," he said, making his shaky way toward the door.

Outside, the cold air made Will feel fractionally more alert, but The Crown's brilliant gaslight forced him to squint. Like most gin palaces, The Crown advertised itself with an enormous light fixture, and the three rows of flickering burners illuminated the street outside the establishment like a fisherman's lure. It was late, though, and there were only two figures standing in the shadows, looking as though they were undecided about where to spend their coin. Even addlepated from the gin, Will noticed that they seemed an unlikely pair. They were both young, but while one was dark and broad and unshaven under a workman's cap, the other was slender, with an aesthete's blond hair worn under a gentleman's top hat. The thought of what might bring those two together brought a flush to his cheeks and made him dart his gaze away.

Ducking into the shadows of the alley, Will leaned against the filthy wall and attempted to unbutton his fly. Damn, he was thoroughly stewed. He didn't want to think about how he would feel in class tomorrow morning.

Being drunk always sneaked up on Will. Normal people had a drink and felt it smooth the rough edges away. *But I'm not normal, and not just when it comes to drinking.* All day, every day, he was constantly, exquisitely, painfully conscious of himself, like an actor in a play who knew he was wrong for the part. Wherever he went, whatever he did, he was goaded by a sly little voice in his head that whispered, "There's a reason you don't feel like you measure up to your brother."

Victor had been the inquisitive one, the bold one, willing to risk bruises and broken bones to investigate what might be hidden in the rafters, and cheerful about enduring the pain if the gamble didn't pay off and he fell. Will had been the moody child, too sensitive, happy to have his adventures within the pages of a book.

One night, he had been seated in a large chair in the library, reading, and his father hadn't realized he was there. "Will should have been a girl," his father told his mother. "But since he's not, you'd best stop treating him like one." They had sent him off to Eton after that, clearly assuming that the company of boys his own age would thrash some toughness into him. Instead, he had found Byram.

Chin up, Will. It's a good thing we get to see the future leaders of our nation before they have the wit to mask how monstrous they really are.

Byram had been the first person to say that Will had a hollow leg. "He looks like a slip of a fellow," he liked to tell people, "but don't try to match him or he'll drink you under the table." It was true, up to a point. The first drink hardly registered with him. Gin was much easier than beer to drink, at least for him, and if he drank the second glass quickly enough, he began to feel a little quieter in himself. By the third drink, he could contemplate his brother and Lizzie without the roiling shame of remembering the night he'd discovered that Victor was alive—reanimated as a Bio-Mechanical. He had tried to shoot his brother that night and had nearly murdered Lizzie instead. They had both forgiven him, but he still felt a twist of misery whenever he thought about it.

Or, at least, whenever he thought about it sober.

By the fourth drink, he could even joke about that night. He could talk about his inability with firearms and his lack of athletic ability as if it were all a huge joke, and look at Byram without worrying that he would give himself away.

Unfortunately, at some point, he always had another.

Five drinks in, and he was all too willing to give himself away. At that point, his legs felt a long, long way from his brain, and he thought about the likelihood that he would fail out of school, or worse, not fail, and have to spend the rest of his life as a mediocre doctor and the genial visiting bachelor at other people's family tables.

He also thought about all the nights when Byram couldn't sleep because his bad foot was aching, and how he used to massage the twisted muscles until they unknotted and his friend's breathing slowed. He thought about the nights he hadn't stopped until Byram's breath grew ragged again. *We're getting a bit old for schoolboy pranks, Will.*

Byram had always been skittish about the times they touched each other, but ever since the night they had walked Aggie home, he had seemed more distant. William didn't know everything that had happened between the two of them, but back at Ingold, he had been jealous of the way Byram looked at Aggie. Then something had changed. What had she said, the other night? *A garden variety pervert.* Will was certain Aggie hadn't meant to insult Byram, yet that evening had marked some kind of change in him.

And now he was romancing this gin-house tart. No, that was unfair. But Will didn't want to be fair, he wanted... He wanted things he couldn't have.

Will came to himself with a start. He must have drifted off, a daft thing to do when you were standing propped against a filthy alley wall with your trousers partway undone. *Time to do your business and then get yourself home,* he thought.

"Having a bit of trouble, are we?"

Will flinched, startled by the voice behind him. "Afraid I'm a bit fuddled," he admitted, not turning around. "I'm all right, though." The speaker sounded like a gentleman, so perhaps he was just checking to make sure that Will was all right.

"Are you certain? Perhaps you need a helping hand?"

Dear Lord, perhaps the stranger was checking on him for an entirely different reason. Will shook his head, buttoning himself up. "Appreciate the offer, but I'm just heading back in." Maybe there would come a time when he stopped thinking about his friend and roommate and considered other options, but this was not the night.

"Don't be so hasty." It was the young man who had been loitering in front of The Crown with his thuggish companion. He was a little too thin, but still good-looking, even if his breath did have a faint, unpleasant, medicinal smell. "What's your name? I'm Oliver Twist."

"William Frankenstein. But I'm afraid I can't stay. My friend is waiting for me inside," said Will, giving the man an apologetic smile as he turned to leave.

"I could be your friend." Now the man was standing directly in front of Will, blocking his way. A prickle of unease penetrated the fog of gin and fatigue around Will's brain.

"Please, don't hurt me."

Twist raised his eyebrows and smiled as if Will had told him a secret. "Who said anything about hurting?"

"I've got some money," Will stammered, reaching into his pockets and pulling out some notes. He felt sick from gin and embarrassment. He wanted Twist to take the money and leave him alone—or, at least most of him wanted that.

"That's obliging of you." Twist stuffed the notes into his own pockets. "Now, what were you wanting to pay me for?" He took a step closer.

"My friend will be looking for me." The bright glitter of the gasworks was just around the corner. There were people, crowds, Byram, just feet away from him.

Twist put one finger under Will's chin and leaned in, and

mingled with his anxiety, Will felt an unwelcome flutter of excitement. "So let him look."

"What the bloody hell is going on out here?" It was Byram, appearing in the alleyway, the girl clinging to him. "Is this man robbing you?"

"Not at all." Twist's smile was wry. "I never made a threat. I made an offer."

"Well, he's not interested, so on your bike, friend."

Twist gave Will an assessing look. "You certain he's not interested?"

Byram lifted the elegant, ebony-handled walking stick he carried on longer walks. "Dead certain." He smacked the cane against his hand.

"Didn't realize he was yours." Twist made a mocking bow, then addressed the girl in the worn red velvet dress. "Seems we were both wasting our time, Nancy."

"Speak for yourself," said the girl with a laugh. "I got free drinks. Come on, Twist, I'm in the mood for a meat pie."

The two strolled off, chatting, leaving Byram and Will alone.

"Thanks, Byram," said Will, but Byram turned on his heel and began walking at a pace that made Will have to run a few steps to catch up. "I wasn't encouraging him," he said, but Byram refused to even look at him.

After three blocks, Byram's bad foot gave out, twisting under him and forcing him to stop. Grateful for the excuse, Will put his arm around his friend's back. "Lean on me."

Without a word, the two walked arm in arm until they reached the row of small houses where most of the medical students rented rooms. Then they slipped apart, even though plenty of the other students stumbled home drunk enough to need a supporting hand.

Later, lying in his bed, Will could hear from Byram's breathing that he was awake and in pain.

"Is it your foot?" For a long moment, there was no response.

Then, with a low curse, Byram snapped, "What were you thinking?"

For a moment, Will was confused. "You mean, in the alley? I was relieving myself!"

"So it would seem. Don't you know the risks, Will?"

Will flushed. "Not like that. I meant…"

After a long silence, Byram said, "I'm going to have to get married someday. You can't lose your head every time I talk to a girl."

Will didn't know what to say. He was tired, and even though he was no longer drunk, he was certainly not sober. "If you want a girl," he said, "what was wrong with Aggie?"

They had never spoken about this before. Byram was silent for so long that Will began to drift off, and when he finally did speak, Will wasn't completely sure he had heard correctly.

"Nothing was wrong with Aggie. She just started to expect too much. Like you. I'm not built to be faithful to one person, Will."

It took a moment for the words to work their way under Will's skin, but once they did, they started stinging. Byram wasn't flirting with girls because that's what society expected of him—he was flirting with girls because Will was not enough for him.

Life would be easier if he could just shut off the faucet of desire and content himself with the arid consolations of poetry and books. He thought of his friend Justine, paralyzed inside an iron machine that helped her breathe. How long had it been since he'd visited her?

I'll see her tomorrow, he thought. He wouldn't have anything alcoholic to drink, either. He would exercise self-control and be healthy and stop wanting what he couldn't have. There was a French expression Byram liked to quote: *If they're not going to feed you, leave the table.*

Tomorrow.

Tonight, however, he just wanted to be able to fall asleep. He had been on the verge of sleep before, but Byram's confession had jangled his nerves. *I'm not built to be faithful to one person.* Why was the one person who upset him the only one who could make him feel better?

"You all right, Will?"

"Not really." He paused. "Can I come sleep with you?"

"Of course." Byram pulled back the covers and made room in his bed.

18

PEOPLE OFTEN MADE THE MISTAKE OF THINK-
ing that just because Justine Makepiece was paralyzed, she was
a sweet, childlike waif, as pure of spirit as she was in body.
They walked into her room and saw her delicate pale face—
the only part of her visible inside the metal cylinder that was
her prison and her lifeline—and thought of her as a lucent,
disembodied mind.

Yet even though she spent most of her day lying prone in an
artificial breathing machine, listening to the rhythmic pulsing
of a vacuum pump, Justine was far from being some angelic
creature. Untouched, yes. Innocent, no. After a mysterious
childhood illness left her with weak lungs and wasted legs,
Juliet's father had become obsessed with curing his only child.

Back in her old room at Ingold, her father kept her isolated
in an attempt to protect her from any possible breath of mi-
asmic air. As the head of engineering, Professor Makepiece
had invented the negative pressure ventilator that helped his
daughter breathe. For at least twenty-one hours out of every

day, she had to lie inside the metal canister that forced air in and out of her lungs. There were only a few scant hours each day she could spend on the outside, free to sit up, use her arms, and speak to people without staring up their nostrils.

Sometimes she felt like a princess who was under some cruel enchantment. But then, she had also been granted some highly unusual gifts, so perhaps it balanced out in the end.

All in all, she felt she had done all right. At the age of seventeen, she had completed a correspondence course in history at Oxford, been published in the editorial section of the *Times* on three different occasions and had struck up a number of epistolary friendships with influential people.

Her body might be trapped in this room, but thanks to her father's experimental electromagnetic treatments, her mind was stronger and freer than most.

Which was why it was so infuriating that she had hours and hours to wait before she could write back to Viscount Haldane. Across the room, she could see her writing desk and chair, the pages of blank paper, a bottle of her favorite dark violet ink and pen. Haldane's most recent letter sat at the front of her decorative metal letter holder. It gave Justine a little thrill of excitement to see a letter from a member of the Privy Council displayed so openly, but she knew that it was safe. If anyone unfolded the missive and read it, it would appear to be an innocuous message about Easter egg decorating, a German tradition that Queen Victoria and her late husband had brought to England.

It was only when the cutout paper mask was placed over the letter, blocking out some of the words, that the true message could be deciphered: *Professor Moulsdale assures Lord Salisbury and myself that the Dreadnaught Class Bio-Mechanical will be rolled out before the kaiser's Easter visit. Have you seen or heard any evidence supporting this claim?*

Haldane, who was likely to become the next Secretary of War, had concerns about whether the Bio-Mechanical program was truly the answer to the burgeoning arms race between Great Britain and Germany. After seeing how her own father had become morally compromised by his dedication to the program, Justine had her own concerns. For now, she was content to observe—and report.

Justine glanced at the clock on the wall. Nearly 1:00 p.m. Lizzie was almost an hour late—or perhaps she wasn't coming at all. *Blast.*

Justine heard the door open. "I was starting to think you weren't coming," she began, and then saw that it was Will.

"What a lovely surprise," she said, meaning it. When she had first met Will, she had thought he looked as handsome as a prince in a fairy tale, with his slender hands and the lock of slippery blond hair that always fell into his eyes. Even now, when she knew better, she felt a little flutter when he smiled at her.

"I realized it had been far too long," Will said, setting down a hamper. "How're you feeling today, Just?"

"About the same, I suppose."

You look worse, though. Will didn't say the words out loud, but Justine heard them all the same—an unexpected side effect of her father's unsuccessful attempt to transfer her mind into Lizzie's body. Makepiece had used the galvanic magnetometer to strengthen the electrical impulses of her brain as part of his plan to free Justine from the prison that did her breathing for her. The treatments had been excruciating, but she did not regret them. In the end, they had bestowed an astonishing benefit—she could read minds. In a way, Justine thought, her father's secret experiments had been successful. Even though it was only her mind that was free, at least she was no longer trapped inside her own head all day long.

Not that she deliberately eavesdropped on other people's thoughts. It was just hard not to hear Will's constant background noise of *Byram, Byram, Byram.*

"What have you been reading these days?" Will unpacked a thermos of tea from the basket, along with two wax-paper-wrapped sandwiches. "I miss the days when I had the time to read something other than medical texts."

"I'm reading the first installment of a new serial novel by Mr. Wells," said Justine. "Martians have just invaded and are attacking Shepperton."

"How fabulous. I'm sure Shepperton will be vastly improved." Will carefully arranged the lunch items he had brought on a tray. "How ever does Mr. Wells come up with these ideas?"

"From the columns of any newspaper," said Justine. "Every day I see a new opinion piece about the dangers of a German invasion." Even though Great Britain still had a vastly superior navy, Germany had been steadily improving its battleships with steam turbines and heavier caliber guns.

"Afraid I'm not much for reading newspapers," said Will, bringing the tray over and then looking horrified as he realized that there was no way for Justine to eat a sandwich or drink a cup of tea while lying on her back. "I—ah—I just realized that…"

"I just finished eating before you arrived," said Justine, figuring that the sweetened egg-and-milk concoction she drank through a metal straw must qualify as lunch. "Why don't you go ahead and tuck in? I won't mind."

"Are you sure?" Will pulled a chair closer to her, then sat a bit self consciously with the tray on his lap.

"Absolutely."

Will unwrapped a sandwich—cheddar with ploughman's pickle. She watched him take the first bite and permitted herself to dip into his mind for a moment so she could vicariously savor the bite and tang of cheese. "So," said Will, "tell me more about your new obsession."

"Actually, I think Lizzie is about to join us." She could hear the clamor of the other girl's thoughts more loudly than her footsteps as she approached the door.

"Sorry I'm so late," said Lizzie, sounding a little out of breath as she came into the room. "I was in the lab and lost track of the time."

"It's all right," said Justine, looking from Lizzie to Will. "I've had a surprise visitor to keep me company."

"Hello, Will," said Lizzie, but as he replied, she glanced over at Justine and thought, very clearly: *Do you want me to go and come back later?*

No, Justine thought back at her. *Stay.* Lizzie was the only person who knew about Justine's secret ability, and so she was the only person to whom Justine could speak, mind-to-mind. Of course, Lizzie was under the mistaken impression that Justine's powers were limited to the two of them. If she knew the truth, she might insist on all manner of tests and soon Justine's telepathy would become another weapon in Moulsdale's arsenal.

Justine did not trust that man enough to give him any more ammunition. This was why she wrote to Haldane, to gather information and assess where the Bio-Mechanical program was headed—and debate whether its ends could justify its means.

"Why is everyone so quiet all of a sudden?" Will walked over to the hamper. "Did you have any lunch, Lizzie?"

"No, and I'm ravenous."

"Go ahead and take mine," said Justine.

Lizzie was already unwrapping the wax paper. "Thanks."

Will poured a cup of tea and then passed it to Lizzie. "So, how is life in the laboratory treating you?"

"It's insane," said Lizzie, taking a sip of her tea. "There's a big push on to create a showstopper for the kaiser, and we've been working on this one Bio-Mechanical who is absolutely huge—we're talking six foot five and muscled like an ox. I think he was a longshoreman."

"Is that his main selling point?" asked Justine. "The fact that he's huge?"

Lizzie, who had just taken an ambitious bite of her sandwich, had to wait a moment before responding. "No, there are other enhancements. Dr. Grimbald is thinking about replacing the creature's right arm with an interchangeable semi-automatic rifle, Victor is experimenting with an alloy that will protect his heart and vitals, and I've been working on a mechanical eye that will increase his visual acuity."

"Enhanced vision? That's brilliant," said Justine.

"Well, it would be brilliant if only the Dreadnaught could make any use of them," said Lizzie, walking across the room to pour herself a cup of tea. "We've been trying different frequencies to stimulate the brain, but so far, all he does is grunt and drool."

"I can just imagine it," said Will, refilling his own teacup.

"Two armies facing off against each other, armed to the teeth, but the soldiers just stand there grunting at each other." He raised his cup in a toast. "Here's to a war to end all wars."

"Unfortunately, it sounds as though the kaiser's Bio-Mechanicals do a lot more than grunt and drool," said Lizzie, glumly contemplating what was left of her sandwich.

"Oh, well," said Will, "German engineering and all that." With a guilty look, he added, "Not that your father wasn't brilliant, Justine."

"Apparently not as brilliant as the Germans," said Lizzie.

They all sat in silence for a moment, considering this.

"All right, ladies, no point in stewing," said Will, standing up and brushing off the front of his trousers. "I'm sure we'll crack this nut. After all, we did it once. And if we managed to turn my brother into a Bio-Mechanical without compromising his intelligence, I'm sure we can do it again."

"Fair enough." Lizzie drained the last of her tea and then placed her cup back in the straw hamper. "But can we do it before Easter? That's an awfully tight deadline."

A terrible thought occurred to Justine. "Tell me something, Lizzie. Has anyone taken Victor to do any tests recently?"

"We don't have any exams right now."

"I mean medical tests. Has anyone asked to check his vitals or his eyesight?"

Lizzie looked as though she regretted bolting down her lunch. "How did you know?"

"I don't know anything. I'm just asking questions." She did not add, *I know because Moulsdale needs a showstopper of a Bio-Mechanical, and he has a limited window of time to add all the new improvements.* The firearm prosthetic, the alloy armor, the sniper-enhanced vision. So far, Moulsdale's team had only managed to produce one superior Bio-Mechanical—Victor. It stood to reason they might start to consider using him to replace their defective Dreadnaught.

Lizzie understood without having any of this spelled out.

"But Moulsdale promised!" Lizzie looked from Justine to Will and back. "That was the deal. I keep quiet about the queen being a Bio-Mechanical, and he holds his peace about Victor. He can't just turn around and decide that Victor's nothing but a machine."

"Moulsdale is a politician at heart," said Justine. "He'll do whatever he needs to climb to the top, and then he'll come up with some reason to justify it."

Will went over to Lizzie and put his arms around her. "Don't worry, Lizzie. We won't let anything happen to Victor."

Justine said nothing. Victor was her friend, and she would do what she could to protect him, but she didn't believe in making promises she might not be able to keep.

11

THERE WAS A SMELL TO OTHER PEOPLE'S LIVES, thought Dodger as he sorted through the latest bundle of stolen handkerchiefs, bowler hats and gloves. An aroma composed of tobacco mingled with homelier ingredients like vinegar and slightly rancid grease, with an underlying base note of stale sweat and unfulfilled dreams.

"What's taking you so long?" Faygie was pinning up a tart's red silk petticoat onto a mannequin so the stained bits didn't show. "If you pickpocketed things as slowly as you put them away, you'd be swinging from the gallows by now."

"We all have different strengths."

"And we can't always play to them. Sometimes, my friend, even a show horse needs to take a turn pulling the cart."

"That's how you ruin a good show horse."

Faygie shook her head but let him have the last word—for the moment. She was only a few months older than Dodger, which meant less than it once had, but she still liked to act the mother of their group. One of these days, Bill was going to refuse to go along with the pretense that Faygie was still in charge, and Dodger didn't know what would happen then—perhaps Nancy would talk him out of the confrontation, or perhaps the group would split in half, with Nancy and Bill going their own way. For now, though, things still felt pretty much as they always had.

"You're awfully quiet," said Faygie as she adjusted the petticoat.

"Just thinking. I like the St. Valentine's Day theme," he offered, indicating her latest project.

"It's absurd. What's romantic about mid-February? It's cold and gray and it gives me the morbids." She stepped back to examine the hang of the petticoat on a mannequin's form. "Hard to make any money from misery, though, so might as well peddle red hearts and romance." Other pawnshops kept the same display year after year, only removing an object when it was sold or redeemed and replacing it with another one. Faygie rearranged her wares constantly, carefully placing the stolen and pawned objects as if setting the stage for a new production. Now, in preparation for the holiday, she was bringing out all the scarlet knickknacks and vermillion tchotchkes from storage, arranging a single garnet brooch in a circle of cheap red glass beads, and propping a gaudy red leather prayer book in the arms of a red china devil figurine.

"Speaking of romance, when do you think Nance and Bill will get here?" It seemed unfair that they were off somewhere, presumably together, having an adventure or cuddling and kissing, while he was stuck with his least favorite part of the job.

"Never."

"Never?"

"I'm answering the question you're not asking, which is, when's she going to come to her senses?" Faygie met his eyes, then went back to sorting red silk flowers from the yellow and white and blue ones in a basket. "And the answer is, she is never going to look at you as though you've got some big secret to happiness tucked inside your mouth and she's only got to kiss it out of you."

Dodger experimented with folding one of the handkerchiefs into a rose.

"You think I don't know that?" he said handing Faygie the folded rose. "I stopped pining for Nancy ages ago."

"Really?" Faygie took a stuffed parrot and positioned it so it seemed to be pecking at the red glass rubies. "As I recall, it was only last week you was lamenting about how girls only love the blokes that treat them badly. And I said to you, 'It's the little bit of goodness mixed in with all that badness that puts the hooks into a girl's imagination.'"

"Maybe she just needs to readjust the proportions."

Faygie's all but invisible eyebrows went up. "That's a thought." She lifted a fringed pink scarf and wound it around the mannequin so it contrasted with the petticoat. "So… you've met someone new, have you?"

Damn, she is sharp. Dodger attempted to fold a white handkerchief into the shape of a swan, but the fabric was too soft.

"Someone who likes you back, for a change?"

He found a starched collar and used it to reinforce the swan handkerchief, letting his hands work out the shape while he thought about Aggie.

It seemed strange to even consider liking another girl. Yet there was something oddly familiar about Aggie. At first glance, she looked nothing like Nancy—Aggie looked like the kind of ripe milkmaid who decorated adverts for cheese and skin cream, while Nancy could have posed for a wild-haired Ophelia. Yet there was some quality that both girls shared. He'd had fantasies of Nancy grabbing him one day, the way Aggie had, and kissing him. He'd never realized how compelling it was, to be wanted like that. In stories and plays, heroes loved the distant, unattainable girl, and heroines loved the fellow who carried a torch for someone else. He'd assumed that nothing could shake his feeling for Nancy, until the shock of being desired had gone through him like a shot of gin and left him burning for more.

Maybe he would pick up some bauble for her and bring it to the hospital when it closed its gates tonight. No, Aggie wasn't the type to be tempted by paste jewels. Perhaps he could convince her to go to the pub for a harmonic evening—but wait, it was a Tuesday, so instead of comic songs and ballads the punters would be debating politics and whether or not the Germans were now a greater threat than the French.

Bloody politics. As if sitting around and arguing ever changed a damn thing that was wrong with the world.

"Don't think I haven't twigged that you're not saying no." Faygie pulled out a drawer of tangled copper and brass chains. "Here, leave off torturing the handkerchiefs. You can tell me the story of this new girl while you set the chains to rights."

This was easy work for his fingers, and he let them follow the knotted links. "No story to tell."

"Has she got her hooks in that deep already?" Faygie shook her head. "Just try to remember my motto—love's just another con game."

"I'm not in love with the girl. I'm just…intrigued." Dodger

focused on freeing one metal chain from the tangle and set it aside to concentrate on a larger one.

Faygie snorted. "Intrigued, is it? That's one step away from snared like a rabbit. Really, Dodger, I would have expected more of a—" She broke off as the bell over the door rang.

Bill brought the cold in with him, and the clinging, sulfurous smell of London fog. He stamped his boots on the doormat as his dog followed him into the room, then lifted the canvas bag from his shoulder and settled it on the ground with a clank. "Foul out there tonight," he said, more to himself than to Dodger or Faygie, as Bullseye shook herself and rubbed at her long snout with her paws. Dodger gave the dog an affectionate scratch.

"That's quite a haul," said Faygie, pulling a copper kettle out of the bag.

"We're all too old to waste our time picking pockets," said Bill. "It's time you and Dodger took it to the next level." Spotting his dog enjoying Dodger's attentions, he gave a whistle. "Oi. Bullseye. Come get warm."

The dog left Dodger and followed Bill over to the potbellied coal stove, her toenails clicking on the floor.

"You know how I feel about burgling," said Dodger.

Bill held his hands closer to the stove. "Yeah, well, sometimes you have to take a few risks."

"We've been through this," said Dodger. "I don't mind risking my own neck. I just don't want to wind up killing some bloke because he came home unexpectedly."

"Fancy a cuppa?" Faygie was already setting the kettle on the stove, eager to forestall any more conflict.

"Yeah." Bill flexed and unflexed his fingers. "Anything to eat? I'm famished."

"I'll put on some sausages." She pulled out a paper-wrapped package and carefully arranged four sausages on a cast-iron skillet, which she set next to the kettle. "Was Nancy with you?"

"Nah." Bill left the stove and sank down into a chair. "She took off on her own."

"Typical," said Dodger. "What did you do, start talking about how you was just friends the moment after you detached her from your face?"

Bill swung his booted feet up onto a table. "Least I'm honest."

Dodger snorted. "Yeah, you're a real prince."

"Dodger," said Faygie, "care to help make the tea?"

She was trying to distract him, but he walked over to the kettle anyway. "You're a piece of work, Bill." Dodger tried to keep his voice light as he spooned tea leaves into the chipped pot. "Why the hell do you keep starting up with her? You must recall what she was like after the last time you broke things off."

"I didn't have to break things off," said Bill. "We were never a couple."

The kettle began to whistle, and Dodger wrapped a cloth around the handle before removing it from the stove. "Is that what you told Nance? Smooth." The last time Bill had gotten Nancy's hopes up before squashing them, she had disappeared for a week. When she was upset, she took chances with herself, and Dodger couldn't help thinking about all the awful things that could happen to a young girl in the East End.

What had Twist said about digging up that poor girl? *If it's fresh enough, the doctors will buy a body piecemeal.*

"Come on, lads," said Faygie, prodding the sausages in the

pan so they gave a satisfying sizzle. "Nancy's a big girl, and we're all in need of something warm in our bellies."

As Dodger poured out the mugs of tea, he glanced at the mantelpiece where Faygie kept three clocks. One was a squat schoolhouse model made of wood, another was flanked by curling ceramic handles and rosettes and the third was made of brass and apparently stolen off a ship. They all kept slightly different times, so all Dodger knew for certain was that it was somewhere between half past six and a quarter past seven. "You think we ought to go look for her?"

"It's not that late," said Faygie, lowering the flame under the saucepan.

"True enough." Dodger handed Bill his mug of tea. "But it's a foul night out, you said."

Faygie turned the sausages, which filled the room with a savory smell. "How is the fog tonight, Bill?"

He shrugged, clearing his throat. "It's February." The fogs were always worse in the thick of winter, when coal fires burned in every house and business that could afford them.

"Last week, fog was so thick, I walked smack into a horse," said Faygie, offering Bill a plate of sausages. "My eyes was burning something awful."

"Your point?" His voice a low grumble, Bill took the plate while Bullseye licked her chops.

Faygie sighed. "My point is, maybe one of you should go and make sure she's all right."

Bill tossed one of the sausages to Bullseye. "Let Dodger go, since he's in such a fret."

Dodger said, "So you're not bothered?"

Bill took a bite of sausage. "Not particularly."

Dodger shrugged, and then, without planning, found himself swinging his arm to shove Bill's feet off the table, making Bill's chair rock backward. The chair overbalanced and the last two sausages went flying off the plate, but Bill was already rolling onto the balls of his feet. He grabbed the front of Dodger's shirt, hauling him up. "You angling for a beating?"

Dodger didn't flinch, even though his stomach was twisting with fear. "I'm just giving you what you want, Bill. You want to be the bad man? Go for it. Hit me." He flicked open Bill's knife, holding it up against the bigger man's carotid. "Or don't."

Over by the stove, Faygie drew in a sharp breath. "Jesus, Dodger, put that down!"

Dodger didn't take his eyes off Bill's. "Tell Bill to put me down, why don't you?"

"Both of you back down! Look at poor Bullseye—she's going to have an apoplexy!"

The dog was wide eyed with anxiety and trembling all over. When Bill and Dodger looked her way, she yawned and stretched and slunk over to them, her tail tucked between her legs.

"On the count of three," said Dodger.

"Sod off." Bill released him abruptly, forcing Dodger to move his hand away to avoid slicing his friend's throat.

"Arsehole." Dodger folded the knife shut and handed it back to Bill.

"Keep it. You need it more than I do, you scrawny bastard."

"Ta very much." Dodger slid it into his pocket. "I won't let it out that you did something nice. Wouldn't want to ruin your reputation."

Bill looked down at Bullseye, who was wolfing down the last of the sausages that had fallen onto the floor. "I'm not trying to be a big man here. I just don't think you can keep rescuing people from themselves. Nancy knows what Twist is. If she's after putting herself in harm's way to prove something and I go after her, then I'm just setting her up to do the same thing next time."

"Great argument, Bill," said Dodger as he shrugged on his wool overcoat. "You've just convinced yourself that sitting on your arse isn't just convenient—it's the right thing to do. Good as a bloody barrister, you are." It was as good an exit line as he was likely to get, and he timed it so he had his hand on the door handle when he said the final word.

The moment the door was open none of that mattered anymore. It took his brain a moment to recognize that the jumble of red velvet on the threshold was actually Nancy, her battered and bloody face pressed to the cold ground.

12

AGGIE WAS AT THE END OF A TWELVE-HOUR shift, the back of her head buzzing with fatigue as she tried to take down a patient's history. That morning, Shiercliffe had made an announcement. As part of preparations for the kaiser's visit, there would be renovations to the main operating theater, the receiving room and two of the wards, which meant extra work as patients were relocated and dust from the repair work was cleaned away.

"I'm sorry," Aggie said, trying to focus on the patient, a pinched-face man in his forties. "Where did you say the pain was located?"

The man looked flustered. "I don't like to say, miss."

That meant either kidney stones or syphilis. "How badly does it—?" She broke off as she caught a glimpse of Dodger striding into the receiving room. She was surprised by the jolt of excitement she felt, seeing him in his shabby tailcoat, battered top hat and red cravat.

"Sorry, mate," said a uniformed proctor, stepping in front of Dodger. "It's too late for any new patients."

"Sorry I couldn't fit my emergency into your schedule," said Dodger, scanning the room until his eyes settled on Aggie. She started to smile, then realized where she was and turned back to the flustered man.

"Now then," she said. "How badly does it hurt when you relieve yourself?"

"Agony," replied the man.

Probably kidney stones. "All right. I'll go tell the head nurse. You'll have to be admitted." She started walking across the receiving room, flinching a little when Dodger called out to her.

"Oi," he yelled, waving his arm. "Aggie!"

Dear God, what if Shiercliffe had heard? She walked over to where Dodger stood arguing with the mustachioed proctor. "I can't talk now," she said firmly.

Dodger put his hand on her shoulder, preventing her from leaving. "Afraid this can't wait."

The proctor grabbed the back of Dodger's jacket. "Hands off, mate," he said, dragging Dodger toward the door.

Dodger twisted and suddenly the proctor was holding an empty jacket and Dodger was standing in front of Aggie in his shirtsleeves. "You offered to pay me for getting you back to your room, remember? Well, consider this payback time." There was no trace of humor in his face or voice; whatever this was, it was serious.

"Fair enough," she said, hoping she could make him understand what he might be costing her here. "I owe you. But there's nothing I can do right now. There are still patients waiting to be seen before the gates shut, two of the night nurses are running late and the back of my head's about to explode."

Dodger's expression remained hard, and for the first time, it occurred to Aggie that he would make a formidable enemy. "Sorry to add to your troubles, darlin', but my friend's been beaten, and we can't wake her up."

"I'm sorry, Dodger. I didn't realize." She glanced at the big mantel clock that ruled her day. Nearly 7:00 p.m. Which meant there was an hour before the front gates closed for the night. *Think*, she told herself. What would Shierclife do? "Is your friend somewhere safe and warm? Is there anyone looking after her?"

"Yeah, but she doesn't seem right."

That didn't sound good, but then again, Dodger might be overreacting. On the other side of the room, Ursula Shiercliffe was deep in conversation with Professor Moulsdale and looking particularly unhappy. "Look, just watch your friend tonight— keep her warm and comfortable—and bring her round in the morning." She turned to leave but his hand on her elbow stopped her.

"The morning might be too late. Her heart's racing, and she's having trouble talking."

Which meant the girl probably needed a doctor or a trained and experienced nurse. Not that either one was likely to show up for her. "I can't leave for another half hour," said Aggie, without consciously making a decision.

"Make it fifteen." He hesitated. "Please."

There were four more patients to be assessed and sent home, and then she was meant to see that the cleaning staff had arrived to sweep the floors and dust and polish the intricate woodcarvings and brass doorknobs and railings. That would be half an hour at the very least.

Taking a deep breath, Aggie said, "I'll do my best." She smoothed her hands over the front of her apron as she approached Shiercliffe, trying to think of a way to frame this that wouldn't sound irresponsible or suspicious. An orderly moved a gurney aside, revealing Professor Moulsdale standing and talking to Shiercliffe, saying something to her that made the head of nursing clasp her hands together.

"...insufficient planning and preparation," Moulsdale was concluding. "The receiving room should be emptied of unseen patients by seven, or we will never be able to get done and have the gates closed by eight. We have a great deal to accomplish before the kaiser arrives."

"I promise you, we are on top of things," Shiercliffe responded, sounding surprisingly meek. "I am overseeing preparations myself."

The Bio-Mechanicals. Sometimes it seemed as though they were all that mattered. Aggie was beginning to resent the program more and more, seeing how real care for real people went by the wayside as the focus on Bio-Mechanicals intensified.

Shifting from one foot to the other, Aggie fought the urge to interrupt to get Shiercliffe's attention. Shiercliffe gave her the briefest of looks and an almost imperceptible shake of the head, which Aggie understood. Whatever her problem, she was not to break into this conversation.

Moulsdale puffed his chest out and hooked his thumbs into his waistcoat pockets. "Forgive me if I continue to have my concerns. What if there is some unfortunate accident in one of the factories, or if a steamship sinks? Are you going to throw all our planning up in the air to bandage wounds?"

"If there is some catastrophe, surely we should do our part—"

"Balderdash. There are other hospitals. What we are doing is more important than the lives of a few rookery rats." With that, Moulsdale walked off with a firm air of authority, no doubt to criticize someone else's performance of their duties.

"I'm sorry to bother you, Matron," said Aggie. "But I have to ask a question."

"Go ahead." There were shadows underneath Shiercliffe's eyes, which were red from fatigue.

"I need to ask if I can leave before the night nurses arrive."

Shiercliffe gave her a level look. "I know you aren't asking to leave because you have some minor ache or pain, which would be my first question to most of the other probationers."

Aggie nodded. "It's just—it's my time of month, Matron. I've been on my feet for the past six hours, and I need to use the facilities."

Shiercliffe rubbed the bridge of her nose, a rare concession to fatigue. "Fine, then. Hand me your logbook."

Aggie turned over the little red-leather notebook and pencil that each student nurse was meant to carry with her at all times. "Thank you, Matron."

Bobbing a quick curtsy, Aggie walked, straight-backed, across the receiving room. Dodger had stopped a few feet away to read a notice about the symptoms of cholera. She swept past him without making eye contact, trusting him to follow her into the cloakroom.

"All right," she said, buttoning her cloak and picking up her battered carpetbag from its hook. "I'm ready."

"Hold up. You got everything you need in there? Bandages and such?"

"We'll have to make do with what I have left." There was no way she could remove what she needed from the medical supply cabinet without Shiercliffe noticing—and objecting.

"Will any of this help?" Dodger opened the left side of his swallowtail coat and revealed a startling array of hooks and pockets, all filled with surgical implements and supplies clearly purloined from the hospital.

"How on earth did you get all of that?" But she knew. The same way he'd snatched her coin purse. He had light fingers.

"Not to mention these." He opened the right side of his coat and revealed a scalpel, a bottle of chloroform and an anesthetist's mask.

I don't really know this boy at all, she thought. "I don't know what your game is, but those supplies belong to the hospital and the poor people who come here for help. I'm not going to allow you to just help yourself so you can make a profit selling these things on to some dirty back alley butcher."

Dodger looked as though he had been struck. "No! It's just for Nancy. Whatever you don't need, you bring back." Dodger opened the front door for her and held it. "Come on, Aggie. Please."

It was the look in his eyes that decided her. She might not be able to trust him, but she couldn't seem to make herself walk away from him, either.

13

AGGIE WASN'T SURE WHAT SHE HAD BEEN expecting, but the pawnshop's bright red Valentine's Day decorations caught her by surprise. The splashes of crimson seemed a bit macabre, especially with the lovely blond girl lying bruised and bloodied on a chaise longue and the smell of sausages still lingering in the room.

She glanced at Dodger and was relieved to see he wasn't about to toss up his accounts. The last thing she needed was for him to get weak-kneed and pass out.

"You brought the nurse for Nancy?" The speaker, a young woman with a strong nose and curly brown hair, was sitting beside the chaise longue and sponging cold water onto the semiconscious girl's bruised face.

"That I did," said Dodger. "How is she, Faygie?"

Faygie looked up, her expression bleak. "I don't know." Her eyes were red and swollen from crying. "Thank you for coming, miss."

"I'm afraid I'm just a probationer nurse," said Aggie, not wanting Faygie to get her hopes up. "But I'll do whatever I can."

Faygie stood up, making room for Aggie. "I've put some cold water on the bruises to try to keep the swelling down."

"You did well." Aggie sat down in Faygie's place, moving the water and cloth aside. "Hello, Nancy. Can you talk to me?" Nancy's eyes fluttered open. She was lying on her back, her scarlet dress ripped and muddied.

"H–hullo," she said. Her bottom lip was split, and the cut on her forehead was still seeping blood into the tightly coiled curls at her hairline.

"I'm studying to be a nurse. Can you tell me what happened to you?"

Nancy opened her mouth but couldn't seem to get enough air. "I," she said. "Hurts."

"And it's difficult to speak. All right. I'm going to check your pulse." Aggie pressed two fingers to Nancy's wrist, then frowned. The girl's pulse was faster than she would have expected. "Nancy? I'd like to check your heartbeat, if that's all right?"

"Yeah."

Aggie pressed her ear to Nancy's chest. The injured girl's heart was racing. *If only I had a stethoscope*, thought Aggie, moving the position of her head so she could listen for breath sounds on both sides.

Nurses weren't supposed to diagnose illness, but Aggie felt an increasing suspicion that Nancy had a collapsed lung—a tension pneumothorax. As the lung deflated, the air filled the chest cavity, and the lungs could shift into the space where the heart was located, putting stress on it.

She looked up to find Dodger watching her. "What's going on?"

"I think she has air filling her chest, which is making it

harder for her to breathe. There's a way to let the air out," Aggie said, "but I'm not trained to do it."

A hulking shadow in a corner of the room stood up, revealing itself to be a big man with a thuggish face. He cleared his throat, nervously twisting a cap in his hands. "She going to be all right?"

Aggie swallowed. "I think we need to perform a procedure to help her breathe." Except that there was no *we*—she was going to have to be the one to do it, or it wouldn't be done.

"What kind of procedure?" The big man's voice was thick and raw and more than a little menacing. His dog gave a low whine.

Dodger put his hand on the man's shoulder, pressing him back down. "Take it easy, Bill."

"All right. I can do this." Aggie unbuttoned the bodice of Nancy's dress, revealing her chemise.

"Do you bloody mind? This ain't a peep show!"

Dodger shoved the bigger man back. "What are you, a lunatic? You couldn't even be fussed to go look for her!"

Bill shook his head. "Don't you start with me."

"Oi! Cut it out, you two," said Faygie. "Outside if you're going to start throwing punches." She looked from one to the other, clearly disgusted. "Pair of bloody arseholes."

Nancy tried to lift her head as she made a horrible wheezing sound. "Don't worry, Nancy," said Aggie as she pulled a thin knife out of her medical bag. "We're going to help you." Except that she didn't have all the equipment she needed. "Does anyone have a pen? I need a small hollow cylinder."

Faygie handed her a fountain pen. "Will this do?"

"Perfect. Thanks." Unscrewing the pen, Aggie extracted the ink tube. "Hand me the carbolic acid from my bag—

That's it, the brown bottle. Now pour this over my hands and the tube."

Dodger tipped the bottle over the pen cartridge, ignoring the brown puddle it made on the floor. "That enough?"

"Let's hope so."

"Do you need my help?"

"I'll need you and Bill to give us a little privacy. Faygie, can you help me hold Nancy still?"

Bill reluctantly stepped aside, casting his shadow over her.

"You're standing too close," said Aggie.

He scowled down at her. "Just want to keep my eye on you."

"You're blocking the light."

Bill grunted and moved so he wasn't blocking the lamp, and Faygie took her place at the foot of the chaise longue. "That's good," said Aggie. "Just hold onto her wrists. Gently but firmly."

"Got it."

Aggie focused on her patient, unbuttoning her chemise so her chest was exposed and placing her fingers over the other woman's right clavicle. "All right. Feeling for the third intercostal space." For a moment, looking at Nancy as she lay there, she felt incapable of piercing her skin. Then she thought about her mother's advice: *When you have a difficult task, break it into smaller pieces, and don't think about anything else except the doing of it.*

Of course, Ma also said to know your limits. *A midwife helps nature along—a doctor tries to fight it.*

So much for listening to her mother, then. Aggie took the scalpel and focused on making the cut at the correct angle, over the rib. Nancy opened her mouth but no sound came out, and Aggie realized she hadn't planned on the blood seeping from the wound. It was soaking into the girl's chemise.

"I need someone to mop that up," she said. "There are sterile bandages in my bag." Dodger was there in an instant, dabbing at the wound. His worried gaze remained fixed on the girl's face, and he did not seem to notice her partial nudity at all.

"That all right? More?"

"No, that's good." Aggie inserted the cartridge into the cut, biting the inside of her lip as she pushed the metal into the wound. Nancy groaned, and Faygie had to hold her tight as she tried to push away from the pain and Aggie. It felt strange and somehow wrong, but as Aggie heard the whistle of air being released, she knew she had done the right thing.

After half an hour, Aggie removed the cartridge and disinfected the wound site before bandaging it up. "That should help, but she should go to hospital in the morning," said Aggie. A strand of hair had come loose from her nurse's cap and was falling over her face. She swiped at it with the back of one arm and it fell back, damp with sweat.

"Here." Dodger had tucked the hair back in place. It felt comforting, his hand on her hair. "I can't thank you enough."

She could feel the tremble in her hands, and suddenly she was shaky and odd. "Just take me home, all right? I want to go back now."

He put his hand on her shoulder. "Of course."

The streets were not empty. There were huddled figures in doorways, and the occasional small fire. A feral dog slinked through piles of refuse, skittishly jogging away when it heard them approach.

Light-headed with fatigue and relief, Aggie found herself stumbling into Dodger as he walked beside her. He placed his hand on her elbow to steady her. "You all right?"

"Just a little tired."

"Can I buy you something to drink? Or eat?"

"I think I just need to sleep." What she really wanted was a slug of gin to steady her nerves, but she fought the urge. She couldn't rely on having a drink every time she treated a patient. Coffee would have been nice, but it was too early for the coffee vendors to be out.

"You look shattered. Here—you can lean on me, if you like." He held out one arm with his elbow crooked, and after a moment's hesitation, she slipped her hand through it. She had never walked arm in arm with a man before, but it was easy to match her pace to Dodger's. She felt as aware of his body as if it were an extension of her own, and it made her stumble again. This time, he drew her closer, slipping one arm around her waist. It was not a respectable way to walk down the street, and she knew she should move away from him.

If only it didn't feel so good to have him holding her as they walked.

She wondered if he was going to try to kiss her at some point, and if she was going to let him.

She could hear her mother's voice in her head: *Careful, my girl. That's how they get under your skin.*

Leave off, Ma, she thought. *I have a right to my own mistakes.*

They were about to turn a corner when Dodger abruptly veered around, his hand dropping down to her side as he placed himself in front of her and the unseen danger. "All right," he said, "I know you're following us."

Aggie stared at him, confused, and then looked into the dark street behind them. "Did you hear something?"

"Someone, not something. I can tell when I'm being followed by something on two feet, so come on out."

A figure lurched out of the shadows at them. "Heard you got yourself a tasty new mort." The gaunt young man doffed his top hat to Aggie, revealing a matt of tangled, greasy blond hair scraggling down the sides. "Evenin', miss. It true you work at the Royal Vic?"

Dodger shook his head. "Sorry, Aggie. This nudnik is Oliver Twist. Twist, it's late and I am taking the lady home, so sod off."

"Don't be like that," Twist said, moving to block their way. "You're a nurse, aren't you, miss? Well, I just need a bit of paregoric to settle me."

Paregoric, or camphorated tincture of opium, was often given to children for a cough, but it could also induce feelings of euphoria in a patient. In higher doses, it could also inhibit breathing and cause a dangerous dip in a patient's heart rate.

"What you need is to get yourself off all those nostrums," said Dodger, guiding Aggie around Twist.

Twist wasn't giving up that easily. "Please, miss," said Twist, following closely behind them. "You don't know the kind of pain I'm in."

Aggie stopped, turning to face Dodger's friend. This close, she could smell the bitterness on his breath. "You're right," she said. "I don't know your pain. But do you know that in a high enough dose, paregoric can be lethal?"

Twist's gaze dropped to her medical bag. "So you do have some!"

Dodger gave an almost imperceptible shake of his head.

"I'm sorry," she said. "I don't."

Twist's mouth contorted. "You're lying." He grabbed the handles of her carpetbag. "Let me see."

"Are you insane?" Dodger gave Twist a shove, but Twist maintained his desperate grip on the carpetbag, pulling it out of Aggie's hands and yanking it open.

"I'm only going to say this once," said Dodger. "Give it back."

Twist ignored him as he pulled a brown glass bottle out of the bag and squinted at the fine print on the label. "What's this?"

"Syrup of ipecac," said Aggie, bending to pick up a length of catgut he had dropped on the ground. "Please. I need my supplies back."

Twist tossed it, then pulled out another bottle. "And this one?"

"All right then," said Dodger. "We'll do it the hard way." Jabbing his elbow into Twist's ribs, he grabbed for the bag, but Twist reacted with surprising speed, and suddenly the two were grappling with each other, lurching into the brick wall as Twist aimed a dangerous rabbit punch at the base of Dodger's neck.

"Dodger, watch out!"

"Don't you worry about me, luv." Dodger threw his shoulder into Twist's midsection, knocking him back into the wall behind him. The bottle in Twist's hand smashed hard against the bricks, shattering instantly into a spray of glass fragments. Taking advantage of his opponent's momentary distraction, Dodger launched himself at Twist just as Aggie felt something pelt her face like hail, followed by an awful, stabbing pain in her eyes.

She froze, ice-cold with terror as everything she had ever learned about eye trauma flashed through her mind—abrasians and lacerations and perforations, the urgency of immediate treatment, the risk of permanent damage.

Then someone slammed into her from behind, throwing her off balance. The last thing she heard was Dodger, calling her name. Her head struck the stones and there was a moment of spangled brightness before everything went dark.

14

AGGIE WOKE UP FEELING MUDDLED AND STRANGE. The room was still dark, but she had the sense that she had slept later than usual. "Lizzie? What time is it?"

"Aggie?" It was Justine's voice that answered her.

"Justine? What are you doing in my room?" Aggie sat up, disoriented. Her eyes were open, but the room remained dark. Wait—was there something covering her face? She brought her hand up to her temples and encountered the rough gauze of bandages.

All right, she told herself. *Think*. What had happened last night? She came up blank, and a stab of panic pierced the lingering fog of sleep. Reflexively, she reached for her bedside lamp and something heavy slid off the table and fell to the floor with a crash. "What was that?"

"Stay calm, Aggie," said Justine. "Someone will be here in a moment to help." There was a bell ringing nearby; someone was calling for help in one of the wards.

Which meant she wasn't in her room. She was in the hospital.

"You've had an accident," said Justine. "You're in my room, and you're safe."

"I'm in your room?" Even as she asked the question, Aggie became aware of the sound of Justine's ventilator and the faint smell of carbolic acid. "Where's Lizzie?"

"Lizzie's probably in the laboratory."

"At this time of night?"

"Aggie—I'm afraid it's not nighttime." Justine sounded regretful. "It's three in the afternoon."

"Three? How long have I been asleep?" With a growing sense of unease, Aggie tried to think back to the last thing she remembered before going to bed. Then it hit her—she didn't remember going to bed. "What day is it?"

There was a moment's pause. "You had an accident, Aggie. You've been unconscious for nearly three days."

Three days. Aggie took a deep breath, fighting a wave of panic. The memories came back in pieces. The alleyway. Dodger's hand on her elbow. The gaunt-faced young man with the lank blond hair—Twist. The struggle over her medical bag.

She must have blacked out when she hit her head. "I think I remember some of it now. How did I get back here?"

For a moment, the only sound in the room was the wheeze of the ventilator, and then Justine replied, "I don't know. Shiercliffe just told me that you had been attacked while seeing a patient in the East End. She asked me if I minded sharing my room, and I said no, of course not."

So Shiercliffe knew that she had not gone back to her room that night. *This is too much to take in.*

"I know," said Justine, and Aggie realized she must have said the words out loud. "Try to stay calm."

That shocked Aggie into silence. No one had ever told her to remain calm before. She was always the one calming other people down. She had never realized that there was nothing less soothing than being told to stay calm.

There was a creak as the door opened, and then the sound of hurried footsteps. "How long has she been awake?" Shiercliffe's voice, a bit breathless from hurrying.

"Just a few minutes, Matron. She's a little confused."

"That's to be expected." Footsteps, then a cool hand on her brow. "Fever's down—that's good. How are you feeling, Agatha?"

"I'm fine," she said automatically, because she was always fine. From the time she was little, she was the child who did not get sick and require nursing. Her brothers dropped hammers on their fingers or got kicked in the leg by donkeys, but Aggie sailed through childhood all but unscathed. *Till now.* "What's wrong with me?"

There was a rustle of skirts as Shiercliffe moved closer to the bed. "Well, to begin with, you've sustained an injury to the back of your head. You were unconscious for nearly three days."

Suddenly, Aggie had a flash of memory: Dodger. The shattered bottle. The stabbing pain in her eyes.

"I'm not going to ask you where you were or what you were doing," said Shiercliffe, in a tone that implied that she did not want her worst suspicions confirmed. "I only know that Henry Clerval brought you here in a hired carriage. It seems you were injured after the gates had already closed for the night, and someone saw fit to bring you to Mr. Clerval for treatment." Aggie noted that Shiercliffe did not call Clerval a doctor, although he styled himself one. "To his credit,"

Shiercliffe added, "Clerval knew enough to bring you here in the morning. Unfortunately, he did not know enough to treat your eyes properly beforehand."

Which meant that Henry Clerval had wasted precious hours when she could have been getting treatment for her eyes. "Matron?" Hearing the quaver in her voice, she firmed it. "Can we take these bandages off now?"

Shiercliffe hesitated. "Not quite yet. Dr. Grimbald will come by to check on you first."

Aggie made herself ask the question. "My eyes. How bad was the damage? Don't sugarcoat it. I want to know the truth."

"Very well, then. The cornea was damaged, by the glass and by carbolic acid. We irrigated the eye and got everything out, but there may be scarring."

Aggie sucked in a sharp breath. "I see." Then, hearing herself, she added, "So to speak."

Shiercliffe didn't laugh. "Was it worth risking your sight and your life for some boy? Don't bother to deny it—I watched you leave the hospital with him."

"It's not like that. He had a friend who needed medical help." True enough. But she'd gone also because it was Dodger doing the asking. Shiercliffe was right. Risking sight and life for a boy? Never again. And here she'd thought pregnancy was her most serious concern.

"And so you left your shift and hared off into the East End?" Shiercliffe's voice, usually so measured, was shaking with fury. "How many people have you already helped? How many more could you help, if only—"

Shiercliffe's outburst was cut short by a brief knock on the door, followed by the brisk sound of confident footsteps.

"Well, well, well," said Grimbald, his voice sounding unexpectedly loud in the room. "I hear our patient is awake at last. Let's get these bandages off, shall we?" He smelled of some bracing aftershave and moustache wax as he bent over her, and then there was the snip of scissors. "Turn up the light, will you, Matron?"

"Of course, Doctor."

"Now, Miss DeLacey, you might want to keep your eyes closed to give yourself a moment to adjust."

Assuming all went well and she could see when the bandages came off. "All right." She felt Grimbald unfasten the end of the bandage. Time seemed to slow as he began to unwrap the gauze until only one thin layer remained between her and the world.

"Ready?" Before she could respond, Grimbald pulled the thin fabric away, removing the last bandage.

She felt a smooth, feminine hand slip over her wrist, slender fingers gripping her hand tightly. Shiercliffe. Grateful for the support, Aggie took a deep breath.

"Aggie?" Shiercliffe's voice was unusually gentle. "Go ahead and open your eyes."

She opened them. The room was a blur, but she could make out the crude shapes and colors of things—a dark blob of something on the walls, the light streaming through the tall windows, the silver dirigible shape of Justine's iron lung. She could see Shiercliffe beside her and Grimbald standing over her, even if she couldn't discern their features.

"I can see," she said, her eyes stinging with tears. "I'm not blind!"

"Oh, don't cry," said Shiercliffe, dabbing at Aggie's eyes

with a compress. "Silly girl. How can you tell us what you can see if you're crying?"

"Perfectly natural response for a girl," said Grimbald.

"As if soldiers never shed any tears," said Shiercliffe.

"Now, don't worry if you're not seeing clearly right away," said Grimbald. His eyes were dark smears, but she tried to focus on them. "Your vision might be a bit blurry at first, but it should improve over the next few days."

She nodded. "Thank you! Thank you so much, Dr. Grimbald."

It was only as the days turned into weeks and Aggie's vision remained the same that she began to understand that blindness might not be an absolute. Her right eye was marginally stronger than her left, but even with that eye, she couldn't recognize a person from across the room. She couldn't measure out a teaspoon or read a book, and in low light, she couldn't even spot her hairbrush sitting on the side table right in front of her.

Lizzie came to visit when she could, but she was preoccupied. She thought she had a good prototype of a Bio-Mechanical eye, but none of the new Bio-Mechanicals was advanced enough to speak in complete sentences or solve a simple wooden puzzle. Moulsdale was beside himself, pointing out that the kaiser was hardly likely to be impressed by a witless Bio-Mechanical, even if it did possess superior vision.

With less than two months left before the kaiser arrived, Moulsdale was becoming increasingly impatient with the lack of progress. According to Lizzie, he had begun to talk about his duty to the Crown and the need to revisit Victor's status.

"I reminded Moulsdale what he had promised me," Lizzie said on a late night visit to Justine and Aggie's room. "The bargain was that I don't reveal what I know about the queen, and he allowed Victor to complete his education." She paused in the act of braiding Aggie's hair.

"What did he say to that?" asked Aggie.

Lizzie tied off the end of Aggie's braid with a ribbon. "He said there are promises made in peacetime that do not apply in times of war."

"I hope you told him that we aren't at war with Germany," said Aggie.

"I did." Lizzie pulled some of Aggie's red hair from the brush's bristles. "He just looked at me and said wars begin long before someone fires the first shot."

"He's not wrong there," said Justine.

"Poppycock!" Lizzie threw the hairbrush against the wall, startling a gasp out of Aggie. "Sorry, Justine," said Lizzie, walking over to pick up the brush from the floor. "I didn't mean you. I just don't see why we can't test the technology on a person who needs it."

Aggie perked up at the prospect. "Like me, you mean?"

"No, seriously," said Lizzie. "Why couldn't we try the new device on you? I'm sure the kaiser would be able to see the military application. We don't need to turn Victor into a showpiece that gets paraded around."

It made perfect sense to Aggie. Why shouldn't the Bio-Mechanical program be used to benefit ordinary people? For the first time in weeks, she felt a flicker of hope.

"Moulsdale will never agree to it," said Justine bluntly, and Aggie felt herself sinking again. "He's a gambler and a showman, and he wants to pull off a big win. That means a British Bio-Mechanical he can pit against the kaiser's model. I don't see him settling for less." After a moment, she added,

"Besides, I'm sure Aggie won't need artificial eyes. She just needs a little more time to heal."

Yet time kept passing, and Aggie's eyesight did not improve.

On rounds, Dr. Grimbald brought the medical students and probationer nurses around to discuss her case and how they were treating it. Corneal scarring could take up to six weeks to improve, he said. Byram, Will and Lizzie always lingered behind for a moment before scurrying to catch up. Aggie knew that Grimbald was telling them things when she was out of earshot. He needn't have been so discreet. She knew full well what he wasn't saying—the longer she went without improvement, the slimmer her chances of regaining her eyesight.

After six weeks had passed without a change, Lizzie made Aggie a pair of spectacles. The lenses were much thicker than Lizzie's own glasses, but Aggie didn't care. If they helped her see more clearly, she didn't care what she looked like.

"Well?" Lizzie perched on the edge of her bed as Aggie looked around the laboratory through the new lenses. "How are they? How does everything look?"

Wordlessly, Aggie removed the glasses and shook her head. There wasn't going to be any miraculous cure for her, it seemed. Funny old world. Before her accident, she had thought the worst fate imaginable was failing out of school and winding up pregnant and married to some local boy. Now she wondered if she was even going to be able to live on her own.

She tried to console herself that she was not blind, if blindness meant living in total darkness. Her world wasn't devoid of light and color.

It just felt that way.

15

DODGER WAITED OUT THE GRAY END OF FEBRU-
ary and settled into the long, blustery month of March, hoping
in vain to catch a glimpse of Aggie. He stationed himself near
her lodging house in the morning until he learned to recognize the pigeons roosting there. When that strategy failed, he
arranged to pass by the gates of the Royal Victoria at eight, so
he could bump into her among the crowd of departing patients.

That plan went pear-shaped, as well.

Dodger couldn't make sense of it. Nancy was up and about
again, though not as strong as she had been, and her injuries had been life-threatening. Surely Aggie should have recovered by now…and yet the image of her, unconscious on
the ground, haunted him. He had brought her to the doctor within the hour, then paid to have her transported to the
hospital. Perhaps she was perfectly healthy but had a different schedule.

Or else she might be avoiding him.

In mid-March, the flower girls that strolled around Covent

Garden stopped selling cloth flowers from their baskets and started selling primroses and daffodils from the countryside, and Dodger faced up to the facts. If he wanted to find out how Aggie was faring, he would have to seek her out at the hospital. At least then he'd know for sure if she'd been giving him the brush-off. Part of him hoped that was the case, that she was right as rain, even if the price for that bit of good news meant some ache for him.

He briefly considered the pros and cons of breaking and entering the Royal Victoria after dark, then quickly concluded that his best bet would be to stroll through the front gates in broad daylight. After all, he was a pickpocket, not a burglar. He might not have the tools for picking locks and muffling the sound of breaking glass, but he knew how to blend in and set people at ease.

Stationing himself at the back of the receiving room, he slipped a young woman a thruppence to pitch a fit, then waited till she began shrieking and thrashing on the floor to walk unnoticed past the front desk. When he happened upon a blank-faced orderly pushing a laundry cart, he pulled a marble from his pocket and tossed it under the wheels. As the orderly wrestled to get the cart back under control, Dodger snagged a white coat off the top of the pile. By the time he'd rounded the corner, he had removed his top hat and donned the white coat and the attitude to go with it. He passed another white-jacketed doctor and gave him a friendly pat on the shoulder. "Saw you in action earlier," Dodger told the man. "Really nice work."

"Oh! Thank you," said the man, confused but pleased, and completely oblivious to the fact that Dodger had just swiped his stethoscope. Walking down another corridor, Dodger deliberately moved into the path of a probationer nurse, apologized profusely in his best posh accent, then asked them where to find Agatha DeLacey.

"Oh, are you a specialist?" The nurse had a slight Jamaican accent. "I do hope you can help her, Doctor. She's in Waterloo Ward."

So Aggie hadn't fully recovered yet. How badly had she hit her head that night? Could she have caught a lung infection? Tamping down his fears, he summoned his most ingratiating smile. "I'm new here, lovely," he admitted to the girl. "Don't suppose you could point me in the right direction?"

She did even better—she walked him to the right door. "Tell Aggie I'll try to visit her later," she told him, and then hurried off.

Clearing his throat, he knocked on the open door and said, "Miss DeLacey?"

"Come in." The voice was so soft that he wasn't entirely sure he hadn't imagined it, but he stepped in anyway. His first thought was that he was in the wrong room. First of all, there was a strange metal contraption with a bellows attached at one end and the fragile head of a young girl sticking out of the other. He also noticed a tray with some disturbingly medical things—rubber tubing, a funnel, and something that looked like a dull scissors. On second glance, he also saw a regular hospital bed, a small table and one chair, and a bookcase that contained *The Rise and Fall of the Roman Empire*.

Surely this couldn't be Aggie's room.

The girl in the metal device was scrutinizing him as carefully as he had observed her room. "How may I help you, Doctor?"

"Ah—hello, young lady." Dodger gave the girl his best

smile, trying to ignore the rampant weirdness of the metal dirigible. "Dr. Dworkin here to see the DeLacey girl. You must be…ah…" He snapped his fingers, as if trying to dredge the name up from memory.

"Justine Makepiece," said the girl. "Aggie's just gone out for a moment. She'll be right back—Dr. Dworkin."

So Aggie wasn't bedridden. That was something. He let out a long breath of relief, then coughed to disguise his reaction. "You're a peach, Justine." He placed his top hat down on a pretty inlaid dresser, allowing his fingers to linger over a silver brush and mirror. The brush had a dent in it but would still fetch a pretty penny.

"You're quite young to be a specialist, aren't you?"

How to respond? "It can be a bit of an obstacle," he replied, allowing a hint of annoyance into his voice. "Some patients and staff refuse to believe I'm qualified till I produce a whole stack of paperwork." He gave a little sigh for the needless prejudice of people, then picked up a small framed portrait of a black cat with what appeared to be electrodes at its neck. "How unusual. Your pet?"

"Back in Yorkshire. She wouldn't have liked London. Where are you from, by the way? I can't quite place your accent…"

"That's because I've trained in so many different places. Edinburgh, Brussels…" He put the cat portrait down. "Amsterdam."

"So what I'm hearing is a Scottish-Belgian accent mixed with Dutch?" Justine sounded thoughtful. "Who knew that could sound so much like Cockney?"

Just then, Aggie appeared in the doorway, sparing him from having to embellish his lies any further. "Aggie!" She was wearing a white blouse and dark skirt instead of her nurse's pinafore and cap, which made her seem even more approachable. He was about to take her hands in his when he recalled that Justine was watching him. "Miss DeLacey. I'm Dr. Dworkin, a specialist from Brighton."

"Dr. Dworkin?" Aggie squinted at him as though trying to place how she knew him. Clever boots, she was pretending not to recognize him.

"You're just in time," said Justine, sounding cheerful. "Your friend here was about to invent a colorful story about his education in Amsterdam."

"Guess that's my cover blown," he said, giving Justine a wink as he strode to Aggie. "How have you been? You look wonderful."

"Thank you." Averting her gaze, Aggie walked carefully over to a chair and sat herself down. "How is Nancy?"

"Thriving, thanks to you." He looked around the room, wishing there were another chair. He didn't want to sit on the edge of Aggie's bed—it seemed too presumptuous—but there was something awkward about standing in front of her like a supplicant.

"I'm glad to hear your friend is recovering," said Aggie. "Wait—who took care of Nancy's wound? You didn't just do it yourself, did you?"

Now Dodger was the one averting his gaze. "There's a doctor works not too far from the pawnshop. New bloke, just opened a surgery." He forced himself to look up. "Sorry—I probably should have gone to him in the first place, instead of bothering you. He's the one who helped you, after you got hurt."

Aggie's mouth firmed into a hard line. "I suppose. If you count calling me a carriage as help."

"Aw, now, he can't be that bad. He trained with the head of your school."

Aggie shook her head. "Henry bloody Clerval is a total incompetent! You'd have been better off tending Nancy yourself."

With a pang of guilt, Dodger recalled his own gut feeling that there was something off about Clerval. Yet the man had seemed so confident in his abilities. "Well," he said, "Clerval might not be as talented as some, but he seemed to know what he was about. I'm sure he helped a bit, at any rate."

Aggie said nothing, but it was clear she did not agree.

Taking a step toward her, Dodger said, "I can't tell you how sorry I am about that night. I could kill Twist for what he did."

"Twist?"

"That insane bugger who took you out." Acting on impulse, Dodger knelt down and took Aggie's hands in his, and the contact with her ungloved palm felt as intimate as a kiss. She couldn't seem to hold his gaze properly, which felt like another kick in the gut. "If it makes any difference, he was beside himself when he learned what he'd done. Says he's turning over a new leaf."

She raised her eyebrows. "Easier said than done."

"That's for sure." He turned her hands over in his, stunned that she was letting him touch her at all. "You—you're not still in a lot of pain, are you?"

"No." She was looking down at their hands. "I'm not in any pain at all."

"Ah, thank God for that. I couldn't live with myself if he'd really hurt you."

She made a small sound that was almost, but not quite, a laugh.

"Tell him, Aggie." Justine's soft voice seemed loud in the room.

"Tell me what?" Dodger looked from Justine to Aggie. "What's wrong?"

Aggie pulled her fingers out of his grip. "Nothing's wrong, Dodger. I'm fine."

"Then why are you in a hospital room, instead of working or studying?"

Aggie shrugged. "My eyes still get fatigued easily, so I need a bit more time before I go back to my studies."

"Ah." Releasing her hands, he straightened up. "But other than that, you're doing all right?"

"Yes. Thank you for stopping by."

Except she wasn't all right. He'd be a piss poor thief if he wasn't able to read such an obvious falsehood. He retrieved his hat from the dresser. "You were on my mind," he admitted, turning as if to place the hat on his head. Without warning, he gave a flick of his wrist and sent the hat flying in Aggie's direction, where it glanced her when she didn't flinch.

"Ouch!" She rubbed her forehead and looked around. "What was that?"

"A test." Walking back over to her, Dodger put his hand under her chin. "Can you see me?"

She pulled away from his touch. "Of course I can see you."

He held up two fingers. "How many fingers am I holding up, then?"

"I'm not in the mood for games."

"How many?"

She swatted at his hand. "Don't be such a pratt."

"You can't tell me, can you?" Now that he was looking at her more closely, he could see a slight line cutting across the green of her left iris.

"I just need a little more time to heal, is all."

Dodger nodded. "So they expect you to get your sight back?"

"Absolutely. It's just a matter of time."

She was a terrible liar. Luckily, he was not, especially when the one he was lying to couldn't see the concern in his eyes. "That's fantastic," he said, reclaiming his hat from the floor at her feet. "I'm so relieved. I'll come back to see you again as soon as I can."

"You might have to wait a while," she said rapidly, barely looking at him. "I'm going to be awfully busy, catching up on my studies, you know. Just as soon as my eyes are back to normal."

"Understood." He gave a little half bow and then turned on his heel and left without looking back, as if the thought of abandoning her to an uncertain future didn't bother him at all.

16

DODGER WAS USED TO MAKING RECKLESS choices, but this time he wondered if he had gone a little too far. Sneaking into Aggie's room in the hospital was one thing. Asking directions to the head of medicine's private office and breaking into it, now, that was a different order of stupid.

If the Head came in while he was here, Dodger knew that his borrowed white coat and stethoscope would probably not snooker the man for long. For anyone who knew how to read the clues, there was ample proof that the occupant of this office was nobody's fool. The framed sheepskin diploma from Oxford University attested to Ambrose Moulsdale's academic credentials, and the handsome ivory and ebony chessboard, paused mid-game, showed that he was a man who knew how to make sacrifices to achieve his ends. (He would now be sacrificing a few of his ebony and ivory pawns along with his knights, which fit nicely into the oversized pockets of Dodger's borrowed white coat.)

The dog-eared copy of Machiavelli's *The Prince* in his bookshelf strongly suggested that its owner considered ruthless-ness a virtue. The book contained a hidden compartment cut out of its pages, which was a bit of a disappointment. Didn't the head of medicine know that fake books in the house and fake stones in the garden were the oldest tricks in the book? Not that Dodger was complaining. Moulsdale had thought-fully spared him the added step of finding which of his lock-picking tools would unlock the desk drawer.

The faster he got out, the better. *Or maybe I should just leave now*, he thought. Something in his gut was telling him to scarper.

No. Five more minutes.

Leaving Aggie, he had felt a restless, gnawing sense that he had to do something for her. It was his fault that she was now as helpless as a mole caught out in daylight, with no hope of becoming a full-fledged nurse.

Money might not solve her problems, but at least it would lessen the impact of being left without a position or a ca-reer. Five minutes in the fancy doctor's office, he figured, would be enough to fill his pockets with all sorts of valuable commodities—fountain pens, medals, pocket money, maybe even a gold signet ring that had become too tight to fit on the man's finger. All he had to do was work fast, pawn the goods and then gift Aggie with the money.

On the other hand, if he got caught, Dodger might just find himself with a new address—Newgate Prison.

He focused on rifling through the contents of Moulsdale's broad, lovingly polished oak desk. Unfortunately, so far all he could see were bills, bills and more bills, and a small bottle of chloroform. Suddenly, there was a shrill ring, making Dodger flinch like a startled cat—it was the telephone, a handsome brass contraption that looked like something out of a moving picture. *That's it*, he thought. *I'm leaving.*

Then a German phrase at the top of a letter caught his eye.

In his long-ago life as Yakov Dworkin, his mother had spoken to him in Yiddish, which was a close, vagabond relation to German. He had never attempted to read German before but found it was surprisingly easy.

My dearest Grandmother, the letter read, *I so look forward to seeing you this Easter, and to showing off my newest scientific breakthrough, the death's-head model of Bio-Mechanical.*

Stone the crows, thought Dodger. The royal crest on the letterhead gave away the correspondent's identity. *Could that be a letter from Kaiser Willy himself to the queen?* Scanning the rest of the page, he caught the phrase *reminisce about our private, heart-to-heart chats when I was just a boy.*

It certainly sounded like it could be the kaiser. If so, maybe the letter could be worth something. Rolling up the page, Dodger was just inserting it into his boot when he heard the sound of a key turning the lock.

Damn it. What to do? Curtains, side table—no time, the door was opening. Bluff it out or hide?

"I don't see the point of this, Miss Shiercliffe." The man's voice was pitched low.

"Just let me make my case, Professor Moulsdale."

Crouching under the oak table with its heavy green felt cloth hiding him, Dodger listened to the door shut with a sinking feeling that he had made the wrong choice.

Sighing, Moulsdale sank into a leather chair. "You have made it already. And while it is, indeed, a shame about Miss DeLacey, nothing you say can change my mind on this matter. The Bio-Mechanical eyes must go to a Bio-Mechanical."

"I am just asking you to consider an alternative."

"We have tried every viable option. No matter how fresh the body, the results always disappoint. And we are out of time. Do you really think our distinguished visitor will be impressed when I show him we've given our most advanced technology to a bit of skirt?"

"But Miss DeLacey is not just any girl, Ambrose." A caressing note had entered Shiercliffe's voice. "She means a great deal to me...and I believe she would be an incredible wartime nurse."

Moulsdale cleared his throat. "A pity then, that she could not govern her own reckless impulses."

"Let us look at this from a different perspective, then." Shiercliffe's tone was brusque once more. "Victor Frankenstein has powerful connections—his family, Miss Lavenza, even Dr. Grimbald. If he suddenly reappears as a Bio-Mechanical warrior, it will raise some uncomfortable questions."

"Indeed. Which is why I have no intention of using Victor. I simply intend to use the lessons learned from his case to produce another, equally promising specimen."

"Professor Moulsdale, I am not certain I take your meaning."

"Don't be coy, Miss Shiercliffe. You know full well what we need to do. The current candidate is proving a disappointment." Moulsdale's heavy footsteps made their way around the oak table, and Dodger held his breath as the man reached over and picked something up from it. "Perhaps the mistake was choosing brawn over brains. This time, let's try someone clever. Find a patient who used to be a lawyer in the old country, as long as he's not too old."

"Professor Moulsdale, I've taken an oath to preserve the health of my patients. We both have."

Cripes. Under the table, Dodger's mouth went dry as he realized what they were discussing: Selecting some poor patient with a minor complaint—a broken arm or a gash that needed stitching, say—and turning him into a freak-eyed corpse walker.

"There are some circumstances under which the Hippocratic oath can be suspended, Ursula. War, for example. Besides, I think I can think of something that might outweigh your scruples."

"And what is that?"

There was a loud scraping sound as the wooden table was shoved back across the floor, revealing Dodger. Moulsdale, moving more quickly than Dodger would have expected from such a large man, yanked him up by the back of his coat and gave him a hard shake.

"Hello, young man," said Moulsdale. "Has no one ever told you that spies would do well to bathe from time to time? It's hard to conceal oneself when one stinks of unwashed clothes and stale beer."

Thinking quickly, Dodger gave the older man a blank-faced look. "Beer?" he asked, with a note of hope in his voice.

Moulsdale pursed his mouth. "Are you a complete idiot, boy?"

Dodger did his best to look like one. "No, sir. Me ma always said I was special."

The head of nursing looked him over. "Wait a moment. I know you. You're the boy who walked off with Miss DeLacey the night she was blinded." Looking at Moulsdale, she said, "He's no fool. He's shamming."

Moulsdale's eyes narrowed. "I see." Suddenly, his soft hands were patting Dodger down. He pulled a chess piece out of Dodger's coat pocket, then moved down to his boots.

Crap. The letter.

"Look, I can explain everything," he said, mind racing as Moulsdale pulled the incriminating paper out of Dodger's boot. He could hardly claim to know nothing, so he might as well claim to know everything. Shifting his accent, he said, "I'm actually Jack Dawkins, agent of the Crown. Lord Salisbury sent me here to investigate."

Moulsdale stroked his neat salt-and-pepper beard. "Did he, now? And why was that, pray?"

"I'm afraid that the prime minister is very concerned that the kaiser's visit go according to plan."

"I see," said Moulsdale. "And what are you intending to report?"

"That depends," said Dodger, tapping the side of his nose. "I think we can come to an understanding."

"Excellent, excellent." Moulsdale beamed at him and threw an arm around his shoulders. "What a clever little slum rat you are."

Dodger squirmed under the older man's heavy arm. "I am no more a slum rat than you are a humble country doctor. Call up the PM, if you don't believe me."

"What a good idea," said Shiercliffe, reaching into the drawer and pulling out a brown glass bottle and a gauze pad. "By the way, Professor Moulsdale? I have decided to comply with your plan, but I have one small request."

Moulsdale smiled at her as his arm moved, becoming a vise around Dodger's throat. "And what's that?"

"You're making a mistake," said Dodger as he tried to jab

his elbow into Moulsdale's ribs. Who would have guessed the man's grip would be so strong?

"Give the boy's eyes to Miss DeLacey," said Shiercliffe, tipping the bottle onto the gauze pad and soaking it.

"An eye for an eye, is it? Done."

Wait, Dodger tried to say. *Stop.* But the chloroform-soaked pad was covering his nose and mouth and filling his throat with an awful, burning sweetness. The lights in the room spangled like fireworks for a moment, before the darkness swallowed them up.

17

THERE WAS AN UPSIDE TO BEING UNABLE TO SEE anything clearly: Aggie couldn't make out the curious faces of her fellow students as the Bio-Mechanical orderly wheeled her into the center of the operating theater. She had never considered what it would feel like, entering this room from a patient's point of view. As a nursing student, she had been grateful for the chance to see operations and irritated by the way the medical students—all male, aside from Lizzie—were given the best seats.

Now, as the cool air rushed past her face and the gurney wheels squeaked over the polished wood floors, she was glad that all she could see was an impressionist's blur of colors, instead of the expressions of her fellow students peering down from the tiered seats to get a better view of her operation.

Suddenly, her gurney stopped moving and then someone said, "Lifting her on three—one, two, three." She had a moment to brace herself before strong hands gathered the sheet underneath her and hoisted her into the air and onto another, harder surface—the operating table.

No one said anything to her, but she could dimly make out the ghostly shapes of doctors and nurses as they moved around, organizing instruments and conferring with one another in soft voices. The hanging overhead light fixture was turned off, then lowered and turned on, and she closed her eyes against the glare.

They should make all the surgeons lie here and feel what it's like, thought Aggie. *Nurses, too.*

Aggie thought of all the patients she had watched—the man with the tumor on the side of his jaw, the woman who required a caesarian section and, saddest of all, a little boy who had managed to impale himself on a fireplace poker.

"Don't allow your emotions to overwhelm you," Shiercliffe had advised. "You must try to remember at all times that you have a job to perform—and part of that job is to present a serene face to the patient."

The job of a patient, it seemed, was to allow others to treat you like an inanimate object. Being a good patient meant being passive and quiet and serene and grateful—and not asking too many questions.

Yet she had so many questions. So much had changed in the past twenty-four hours since she had discovered Dodger in her room. If only she had been given a little advance warning to prepare herself…but then, maybe that would have only made it worse.

Even now, lying in the operating theater, stomach coiled tight with nerves, she found herself thinking about Dodger. She kept flashing back to the moment he had touched her hands and asked whether she was still in a lot of pain.

Stupid boy, stupid question and what a stupid girl she was for wanting to cry when he asked it.

After he had left, she'd felt a wave of anger at Justine. "Why did you do that? Tell him there was something wrong with me?"

"I didn't tell him anything—I urged you to tell him," Justine had replied. "Why are you trying to protect him? He ought to know the consequences of his actions."

Aggie had gone over to her bed and removed her shoes. She hadn't been trying to protect him. She had been protecting herself, as best she could. His pity would have crushed her.

"Are you going to sleep now? Aggie?"

She pulled the covers over herself. She had always admired patients who were good-natured and sunny and didn't make a fuss, and had imagined that if she were ever sick, she would be that kind of patient.

She was not. She was tired and angry and not sure she even liked herself anymore. Nursing student Aggie would have found patient Aggie a nuisance and a bore.

"Aggie?" The next time, it had been Shiercliffe's voice, but Aggie had kept her eyes closed.

"I'm just resting," she said.

"Good," Shiercliffe responded, surprising her. "You'll want to be well rested for the operation."

She had opened her eyes then, to see the indistinct oval of Shiercliffe's face looking down at her. "What operation?" For a moment, she thought Shiercliffe meant that Aggie was supposed to observe someone else's surgery, and then she sat up. "Tell me, please."

Shiercliffe's hand had clasped hers in an unexpected display of affection. "You're going to receive a corneal transplant. We've found a donor."

"A donor?"

"Yes. Young and healthy and with perfect eyesight. We'll operate first thing in the morning."

Now it was morning, and she was lying in the middle of the operating theater, dimly aware of the presurgery bustle of preparations going on around her—footsteps going back and forth, abbreviated questions and shorthand answers, the clatter and clink of instruments being arranged, the odor of carbolic acid and fresh linens. No one spoke to her or told her what was coming next, and even though she was ostensibly the focus of all this activity, she had never felt more alone.

"Aggie." She was surprised to hear Victor's voice. "Would you prefer a local or a general anesthetic?"

Her heart began to pound. "Local," she said, even though she yearned to escape into darkness. *That's not who I am, though.* She could just imagine herself as a spectator in the bleachers, craning her neck to catch a glimpse of this pioneering new procedure. It was for the sake of that other self—her true self, the one she hoped to be again—that she chose to remain awake and aware during the operation.

"All right, then. You'll feel a bit of cold now...this solution will numb your eye."

Aggie smiled up at him. "You're much better than Grimbald at this part," she said. "I doubt he'd explain anything to the patient."

"Um... Aggie..." Victor sounded uncomfortable.

"Point taken," said Grimbald. He must have been standing right behind Victor.

"Sorry," she said.

"With any luck, you'll be able to see whom you're insulting by the end of the day," said Grimbald.

As the cold numbing agent trickled into her left eye, Aggie

thought that Victor must be pleased to be at his mentor's side again.

"You must be so pleased to be back in the operating theater," she said.

"I am—though I think Grimbald was motivated more by necessity than by choice," admitted Victor.

"Is the procedure so complicated?" When Shiercliffe had described how they would replace her cornea, she had assured Aggie that the process was both straightforward and simple.

"No," said Victor. "There's another procedure going on at the same time, in the other operating theater."

Before Aggie could ask anything more, Grimbald cut in. "Is the eye numb yet?" He leaned over her, and Aggie nearly sneezed as the strong scent of Bay Rum moustache wax filled her nose.

"It should be," said Victor.

"All right, then. Time to address the students, and then we begin."

A new blur appeared beside Aggie. "How're you doing, Ags?"

"Lizzie?" For a moment, Aggie was so overcome with relief at the sound of her friend's flat American accent that she couldn't speak. "Aren't you going to get in trouble for being here?"

"I'm only here for a moment. I'm actually supposed to be over in the other operating theater, but I wanted to take a moment to see you before your surgery."

"Oh, that's nice of you."

"Hello, Miss Lavenza." Shiercliffe's voice carried a slight undertone of censure. "I do believe you are wanted in the other room?" She gestured at something, but to Aggie, anything farther than two feet away might as well be invisible.

"Of course, Miss Shiercliffe. Ags, don't worry about a thing."

"Oh, these new nurses!" Shiercliffe was fussing with something at the periphery of Aggie's vision. "They've left a knot on the length of the IV tubing. Must I do everything myself?"

She's nervous, thought Aggie, surprised by the realization. "Matron?"

Shiercliffe continued to fiddle with the IV stand. "It will just be a few more minutes, and then we'll begin."

"Tell me something about the donor. Who is he?"

"Just an ordinary East End boy." There was an edge to Shiercliffe's voice.

There were thousands upon thousands of East End boys, and a myriad of ways for them to die—of cold, of hunger, of the many diseases that cold and malnutrition caused. There were countless ways for a poor boy to come to harm. Yet Aggie felt a chill race down her arms. "What happened to him?"

"Exsanguination," said Shiercliffe. "He died of blood loss."

Heart racing, Aggie forced the next question out. "Do you know anything else about him?"

A beat of hesitation. "He was a thief and a pickpocket—not a life conducive to longevity, I'm afraid. One of his lowlife companions did him in just as he was leaving this hospital, as a matter of fact. Some kind of retribution, I imagine, but on the bright side, because he was attacked on hospital premises, he was able to receive the very best care." Shiercliffe gave her an awkward pat on the arm. Presumably, it was meant to be comforting. "It might not have been sufficient to save his life, but it's enough to save yours."

Aggie understood. She was going to see again—*with Dodger's eyes*. In an ironic twist of fate, something had happened to him on his way out of the hospital, and now he was gone. But she had another chance at the life and career she had planned.

But wait—hadn't Shiercliffe just contradicted herself, changing her version of what had killed Dodger? *Perhaps I'm just confused*, thought Aggie. The operating theater, the impending surgery, even her impaired vision might all be muddling her memory.

In the end, though, what did the details matter? He was dead, with all his vitality and mischief and unexpected sweetness snuffed out. She felt a hollow ache at the thought that he was no longer out in the world somewhere. Yet now he would always be a part of her. There was a biblical proverb that said that eyes were the windows to the soul—or the mirrors, Aggie couldn't recall which. It seemed an important distinction, though. After this procedure was complete, would she see the world differently through the lens of Dodger's eyes—or would she look into a mirror and see a stranger reflected there?

18

WILL FOUGHT THE URGE TO RETRACE HIS STEPS when he saw the sign for the morgue. It was a shameful thing for a medical student to admit, but dead bodies made him deeply, viscerally uncomfortable. Admittedly, the fact that he was badly hungover from the night before wasn't helping matters.

Maybe, said the little voice in his head, *I ought to be pursuing some other career.*

Of course, that would mean leaving Byram as well as his brother. Not that he saw that much of Victor. They weren't in any of the same classes, and on the rare occasions they met up for dinner, it seemed easier to talk to Lizzie about her inventions than to try to bridge the gap between Victor and himself.

But now Victor had sent him a note. *Come down to the overflow morgue. Tell no one.* And then, as an afterthought: *Bring something to eat.*

So here he was, carrying a scone and a thermos of lukewarm tea he had scavenged from the student lounge down into the bowels of the hospital, trying not to jump at every rumble of the boiler and hiss of the gas sconces along the wall. He hesitated outside the morgue, wondering if the overflow morgue had a sign that said Overflow Morgue, and realizing how ridiculous that was.

You're going to have to go inside.

There was a painful knot just below Will's breastbone—fear always gave him heartburn—and he wished he had thought to bring a bit of brandy to bolster his courage. Hair of the dog—wasn't that supposed to be the cure for drink-induced ills?

Of course, these days, he'd been having enough hair of the dog to create a whole other dog, which was why he had decided to drink tea instead.

You're procrastinating, said the little voice of his conscience, which sounded a lot like Byram's voice—darkly amused. He tried not to think about the fact that Byram was hardly speaking to him these days.

He's gone off me. Any day now, Will knew, Byram would be requesting another roommate.

But what was the point of worrying about that now? He forced himself to push open the door. Inside, the morgue was cold and dark, so he held the door propped open.

"Victor?" He could just make out a wall lined with drawers, and a body on a slab—a middle-aged man, his skin fishy white and wrinkled as if he had been submerged in water, his toes and fingers missing. Behind him, there was another body on display. This one was in even worse shape—it was missing its limbs and head as well as part of the outer layer of skin, and Will had the unwilling association of a cut of beef. He shuddered violently, and not just from the chill. A large slab of ice had been placed in the corner of the morgue, but there was still a sickly sweet, meaty smell mingled with the acrid, chemical tang of formalin.

His gorge rising, Will backed out of the room. Why did Victor have to send him that note? Surely Lizzie could have brought him whatever he needed.

I'll give it one last look around the corner, he decided. If he didn't find Victor, he was going back up to his own room to wash his hands and face until he stopped wanting to vomit.

Will rounded the corner and saw a smaller, hand-written sign that read Waiting Mortuary. Will wasn't sure whether that meant the same thing as morgue or not, but he knocked twice, just for form's sake, and was turning to leave when the door opened, making his heart slam into his chest.

"Will? That you?" Victor peeked out, looking unshaven and a little red-eyed. "Thank God, I'm beginning to fade. Come on in."

Will reluctantly stepped into the waiting mortuary. This was a much smaller room than the first, and there was no ice bringing the temperature down and reducing the sour smell of the bodies. There were three cadavers, all laid out on slabs. Two of them were naked, with stocky, once-muscular bodies gone slack with death. One had the sickly greenish-gray pallor of decomposition; the other had gone the mottled bluish-purple of a bruise. The metal plates that covered their left pectoral muscles looked like scrap metal, and the heavy black stitching that crisscrossed their bodies suggested they had been cobbled together from multiple sources.

Will recognized the third body, off to one side on a gurney, from the Bio-Mechanical procedure he had observed earlier in the day. This corpse appeared far less offensive than its companions. In fact, the slender young man might almost have been sleeping—except for the metal armor plating his chest and the electrodes at his neck.

"Have you been down here before?" asked Victor. "My first time, I thought I was going to decorate the walls with the remains of my last meal. Now I'm so used to it, I'm perishing with hunger."

"Oh, sorry. Here— Sorry, this was all I could find between meals." He handed the scone over, still staring at the body of the young man, who looked like he was—had been—Will's age. There were dark bruises under his eyes and over his ribs.

"Thanks," said Victor, unwrapping the scone and taking an enormous bite. "And that's tea, I presume?" Victor eyed the thermos as if it were a long lost love.

"What? Yes."

Victor smiled as he poured himself a cup and then took a sip as if it were sacramental wine. Instantly, his expression fell. "It's cold."

"Terribly sorry about that, I was rushing and just took what was left in the pot…"

"It's fine, really." Victor took another swallow to prove it. "Have a seat."

The only other stool was occupied by a black bulbed trocar, its metal tip stained a dark brown. *Don't be squeamish*, he told himself, lifting the instrument used for syphoning off bodily fluids and placing it gingerly on the slab next to the greenish body.

Victor took a last bite of the scone. "That's better. Say, do you happen to know what time it is?"

"Around teatime."

"Two hours since the operation, and that took the better part of six hours. Christ, no wonder I'm dead on my feet."

"I can imagine," said Will. "It was hard enough to watch from the bleachers."

"Did you catch Aggie's op first?"

"I just observed the other procedure," he admitted. "Watching Aggie felt a bit too personal, and truth be told, I had to look away from most of the Bio-Mechanical surgery."

Of course Victor, the star student, hadn't just observed both operations—he had assisted in them.

I'm not cut out for this.

"I don't know, Will," Victor said, shaking his head. "Are you sure you're in the right school? Or did you get lost on your way to Oxford and were just too polite to tell anyone?"

No, thought Will with a burst of anger, *I'm here because our father thought you were dead and so I was supposed to take your place.* It made no sense, he knew. Why should he be stung that Victor had voiced the very thoughts he had about himself? Yet still, it rankled to have his perfect older brother questioning his fitness to be here.

Except he's not so perfect anymore. Now, when they went home, it was Victor who made their parents uncomfortable, who seemed subtly but unmistakably other.

"Assuming you're right and I don't belong here," Will said, unable to keep a hint of defensiveness from his voice, "where do you suggest I go? Our father would happily foot a transfer into finance, but I dislike numbers even more than I do blood."

"How about the law? I can see you as a barrister, eloquently stating your case."

"I'd have to wear a white wig, though. Not sure how I feel about that." It was not an altogether terrible idea, though. The law was respectable enough for their father to consider, but it also involved stories, and Will could imagine himself doing quite well in a discipline of stories and ethics.

On the other hand, it would also mean leaving Byram behind for the first time since they had become friends, at the age of seven.

"You know, Will," Victor began, but whatever he began to say was cut off by a low groan from one of the beds.

"Oh, Jesus, is it waking up?" Will jumped to his feel, icy fear coursing down his spine.

"Possibly." The greenish-tinged body shuddered and gave a long-drawn-out sigh.

"I think that's a definite yes."

"It could just be built-up gas escaping from the body."

"I don't know which is worse." Keeping his eye on the green body, Will stepped back as Victor moved around it, fastening the leather restraints to its arms and legs.

"What are those for?"

"Just a precaution. They tend to wake up disorientated. We restrain them so they don't accidentally injure themselves—or anyone else."

"Then why were they not restrained to begin with?" He glanced at the other two bodies and had a nightmarish image of the big, bruised one sneaking up on him from behind.

"It impedes circulation. Besides, it's often not necessary. Over 75 percent of attempted Bio-Mechanical procedures end in failure."

"Oh," said Will, his voice coming out small and thin.

"Not convinced? Here." Victor placed his stethoscope onto the cadaver's chest. "Nothing. Must have just been natural gases escaping during decomposition." He picked up the chart, checked his fob watch and jotted down the time.

Will approached the young man's pale body. "What about this one?"

Victor picked up the chart by the bruised body's slab and added a note. "Our showcase project? We're hoping this one does a lot more than just open his eyes and grunt. Otherwise we're not going to have anything to impress the kaiser. But we got him immediately after death, so his prospects are good."

Will shivered in the cold air. "Can't we cover him with a blanket or something?" Will tried to think of the right word to describe the pale body lying exposed on the gurney. Despite the electrodes visible at his neck and the brass chest plate, he looked all too human.

"Just don't look at him, if it bothers you that much."

"It's not that. He looks cold, Victor."

"Hang on. You worried he's going to wake up and attack you, or concerned he might catch a chill?"

Will considered the bruises visible on the dead man's ribs. "Um...a little of both?"

Victor chuckled. "Don't ever change, little brother." Walking over to the body, he secured the leather restraints around its arms. "You know, you're not the only one who gets a bit spooked by them. When we were operating, I had this sudden pang— What if he's not really dead? What if he's just paralyzed, like I was?"

"Did you say anything?"

Victor moved around to fasten the ankle straps. "I thought about it. But then I realized that Grimbald and Shiercliffe wouldn't make the same mistake twice."

Will noticed his brother did not include Moulsdale. "I know it might sound absurd, but can we give him a blanket?"

"Not absurd at all. They're on the shelf there."

Will pulled a gray wool blanket down from a shelf and un-folded it over the body.

Victor watched him, looking amused. "Why not add a hot water bottle, while you're at it?"

"That's not a bad idea."

"Foot massage? Fox-fur stole? Perhaps some hot tea with rum? I wouldn't mind a nip of that, myself."

Will shot his brother an annoyed glance. "Oh, do shut up." He picked up Victor's medical book and began reading about the importance of calculating the rate of anesthesia during an operation. *I am never going to understand these equations*, he thought.

Suddenly, Victor got to his feet. "Egads, Will, I think your blanket idea's working—our patient's waking up!"

Will did not put down the textbook. "Have I mentioned how unfunny you are?"

"No, really. Turn around."

Will shook his head. "You must think I'm still eight years old."

"Hang on to that thought." Victor moved with athletic swiftness, shouldering Will aside.

"Hey, do you mind?" said Will, turning as he added, "This isn't rugby—oh my God!" The young man who had been as still as a corpse a moment earlier, was now gasping, his muscles tense as he strained against his straps. "You weren't funning me!"

The Bio-Mechanical's eyes were open and flicking wildly around. There was something strange about them—a glint of silver in the green of the iris—and something stranger about the way they moved, the pupils expanding and contracting at extraordinary speed, the eyes flicking much faster than was typical and then—dear Lord—oscillating inside their sockets.

"What's wrong with it?"

"Not a thing. That's Lizzie's newest invention—telescopulars. They can magnify up to one hundred times more than your eyes or mine, and they can see in low light the way a cat can. They can even record things they see."

"But why are they spinning like that?"

"No idea. Lizzie should be down here soon, but she wanted to check on Aggie first."

The creature closed his eyes and began to pant like an injured animal. "Um... Victor...the way he's breathing...is any of this normal?"

Victor made another note in the chart. "I don't know. I've never seen one actually wake before—and I don't have any memories of what I did when I first became conscious again." He waited a beat, and then added softly, "I don't suppose any of this could ever be called normal."

Something in his brother's voice made Will turn to look at him. "Don't you feel normal now, Victor?"

Victor met his eyes. "No. I can pass for normal, but I'm an aberration."

I'm different, too, Will longed to say. For one absurd moment, Will thought about telling Victor about his feelings for Byram. Perhaps Victor would even understand.

Yet he couldn't bring himself to do it. Perhaps, if they had been closer before Victor's transformation. But it had been years since they had slept in the same nursery bedroom, and in many ways, his brother felt like a stranger who already knew too many of his embarrassing secrets.

The creature made a sound of distress, his head moving

in a circle, like a stunned calf awaiting the killing blow. On impulse, Will reached out to him, placing one hand on his forehead to calm him. Now the spinning metal-and-glass eyes focused on Will and the creature took a deep, shuddering breath. Its eyes settled like a roulette wheel finally coming to a stop.

Will looked steadily into the boy's uncanny eyes, hoping his tone would reassure him, even if he could not comprehend the meaning of his words. "Welcome to your new normal."

19

THE FIRST FORTY-EIGHT HOURS AFTER AGGIE'S surgery passed like a fever dream as she drifted in and out of sleep. Her eyes were bandaged to prevent any inadvertent rubbing and she was told to remain lying on her back, keeping as still as possible. Aware of Justine in the iron lung beside her, Aggie didn't want to admit how trapped she felt as she slipped from memories to dreams and back again.

Sometimes Justine talked to her, mainly about politics, which sent her off to sleep again. At other times, Shiercliffe or one of the other nurses woke her to put drops in her eyes. Some of the drops burned, but this was to be expected.

At one point, Dodger came by to take her on a guided tour of the East End, but wound up getting them both lost in a maze of narrow, winding streets as a fog rolled in, obscuring everything.

"Don't worry," he said. "I'm blind, anyway." He turned to her, revealing marbles where his eyes ought to have been.

She woke up in a cold sweat from that dream, only to find

Dodger sitting on her bed. "You're not dead," she said. "I dreamt you were dead."

"Me? Nah," he said, taking off his top hat. "Never happen. Want to know why?" He pulled an eye out of his hat, then another, and held them up to show that they were all Bio-Mechanical eyes that could blink at her from the palm of his hand. "I got eyes in the back of my head."

She woke up with a shout, then lay there, feeling her own hands and throat, trying to decide if she was in another dream.

The bandages came off, and at first Aggie assumed the transplant had failed, because her vision was as blurry as it had been before. "Be patient," Grimbald told her. "It will take at least a few weeks to see any improvement. As long as you're not experiencing any new pains, we're considering this a success."

She was allowed to attend lectures again, wearing a pair of dark tinted glasses to shield her eyes, but not permitted to read or take notes. She kept the tinted glasses on all the time, even though they dimmed all the colors in the room and made her feel as though the world was permanently stuck at fifteen minutes before sunset. They protected her eyes, and that was more important than seeing colors.

After a fortnight, Aggie thought she noticed a slight sharpening in the outlines of things, and Grimbald proclaimed her well enough to remove the stitches.

Then, to her dismay, he ordered her back to bed rest for another twenty-four hours. She compromised by resting in the recovery room for an hour, and then removed the bandages from her eyes and began getting dressed. Lizzie knocked and opened the door to the recovery room without waiting for a response, making Aggie clutch her petticoat to her chest.

"Oh, thank heaven," she said. "Thought you might be Grimbald for a moment."

Lizzie walked over. "Turn around and I'll do up the back of your corset. I didn't expect you'd be up and about so soon. How are you feeling?"

"Fine. I couldn't bear just lying there another minute." Aggie sucked in a breath as Lizzie tied her corset strings.

Lizzie stepped away, frowning. "Wait a minute—you were cleared by Grimbald, right?"

"He's got other things to attend to." Aggie went over to the wardrobe and removed her lavender overskirt. "Besides, I know how to take care of myself. I'm keeping my dark specs on."

"Have you taken a look around without them yet?"

Aggie removed her blouse from the closet. "Not yet."

"Well?"

Aggie focused on doing up her shirt buttons before responding. "All right." She sat down in the room's only chair. "Let's do it." She pulled the glasses away from her face, and watched light and color return to the room. Everything was so sharp and clear that she felt a little dizzy.

"How is it?" Lizzie asked.

"I think... I think it may be clearer than before the accident."

"That's incredible." Lizzie looked down at Aggie, shaking her head in wonder. "No one would ever know they weren't your eyes. Except for the color, of course."

Aggie brought her hand up to her face. She had avoided mirrors since the first operation. "The color? But that's impossible." The cornea was a clear lens covering the colored iris of the eye, and transplanting it shouldn't have changed the color of her eyes.

"I'm afraid it's not. Here, take a look." Lizzie grabbed a hand mirror from the side table and held it up to Aggie before she had a chance to respond.

Aggie stared at her reflection in shock. "My eyes are dark." Before, they had been a clear, pale green. Now they were brown—no, on closer inspection, they were a mixture of brown and green. "I don't understand."

"Maybe the eye drops have darkened the iris?"

"I suppose it's possible." Peering more closely at herself, she had another, completely unscientific thought: *Dodger's eyes had been dark brown.*

Suddenly, the room began to spin like a roulette wheel, and Aggie grabbed for something to steady herself before losing her balance. She heard Lizzie's startled shout, but the sound seemed as if it was coming from far away. She felt as if she were tumbling down a long well, and then she landed in a dark, damp room with a packed dirt floor.

"Don't get up yet," said Lizzie, holding the cool compress to Aggie's forehead.

"I'm fine. Just hand me my spectacles?" Lizzie placed them in Aggie's hand, and a moment later, she was looking at the recovery room through the familiar filter of the gray lenses. "There," she said, standing up. "No dizziness." Bed, side table, small watercolor of a sunset—everything was where it ought to be.

"I really think we need to get Dr. Grimbald in," said Lizzie.

"I don't want to waste his time, when he has so much on his plate right now." It was the perfect excuse. With less than a fortnight before the kaiser's visit, there was an air of contained panic among the hospital staff.

"I don't care what else he has to do. You fainted."

"It was just the blood rushing to my head." Aggie didn't understand herself exactly what had happened, but she did know that it had felt as though for a moment, she had been looking out of someone else's eyes. "Please, Lizzie. Don't tell Grimbald about this. It was a fluke, nothing more."

"A dangerous one. What if you had hit your head?"

Aggie smoothed back a lock of hair that had fallen out of her bun. "You'd yell at me even more."

"Very funny." Lizzie picked the cold compress off the chair and placed it near the basin. "You're not a machine, you know."

"Don't sound so disappointed."

Lizzie made a noise halfway between exasperation and laughter. For a moment, Aggie considered telling Lizzie the truth about what had happened. The only problem was, it sounded so insane. No, it *was* insane. Clearly, her mind was playing tricks on her.

Lizzie put the back of her hand on Aggie's forehead. "Well, at least there's no fever. Why don't you lie back down in bed and I'll fetch you some lunch?"

"I'm fine sitting here in the chair till the nurse comes back," said Aggie. "And please don't think you need to babysit me. I know you have to get back to your own work."

Lizzie smiled a bit ruefully. "I must admit, I am curious to see how our Dreadnaught is coming along. His progress has been pretty remarkable—he's learning to speak even more quickly than Victor did. I think it must be the new electro-cranial stimulation protocol."

Aggie tried to look enthusiastic as Lizzie launched into a complicated explanation of brainwave frequencies and how they impacted the endocrine system. "That's fantastic," she said. "Keep me posted." It was only when the door clicked shut behind Lizzie that Aggie allowed herself to sink into the chair and succumb to exhaustion.

Maybe something did go wrong with the transplant, she thought.

No. It was a hallucination, she told herself. Some aftereffect of anesthesia or guilt or both.

Groaning, she closed her eyes and wished she could just go to sleep for a week.

But they aren't your eyes, she thought. *They're someone else's. They're Dodger's.* Somehow, she would have to learn to live with the guilt of that so she didn't wind up losing her mind.

28

HE WASN'T SURE WHAT WAS REAL AND WHAT was a dream. Had there really been a whirling merry-go-round room filled with dead bodies and a fair-haired boy with kind eyes? No, that must have been the drugs. A witch of a nurse, dressed all in black, kept giving him injections of some bright green liquid that burned as it made its way through his veins.

There were other things they did to him, as well, things that made his muscles twitch and then convulse. He tried to keep his eyes open, but the light hurt too much for him to keep them that way for long. There was a sound, a hum of machinery that increased to a whirring whine, and then a tingling, stinging wave went through his whole body. Worst of all, his eyes felt as though they were spinning in their sockets.

If it was a dream, he wanted to wake up. If it wasn't... Well, then. He wanted to dream something else.

He took a mental inventory of his injuries. First and foremost, his eyes felt dry and scratchy, as if someone had thrown sand in them. Opening them took an effort he couldn't muster very often. His head ached, too, and so did his neck and chest. There had been a fight, presumably. Or an accident. Maybe he'd been run over by a stagecoach. He sure felt like he'd been trampled by multiple horses, but he couldn't recall any details. Maybe he could ask one of the people who came into his room to poke and prod at him and make brusque, incomprehensible comments. Problem was, he couldn't keep his eyes open long enough to get a good look around—the light was bloody painful—and once his eyes were shut, he kept drifting in and out of consciousness, trying to grab hold of something to anchor him in place but always slipping back under.

"Extreme photosensitivity," said a man who sounded like a drill sergeant. "Why the hell were there no bandages covering his eyes when he woke up, Victor?"

"Sorry, Dr. Grimbald. Must have been an oversight," responded Victor.

"I must have expected too much of you," said Grimbald. "Next time, I'll spell everything out."

Something dark and cool and moist was placed over his eyes, and he fell back into the cool darkness.

When he surfaced again, he was burning up.

"His temperature is spiking. Postoperative fever." That voice—stern, female, older—raised a prickle of alarm along his skin. That was the witch nurse.

"We don't have the time to waste nursing him like an infant," insisted a man with a posh, deep, rich baritone. "He needs to get used to those telescopulars in time to train for the exhibition. I want him up and about in the next forty-eight hours."

No one asked him what he wanted. To know his name, for starters. To know what had happened to him. And last but definitely not least, to know what they wanted to train him to do.

Sometimes he remembered fragments of things, like walking with a pretty redhead through a maze of dark streets and narrow alleys.

"And who are you meant to be then?" The redhead's accent was working class, from the north.

He doffed his top hat and executed a courtly bow. "The Artful Dodger, successful man of business, at your service."

That name. It felt like the clue to a riddle, a jacket plucked out of a secondhand pile that fit like it was custom made.

Except he hadn't managed to dodge whatever twist of fate had landed him here. Maybe he was the Artless Dodger now.

This was a dream. He was pretty sure it was a dream, at any rate, because he was a child again, and he had a sense that he hadn't been a child in a while. He was clinging to his mother's cooling body in their icy basement flat. He wasn't shivering anymore, and the part of him that was not a child knew that this was a bad sign. The room was so cold that he could see his breath, and he had been lying still for hours. The fact that his younger self was no longer feeling chilled was a sign that his body was starting to shut down.

Someone was pounding on the door, and then there was a crash.

"Ugh," said a man, pulling a handkerchief over his mouth. "They really are like animals."

"Worse than animals," the other had replied, his lip curling. "Even dogs know better than to cuddle up to a corpse."

He didn't speak much English, but he understood a fair amount—and the word for *corpse* was the same in both languages. But his mother couldn't be dead. She had promised she would get up in a minute. "Just let me rest a little, Yakov."

He tried to explain to the men that his mother wasn't dead, just sleeping, but they pulled handkerchiefs over their faces and pulled him away from her. Standing over her, he could see how pale she was. Her skin had a waxen look, and there was something stiff and strange about her mouth. He should never have let her rest for so long. At one point in the night, she had made a gasping, rattling sound, deeper and more desperate than her usual snores when she took too much of her medicine. Stupidly, he had been relieved when it stopped. He should have kept shaking her, forcing her to keep her eyes open—but in the end, it would not have changed a thing. She had let go of him long before he had let go of her.

Dodger opened his eyes and the memory vanished. *I'm cold*, he thought. *That's what made me dream about that day.* Then he realized something else: his eyes were open, and there was no more discomfort. Shivering, he sat up on the thin straw pallet, pulling the threadbare gray blanket over his shoulders. He was in a windowless room with stone walls and a dirt floor—a poorer room than the one from his dream, and that was saying something. Dodger's stomach growled, making him aware that he hadn't eaten in… Wait, how long had it been? He couldn't recall. In fact, he realized with dawning shock, he couldn't seem to recall much of anything that had happened before waking up in this cold prison cell of a room.

There were voices coming from outside the door to his room.

"And how is our newest patient?" The speaker had a deep baritone and sounded somewhat familiar.

"Oh, 'e's fine, Professor Moulsdale. Asleep, most likely." There was the rattle of keys as the door was unlocked, and then two men walked in. One wore some sort of navy-and-scarlet uniform and had a thick, gray-and-brown walrus moustache and thin, wire-rimmed spectacles. The second man, presumably Professor Moulsdale, wore an expensive suit tailored to hide his girth. He had a pale, doughy face and small button-black eyes that gleamed with satisfaction as he stroked his neat Vandyke beard.

"He's awake," he said, sounding pleased. "This bodes well for recovery." Nodding at the guard, Moulsdale said, "Mind you take good care of this one, Wiggins. He's our prize specimen, and we have just under eight weeks to get him in top-drawer condition to impress the kaiser."

That rich baritone voice, thought Dodger. *I know it. How do I know it?*

"Don't you worry, Professor," said the guard. "I'll whip him into shape."

"Tell me something," said Moulsdale. "You're a former navy man, aren't you, Wiggins?"

"Boer War," said Wiggins. "Was going to make sergeant, but there was a bit of bother about a girl." He did not explain what sort of bother.

"Well, then," said Moulsdale, as if he had not heard. "You know how to get a soldier in shape, correct? So, there will be a few bob extra in your pay packet if you bring the subject along in his training more quickly."

Training, thought Dodger. *What kind of training do prisoners get in this place?*

Then the door to the cell was closed and Dodger was alone with the guard. "Right then," said Wiggins, taking his nightstick off his belt and smacking it across his palm. "First lesson—pay attention." Without warning, the nightstick lashed out, slamming into Dodger's thigh.

As Dodger gasped at the shock of pain, Wiggins cocked his head to one side. "Aw, there, there. Don't look so glum, mate. Remember, 'that which does not kill us, makes us stronger.'"

Dodger got stronger.

Days passed. Some of them were better than others, but even the best of them were bad. The dirt floor and stone walls of his cell let the damp in. A lone, barred window revealed that the room was below ground level, but if he peered up, he could see an inner courtyard where lines of white sheets were sometimes left out to dry in the patchy sunlight.

He was still not certain where he was being held prisoner, or what his crime had been. Three other blokes were brought in to share his cell, but none of them seemed able or willing to talk. One, a rough-looking brute with a bald head and a patchwork of thick scars across his face, responded only in grunts and clicks. Another fellow, mummy-thin and leathery as an old boot, had a habit of nervously licking his lips when addressed. The most normal looking of the three had deep-set eyes and the shadowed, flat look of someone who had seen unspeakable horrors. He could say one word—*no*—which he repeated often, but only to himself.

The guards—or porters, as they were called—were mostly nasty pieces of work, prodding him with their heavy wooden clubs and talking to him as though he were an idiot. "Pick up shovel," they would shout, jabbing at him. When he didn't instantly understand what they wanted him to do—shovel coal into the oven or remove old coals—they shouted more loudly and jabbed harder.

Wiggins was the worst. For some reason, he liked to quote some bloke called Neecher.

"Now, some might say that your situation is quite unfair," said Wiggins one day as he ladled out the evening's soup into their tin cups. "After all, what right have we to deny you your natural slumber in the earth? But that is what Nietzsche would call a slave's sense of morality. Slaves tend to concern themselves with consequences. A superior man, on the other hand, has a will to power. There are different rules, you see, for the likes of you and the likes of me."

That left Dodger to wonder. *Am I slave? What sort of man am I now?*

The next day, Wiggins escorted him up three flights of stairs into the laboratory—a room that looked like a cross between the large kitchen of a busy inn and an apothecary's larder. A tall, posh, good-looking bloke named Victor and a lively young girl named Lizzie brought out a machine that made that awful, familiar whirring sound, and Dodger felt a terror so sharp it made the room tilt and spin. It took the two white coats a while to talk him down, but after a while, he began breathing normally again.

"We won't do anything until you're ready," said the girl in her flat Yankee accent, and even though he didn't understand the rest of what she was saying—recalibration and magnetic field integration and bioelectric stimulation—he did believe that she was trying to help him.

"It won't hurt," said the man. Victor. "I know it did before, but I swear to you, that part is over." Something in the man's eyes made Dodger believe that he was telling the truth, and he allowed Victor to hook him up to the machines.

That was the first of several sessions, repeated over a course of several weeks. Dodger couldn't say he enjoyed the way the machines made him feel—sometimes, they set his eyes spinning—but Victor and Lizzie talked to each other with an undercurrent of humor and affection that seemed to spill over into the way they talked to him.

"He seems more aware," said Lizzie, removing a clamp from his neck and dabbing some sort of ointment there. "How much do you think he understands?"

"Not too much, I hope," said Victor, making a note in a black, leather-bound notebook. "There's a fine line between knowing enough and understanding too much. He'll do better if he comprehends just enough without understanding so much he starts to ask questions."

Dodger hesitated. He had very few cards to play, and he hated to reveal his hand too soon, but it was irresistible. "Actually," he said, "I do have some questions."

Lizzie stared at him for a moment, but before she could say anything, Moulsdale entered the room, panting a little. "And how is our little gutter rat turned show horse? Coming along nicely?"

Lizzie and Victor assured him that Dodger's progress was

remarkable, while Dodger instinctively stared straight ahead. Trusting Lizzie and Victor was one thing. Trusting Moulsdale was a far thornier proposition.

When Moulsdale left, admonishing them to hurry along so they did not miss a lecture, Lizzie turned to Victor. "Maybe we need to find a less public place to continue these treatments."

He got no answers that day.

It occurred to Dodger from time to time that he might be living in a loony bin. His cellmates certainly looked like lunatics, and he felt like one.

Sometimes his head ached and he had dizzy spells that left him with the dazed impression that he had escaped his dark cell of a room and been transported to another place.

One time he had been in a room filled with billowing clouds and long white robes—heaven, he thought, until he saw a red-faced wench wrestle a sheet out of a mangler while another, older woman stirred a steaming tub of laundry. Another time, he had thought he might be in quite a different location, as he had clearly seen a shapely female calf emerging from a stocking that was being rolled down to the ankle. That appealing show was cut abruptly short, however, and his distraction had earned him a cudgel blow from one of the porters who objected to how slowly he was shoveling coal.

Stranger still, there were moments when he felt the flutter of some feminine presence in his head—his dead mother's ghost, perhaps, visiting him from beyond the grave, or some sympathetic angel come down to comfort him in his hour of need.

On the other hand, it was a lot likelier that he was simply losing his marbles. One day, when he was about to bite into the bit of moldy cheese that was meant to be his lunch, he saw a bizarre monster, like a deformed eyeless hedgehog.

It was only when he flung the cheese away that he realized he had seen this creature before: through the lens of a microscope exhibitor who used to offer glimpses through the eyefinder for a ha'penny.

"Behold," the man intoned, "entire Lilliputian worlds inside a strand of hair, a handful of dust, a sliver of cheese."

"Cor," said his younger self, "am I consuming those horrible mites every time I have a bit of cheese?"

"What the eye cannot see, the heart never grieves," the man had replied. So what did that mean now that he had telescope eyes and could see all the hidden monsters?

21

THERE WAS SOMETHING NEW IN DODGER'S
schedule. After a week of Wiggins's crude training sessions—
a battery of chin-ups and push-ups followed by a timed climb
to the top of a rope suspended from the ceiling—he was told
he was to have a different instructor, Dr. Grimbald. Grimbald, a spare man in his late forties, had a handlebar moustache and some nasty-looking burn scars on his forearm, and
his eyes were cold and distant.

"Come," he commanded, barking out the word as though
Dodger were a dog before turning to stride down the corridor. He opened a door that led out of the hospital into a small
courtyard. For the next hour, Grimabld never looked directly
at Dodger, as if working with him were an unpleasant but
unavoidable chore. Unlike Wiggins, however, Grimbald appeared to have specific skills in mind.

He taught Dodger to crawl along the ground, head and
elbows down, moving in small increments so that he barely
seemed to be moving at all. He demonstrated hand gestures

for words like *attention, advance* and *withdraw.* He taught him *affirmative, negative* and *wait.* There were other signs for objects like *soldier, gun, horse* and *enemy.* After rattling these off, Grimbald asked Dodger to do them again, from memory. Dodger was trying to remember the first word when Grimbald expelled a sigh and checked his pocket watch.

"What's the point? I might as well be talking to a monkey." Apparently, this last comment was directed at himself.

Feeling a spark of mischief, Dodger scratched himself like a monkey and made the appropriate simian noises.

"Dear Lord," said Grimbald, actually focusing on Dodger for the first time. "Can you understand me?"

Dodger gave the signal for *affirmative,* and then, because it seemed silly not to, he added, "'Course."

Grimbald stared at him as though he'd grown an extra head. "You can speak!" Then, squinting as though he suspected a trick, he said, "Say something else."

Puzzled by Grimbald's response, Dodger shrugged. "Like what?"

"Uncanny." Grimbald made a note in Dodger's chart. "Well, now," he said, giving Dodger an assessing look. "Seems we need to step up the pace."

After that, Grimbald seemed to take more interest in his pupil. In their next session, he brought a detailed picture of a field at the edge of a forest. "Look closely at this picture," he instructed. "Now look at this one," he said, holding out what appeared to be an identical image. "What has changed?"

All Dodger saw was grass and a few fir trees.

"Come on," said Grimbald. "Focus. What's wrong with this?"

At first, Dodger was baffled. He had no memories of the

countryside, something that made him five kinds of fool, according to Grimbald. But bit by bit, he learned. The next time they met, he spotted something. Sometimes there were skid marks in the grass—signs that a lorry had been driven there not long ago. Or else there was swamp grass in the field, where no swamp grass ever grew. That could mean a blind, concealing an enemy soldier. Dodger learned to spot when a tree at the edge of the forest was missing its top—a sign that a sniper had cut off the uppermost branches to use as camouflage.

Mostly, Grimbald shook his head and looked disappointed. "It's not enough to just see something better than the next soldier," he said. "You've got to know how to estimate distances and interpret what you see. Is the target three hundred meters away? Or is it four hundred? Is the target shorter than average, which can fool you into thinking he's farther away than he really is? You need to adjust for distance when something is up a tree—it's easy for a sniper to overestimate."

A sniper. Were they going to ship him off to serve in some war on the other side of the world then? Grimbald refused to answer his questions. "You're not meant to understand," he told Dodger. "You're meant to follow orders."

That night, Dodger couldn't sleep. Staring up into the pitch darkness of his cell, his thoughts whirling, he found his eyes spinning. He closed them, and when he opened them again, the room was still—but he could see the shapes of his cellmates, like orange fires in the cool darkness of the room.

All right, thought Dodger, his stomach churning with anxiety. *Sod this*. Nothing made any sense, and the not-knowing was worse than the worst thing he could imagine. The next time he saw Victor and Lizzie, he was going to ask some questions.

★ ★ ★

Dodger tamped down the surge of excitement he felt as Victor and Lizzie led him out of his cell the next day. Instead of bringing him to the stairs that led up to the laboratory, they walked down a long corridor lined with hot water pipes that peeled gray paint like shedding snakes. They stopped in front of a dark green door where the word *Storage* had been clumsily painted over with the words *Department of Neuroscience*. A sign nailed to the door read, *Please contact the superintendent before depositing items. No combustible chemicals, flammable items or perishables. Do not remove items without permission.*

Definitely a less public place than the laboratory. Which meant he had a good chance to ask his questions again—and quite possibly, get some answers.

Inside, the room was a jumble of discarded furniture and oddities. A broken chaise longue, listing to one side, supported a burnt lampshade, a splayed-out umbrella with broken ribs and the skeleton of a two-headed calf. Nearby, a rusted perambulator contained a taxidermy dodo the size of a small dog, its expression as pathetic as its limp, dusty white feathers. Along one wall, a shelf displayed a series of mason jars containing miniature monstrosities, their stunted limbs and curled faces like something out of a child's nightmare.

On a lovely but chipped rosewood desk, Victor fiddled with two small copper-paddled wheels while Lizzie untangled the electrical leads. "Ready for the phrenologic mesmerator?"

Dodger picked up the dodo, which was surprisingly hefty, before seating himself carefully in a chair with a partially ripped wicker back. Distracting himself with the stuffed carcass of the extinct bird, he allowed Victor to put a small device, like an earmuff, over each of his ears. On his right side, one of the paddlewheels began to turn clockwise, emitting a rhythmic pulse, while on his left, the second wheel turned in the opposite direction. Victor had explained the device to him—something about batteries and magnetism and alternating frequencies that stimulated communication between his brain's two hemispheres. It wasn't painful, but at first, the sessions with Victor had left him with headaches and a vague, unsettled feeling. Now, the brain-tuning treatments didn't bother him at all—although they did seem linked to strange flashes of memory and those topsy-turvy moments when he felt as though he were looking out of someone else's eyes.

Dodger trained his eyes on the faded portrait of the queen as a young woman and tried not to worry about the fact that his brain wasn't just being tuned—it was being reconfigured.

"And that's it," said Victor, when a small alarm went off. "Your progress has been nothing short of remarkable," he added as he removed Dodger's earpieces. "I can't believe that you've regained the ability to speak in less than a fortnight. And your dreams… Just incredible. Do you remember anything more today, Dodger?"

Dodger shook his head. "Sorry."

"Ah, well, the brain's a mystery, and every injury provides us with another clue." Victor began to pack away his papers and puzzles.

There was a pencil on the desk, and Dodger picked it up with his right hand and idly began to pass it from finger to finger. "You said something about the brain and injuries. Did I have an accident?"

Victor paused, then closed the case. "Yes. You were injured—badly, I'm afraid. And I'm sorry to be the one to break it to you, but you didn't make it."

"Beg pardon?"

"You died."

Dodger let the pencil drop from his fingers. "I'm missing something."

Victor tugged at his cravat as if it were constricting him. "I know, it sounds a bit unbelievable."

It sounded insane. "Are you trying to tell me—what? That this pokey little office is the afterlife?"

"No, of course not." Victor's foot jiggled the table. "Elizabeth? Maybe you had better jump in here."

Lizzie shook her head. "It's better coming from you, Victor."

Dodger folded his arms. "Let's go back to the part where I died, shall we?"

"I should have planned this out better, but when I came back to myself, I sort of pieced it all together on my own." Victor snapped and unsnapped the buckles on the leather case, revealing his discomfort with this topic. "Of course, I already knew all about the reanimation procedure, so that was an advantage."

Suddenly, old memories came flooding back. Visiting Aggie in hospital, sneaking into Moulsdale's study—and receiving the injection that left him awake and aware of everything said and done to him in the operating theater, but unable to move a muscle or speak a word.

Bloody hell. They said they were going to turn me into a Bio-Mechanical, he thought, his mouth going dry at the memory. Yet here he was, in some sort of prison, perhaps, but hardly a mindless hulk of rotting flesh. He looked down at his hands and arms—they seemed unchanged. Had they changed their minds about him? Then he ran his hands over the sides of his neck and felt the cold metal. Electrodes. They had turned him, then.

A sour taste filled the back of Dodger's throat. "Oh, cripes, you're saying I'm a corpse walker."

"You're a Bio-Mechanical," Victor corrected. "And a very special one at that. In two weeks' time, you're going to meet the Queen of England and the Emperor of Germany. You, out of all the Bio-Mechanicals in England, are going to represent the best of what our government can accomplish."

Dodger pulled off his flat workman's cap and scratched his head, befuddled. "I'm a bloody show pony? Is that what all this training's about?"

"It's very important," said Lizzie. "The kaiser is bringing his best Bio-Mechanical, and the two of you will be pitted against each other in various tasks. It's like the Olympics."

"The what?"

"Modern version of the ancient Greek games?" Victor seemed astonished that Dodger hadn't heard of it.

"That's not important," said Lizzie. "What matters is this— you're meant to convince the kaiser that British technology is superior to his and that there's absolutely no point in start-ing a war, because his side would lose."

Bloody hell, thought Dodger. Maybe he wasn't the one who belonged in a loony bin. Maybe the rest of them ought to have their heads examined.

"I don't know," said Dodger. "Strikes me that when a bloke is looking for a fight, he always seems to size up his opponent and think, yeah, right, bet I can take you, even if the fellow is a bruiser twice his size."

"That may be true of a pub fight," said Victor. "We are talking politics on the world stage."

Dodger sniffed. "Whatever you say. And you're certain I don't need to actually fight this triumph of German engineering?"

"No one's going to want to risk their newest model of Bio-Mechanical soldier in a fight," Victor assured him. "There will just be a demonstration of skills and strength."

Dodger replaced his cap. "Right, then. And once I'm done showing off, do I get to go home? Go back to me own life?"

Lizzie and Victor exchanged uncomfortable glances.

"Look at it this way," said Victor. "Whatever you were in your former life, you are now a very valuable part of Her Majesty's defense. Now, isn't that something to be glad about?"

"Yeah," said Dodger, thinking that these two would make bloody awful card players. "Lucky me."

22

IT WAS ALMOST THE MIDDLE OF MAY, MORE than seven weeks since Aggie's operation, and there were fewer than five days left before the kaiser's visit, yet Aggie was still not permitted to do anything remotely useful. It was maddening. Outside the Royal Victoria's gates, spring had managed to infiltrate the grim brick buildings of the East End, and a lone mulberry tree was proudly displaying its pink blossoms. With almost no time left, preparations for the kaiser's visit were going into overdrive.

Mouse droppings had been spotted in one of the dumb-waiters, and now traps had to be placed in various corners. The long, wheat-colored curtains in many of the wards were deemed filthy and had to be removed and washed, rooms had to be repainted, and exterior stairs and building facades had to be repaired and cleaned. All this meant constant reshuffling of patients and staff to accommodate the renovations.

One of the first rooms that had been refurbished was the Blue Room. One of a handful of private rooms, the Blue

Room overlooked the small garden area outside the kitchen and was always reserved for special patients—former doctors, genteel but impoverished society ladies, retired generals and famous artists.

Shiercliffe would not name the room's current occupant, but it was an open secret among the nursing students that the lady in question was none other than the elderly Queen Victoria. The Queen had been brought into the hospital for observation and care shortly after Aggie's operation, under the cover of night. Word had it that the octogenarian monarch's temper was as fiery as it was unpredictable. Victoria had attempted to punch one nurse while she was trying to help the queen out of bed, screamed that a second nurse was attempting to assassinate her during a sponge bath, and had overturned her chamber pot when a third nurse informed her that sausages were not on the queen's permitted food list.

According to Lizzie, who was unofficially tasked with giving the queen treatments with the magnetometer, Shiercliffe was at her wit's end trying to find a nursing sister whom the queen would tolerate.

Yet Aggie was not permitted to help.

Because of her accident and surgery, she had missed five lectures, an anatomy test, a practical exam on bandaging and a quiz on digestion, but she was only permitted to read or write for an hour each day, so as not to tire out her new eyes.

At first, Aggie had felt frustrated by these restrictions, but for the past few days, she had begun to slip into a sluggish melancholy. Sometimes she found herself missing Dodger with such unexpected intensity that she began holding conversations with him in her mind.

What if Shiercliffe never allows me back to a regular schedule? she would ask, and she could almost hear his derisive snort.

Never happen, she imagined him saying in response.

She confided in her imaginary Dodger things she was too embarrassed to confess to Lizzie or Justine, like her fear that by the time she was given the all-clear, her classmates would be so far ahead of her that she would be forced to begin again, repeating her first year with a batch of new students.

Then, to Aggie's delight, Lizzie had slipped her a note saying she needed Aggie's help in the Blue Room. Finally, a chance to do something, instead of being coddled like a hatchling chick.

Yet as she walked as quickly as she could down the corridor, Aggie felt a wave of disorientation as the walls seemed to tilt and shift. For a moment, when she opened her eyes, she was in a cramped little office, staring at an odd assortment of cast-off objects.

She closed her eyes and counted to three before opening them again. Everything was normal again, and the nurse walking past her didn't appear to have noticed her lapse.

This had happened before, but only when she wasn't wearing her spectacles. One time, she had watched a shovel raking coals into a huge boiler and it had felt as though she were the one doing the shoveling. Another time, she had seen a bowl of watery soup and a piece of stale bread. If she was very tired, the strange, out-of-body interludes lasted longer and seemed more vivid.

She didn't dare tell anyone, in case they thought she was going mad. It was probably just her nerves, playing up. Or her guilty conscience.

Or else her donor's eyes were giving her glimpses of things that Dodger had seen when he was alive.

No. That was a daft thought. Victor might have absorbed some of the personality of Jack, the donor who had supplied his left arm, but that was different. A cornea was a tiny sliver of membrane, not a whole limb.

She was probably just experiencing pangs of guilt, which was absurd. After all, it wasn't her fault that Dodger had gotten himself killed by one of his thief accomplices. It was nothing more than an unfortunate coincidence that his bad choices had caught up with him just after he had sneaked in to visit her.

It was her bad luck that she couldn't stop dwelling on the fact that she would never see him again.

Shoving thoughts of Dodger aside, she pushed her dark specs farther up her nose and gently rapped on the door of the Blue Room.

"Aggie! Thank God." Lizzie stuck her head out of the door and looked around, checking to see no one else was around to witness this. "Hurry up and get in here."

Aggie stepped into the room, which had been refurbished with Persian rugs, a Georgian armoire and a velvet-draped four-poster bed that seemed far too large for its diminutive occupant.

"Incendiary wench," said Queen Victoria, her voice sounding far frailer than Aggie remembered. "Unblind shadow eyes."

She must mean the tinted glasses. "Your Majesty, if you please, I would rather not remove these. They protect my eyes, you see."

"Unsubstantiated!" In a sudden burst of rage, the queen hurled a teacup at Aggie, followed by a thermometer and a diamond brooch.

Frightened the queen would hurt herself, Aggie removed her dark spectacles. "I beg your pardon," she said, dropping into a little curtsy.

"Beggars and thieves," said the queen, subsiding back into the pillows and closing her eyes.

Aggie picked up the thermometer. Luckily, the glass hadn't broken—mercury was impossible to clean up properly. "I don't think she likes me much," she said in an undertone.

"Are you serious?" asked Lizzie. "This is her version of a royal medal. Besides, she asked for you."

Aggie replaced the diamond brooch on the queen's bedside table. "I find that rather hard to believe."

"Not by name," admitted Lizzie. "She requested the puppy finder."

"And Shiercliffe still didn't ask me to help?"

"Ridiculous, right? And now I'm supposed to give a naso-gastric feeding, only I've never done it by myself before." Lizzie indicated a length of rubber tubing, a funnel and a mixing bowl. "You're a lifesaver."

This was typical Lizzie. Ask her to diagram the pathway of food down the alimentary canal and she would draw you a masterpiece, complete with detailed long-form essays on the processes of digestion. Ask her to locate a vein, stitch a wound or cauterize a nosebleed, however, and she would start stumbling around like a pastor in a bawdy house.

The only problem was, without the dark glasses on, Aggie could feel the slight tilt and shift of the walls. "Perhaps I can talk you through the procedure?"

"No, no, I'm terrified I'm going to pass the tube down her airway by mistake and kill her."

Queen Victoria, hearing this, opened one pale and frightened blue eye.

"Don't you worry," said Aggie, patting the monarch's arm. "We're just using nursing lingo. 'Killing' something means doing it perfectly the first time." She gave Lizzie a look of rebuke as she fitted the funnel into the catheter. "Now, Lizzie, I'm assuming you've got the feed all ready? And it's not too hot?"

Lizzie looked back at her, blank-faced.

"Oh, for crying out loud. What were you going to pass through the tube once you got it in? Thoughts and prayers?"

Lizzie looked sheepish. "I told you I needed your help."

Aggie rubbed her eyes. "All right, check the patient's chart and then start preparing the feed."

"Two pints of milk, three eggs, one pint of beef broth." Lizzie pulled a large jug out of the icebox. "This has the name Mrs. Windsor on it, so I guess we just insert the tube and bob's your uncle."

"Um, no. First of all, that's cold. More important, you're holding the amount for a twenty-four hour period."

"Are you sure?"

"Think about it. How would you like three eggy pints of fluid shoved up your nose all at once?"

"When you put it like that, not at all."

As Aggie talked Lizzie through the process of heating up the egg-and-milk mixture without scalding the milk and curdling the eggs, she decided it was probably for the best not to mention to Lizzie that she had never actually performed a nasogastric feeding on her own, either. She knew she could count on herself to keep a steady hand, and at the end of the day, if someone was going to kill the queen by accidentally funneling eggs into her lungs, it might as well be her.

She closed her eyes as she began to pass the tubing into the patient's nostril, trying to feel her way, when a wave of dizziness hit her so strongly that it seemed as though the floor was shifting under her feet. Opening her eyes with a start, she found herself looking at the forlorn, leathery face of a dodo bird. Then the bird moved, and she realized it was a taxidermist's model, held in a pair of lean, masculine hands.

The hands put the bird down, revealing a small room filled with broken desks and chairs, old books and chamber pots and a machine attached to two small wheels, like miniature windmills with copper paddles. She saw Victor's face as he leaned over, adjusting something—an electrical lead—and then the paddled wheels began to turn, causing Victor's image to flicker like the illustrations in a flipbook.

Then everything went black.

It was over in an instant and Aggie opened her eyes to find herself lying on the floor in a puddle of viscous, eggy milk, while Lizzie called her name.

"Are you all right? What happened?"

"I'm not sure."

"You fainted. Again."

Aggie did not correct her friend, but she knew the truth: She hadn't lost consciousness. She had shifted perspectives. It felt *real*. "How long was I out?"

"Just a moment, no more."

She shook her head, remembering the dodo and the hands and Victor's face. Had it been a hallucination? Why would she hallucinate Victor, of all people? Lifting her hand, she found it wet from milk and egg. The feed. She must have lost consciousness while trying to pass the tube up the queen's nostril. "Oh, God, the queen," she said. "Is she all right?"

"She's fine. She's sleeping."

Aggie looked up at the bed, where Queen Victoria was emitting little snuffling snores. No rattle of aspirated fluid in the lungs. "Oh, thank heaven." She tried to stand up and nearly slipped.

"Careful. I still need to mop the floor." Lizzie offered her a hand, which she reluctantly accepted. Luckily, this room was private, so no one else had witnessed her mishap.

Still, she was going to have to find a way to stop these strange fits before someone observed her at the wrong moment. "All right, then," she said out loud. "Now, all we need to do is clean up this mess and get the sterilizer going while I mix up a fresh feed." Lizzie's hand closed over her wrist, preventing her from moving.

"Not so fast. You fainted a few weeks ago when I was with you. How often has this been going on?"

"Nothing's going on. I just felt a little light-headed."

"Is that lie for my benefit, or yours?"

Aggie hesitated, then said, "I'm not lying. I'm just really, really tired from trying to catch up."

Lizzie changed her grip so that instead of holding onto Aggie's wrist, she had laced her fingers through her friend's. "I'm your friend, Aggie. Don't you trust me at all?"

She hesitated, wondering if she dared reveal her secret when the sound of heeled shoes walking briskly in the hallway outside the queen's room made both girls look at each other, and then swiftly separate. Aggie grabbed the mop, while Lizzie lifted the funnel and tubing off the floor.

Please, Aggie prayed, let it be a ward nurse and not Shiercliffe. The door opened with quiet efficiency.

"How are you coming along with the feeding, Miss Lavenza?" It was Shiercliffe. "And Miss DeLacey," she said, cocking her head. "I was not expecting to find you here, considering that you are supposed to be a patient yourself."

"It's my fault, Matron," said Lizzie. "I was having a bit of trouble administering the feeding."

Shiercliffe pinched the bridge of her nose and sighed. "I can see that."

"Aggie here was doing her best to talk me through it."

Shiercliffe looked at Aggie. "I take it the patient coughed the tube out?"

"Afraid so."

There was a snort from the bed. The Queen was observing them from the bed, her eyes bright in her wizened doll's face. *She's going to rat me out*, Aggie thought. And who could blame her?

"Don't worry, Your Majesty, you'll get your feeding," said Shiercliffe. "DeLacey, I'll handle this. You and Miss Lavenza may observe. Perhaps you'll learn something."

"That is unacceptable."

Shiercliffe turned in surprise to face the queen. "Your Majesty?"

"I desire the ministrations of the Argus." With the electrodes at her neck concealed by the high, frilly collar of her nightgown and her white hair covered by a silk mobcap, Queen Victoria looked like an innocent grandmother—but her pale, slightly protuberant eyes gleamed with wolfish schemes. Aggie wondered what the kaiser would think when he found his beloved Granny so altered.

"You mean Aggie?" Shiercliffe looked uncharacteristically indecisive. "But she has only just begun to recover from her own surgery."

"My eyes feel fine, Matron. I haven't had any problems with them, really." Aggie had no idea why the queen was requesting her assistance, especially after she had botched the tube feeding. Perhaps she was still grateful for Aggie bringing her the puppies.

Shiercliffe pursed her lips, considering. "I'll have to consult with Dr. Grimbald and Professor Moulsdale, but if you're sure that you're up to it…"

"I am."

"All right, then. I suppose you can handle the rest of the feeding, DeLacey. Considering Her Majesty's improvement, perhaps spoon-feeding will be sufficient." With a last stern look at Aggie and Lizzie—*do not mess this up* was the wordless command—Shiercliffe left the room, shutting the door behind her.

"Well," said Aggie. "That turned out much better than I expected."

"There's only one problem," said Lizzie, folding her arms. "You're lying. There's something wonky going on with your vision, and we need to figure out what it is before something goes badly wrong."

"Sausage," said the queen, but whether this was a response to Lizzie or a dietary request remained unclear.

23

"SO, LET ME BE SURE I UNDERSTAND THIS," SAID Victor. "You've been getting visions which make you feel as though you are no longer in your body?"

"Exactly," said Aggie. "It happens mostly when I remove my dark spectacles. But Her Majesty won't let me wear the tinted lenses in her presence." *Lord, it's hot in here*, she thought. The sign on the door said *Department of Neuroscience*, but the windowless room still looked and felt like a spare supply room.

Victor leaned forward in his chair. "And when you fainted earlier today, you had just removed your spectacles?"

"That's right," said Aggie. "Her Majesty demanded that I take them off, so I…" Out of the corner of her eye, she caught the wilted, grayish-white feathers of a taxidermy dodo. "Oh, Lord. I think—I think I was in this room."

Victor's eyebrows rose. "This room? Are you certain?"

She looked around her at the mismatched furniture, the jars of fetal animals and the two copper-paddled wheels. "I think so. I couldn't see the entire space, though, so it's difficult to be sure." On the walls, a peeling portrait of the young Queen Victoria sulked while a devilish-looking man in a Puritan collar and Vandyke beard looked down at them with thinly veiled amusement. "I know I saw the dodo, though. And I'm pretty sure I saw the portrait of the young Queen."

"Almost every room at the Royal Victoria has a portrait of the young Queen," said Victor. "As for the dodo, well, it's not exactly conclusive evidence."

"Well, then, what is?" Lizzie looked up from a folder of notes. "Aggie's not the sort to start imagining symptoms."

"I'm afraid the mind can play tricks on all of us."

"What if it's not a trick?" Lizzie put down the folder. "What if these visions are actually images from the donor of the corneas she received?"

Victor rolled his eyes. "That's a bit of a stretch."

"But why?" Aggie wasn't sure how she felt about receiving impressions from a dead boy's eyes, but it certainly seemed a plausible explanation. "Isn't that essentially what happened with you? When they attached someone else's left arm onto your body, it brought part of his personality along with it." She felt a bit awkward, bringing it up. These days, Victor seemed to be the one in control, and referring to Jack seemed rude somehow, as if she were bringing up an ex-beau of Lizzie's.

Which, in a way, is what Jack had been.

"The cornea is an extremely thin membrane," said Victor. "We're talking about just a few cells."

"But they're important cells," said Lizzie. "And the phrenological mesmerator is meant to increase the connections between the brain's two hemispheres. What if it's doing something else? What if it is forging a connection between Aggie and Dodger?"

Aggie swallowed. "Wait, what did you say?"

Lizzie looked confused for a moment. "Um, I wondered if it was forming a connection between you and Dodger."

Aggie stared at Lizzie, stunned into silence.

"You know," Lizzie prompted. "Dodger, your corneal donor."

"I know that," Aggie said. "But how do *you* know that?"

Lizzie looked at Victor, who held out his hands and shrugged. "Because," Lizzie said, "he's the recipient of the Bio-Mechanical eyes."

Present tense. Lizzie was talking about him in the present tense. Aggie felt a moment of elation so pure she could have gotten drunk on it. "Are you telling me—he's alive? Dodger's alive?"

Lizzie nodded, as if this were common knowledge.

"Why haven't you mentioned this before?"

Lizzie's shoulders stiffened. "I had no idea you knew him. How *do* you know him, Aggie?"

She felt as though she were melting in the airless room. "He helped me find my way through the East End the night Jenny was injured. He's a friend." She hesitated. "He was also with me the night I lost my sight."

"Why haven't you told me this before?" Lizzie looked stung, as though Aggie was the one in the wrong here. "I thought we were friends."

"It's not as though you've been telling me what's going on with you, either," said Aggie. "Why didn't you mention that Dodger was your patient?"

"Because we *are* friends," said Lizzie. "You were so upset

about not being allowed to go back to your nursing studies, and I didn't want to rub it in about all my new, exciting
projects."

Dodger was Lizzie's project. For a moment, this made no
sense, and then it seemed so obvious that Aggie was astonished she hadn't made the connection before. "So Dodger is
a full-on Bio-Mechanical now?" With a rush of relief, Aggie
imagined him restored, like Victor, to the person he had been
before. Then she remembered—Victor was the only Bio-
Mechanical who could remember his former life. The rest of
them were empty-eyed, shambling husks. "What is he like?
Can he remember anything? Can he speak?"

Lizzie's smile was a complicated thing. "Your friend is
rather remarkable. He's the project that Victor and I have
been working on to show the kaiser. The Dreadnaught."

Aggie let out a shaky breath she had not realized she was
holding. She wanted to run away to a dark room to sort
through the tangle of her emotions.

"You can't tell anyone," said Victor. "The whole project is
supposed to be top secret. But considering everything, perhaps we should—" He broke off at the sound of a knock on
the door. "Bloody hell, is it five already?"

Still reeling from the news Dodger was alive—reanimated—
Aggie didn't understand why Victor was rushing to get to the
door as it opened. "Listen," he said, "something's come up.
We're not going to have a session today."

It was too late. Dodger was already standing on the threshold of the room, instantly recognizable but subtly altered.
His lean frame was perhaps a bit more athletic than before,
and instead of a top hat and swallowtail coat, he was wearing a flat-brimmed cap and roughspun tunic. But then he

raised his gaze to hers, revealing the biggest change—his new, strange, glass-and-metal eyes. As his eyes locked with hers, they brightened, gleaming with the luminescent green of ichor. "You're the girl from my dreams," he said, and then listed abruptly to one side.

Still dazed, Dodger stared up at the redhead from his dreams. For some reason, her eyes were concealed behind small dark glasses. "Is it really you?" He felt as though he couldn't draw enough air into his lungs. The air in the windowless room felt thick with unseen currents and unanswered questions. "Take off your specs so I can see you."

She hesitated a moment and then removed them, revealing her familiar, lovely face—and the fact that it had changed.

"Your eyes. They're not green."

"It's the eye drops," she said, replacing the glasses. They were seated on the floor, he realized, and his head was in her lap.

"No." Dodger struggled upright, but his eyes had begun a frantic oscillation, making him sink back down again. "You were blind," he said. "I remember now. That witch of a nurse said they was going to give you my eyes."

The redhead frowned. Aggie. Her name was Aggie. "They gave me your corneas."

"You stole my eyes and turned me into a monster." The words came out more bewildered than angry. He tried to focus on her face, but his head was pounding, and his whirling eyes locked onto a hideous furred beast with two large, beady black eyes and four smaller ones.

Spider.

Aggie's cool hand touched the side of his face, and his eyes refocused, reducing the magnification so now he could see the small wolf spider was crawling up the wall. "I'm sorry," she said. "I didn't plan for any of this."

"Maybe I deserved it." He sat up, cradling his aching head in his hands. "I was a thief, wasn't I?"

"Maybe we've been straining his brain with the phrenologic mesmerator," said Victor.

"No, the treatments are working." Lizzie's shadow fell over him. "Are you remembering something?"

What did he remember?

He remembered this: the sense of being outside the rules that fenced regular folks in and kept them docile. The reckless joy of moving through a crowd, sizing up the gulls and the saps and moving in on them. The sense of moving fast and nimble while everyone around him trudged like cart horses toward the glue factory.

Perhaps this was fate's way of serving him his comeuppance. For every purse and pocket watch and stickpin he had snatched, there had been a divine reckoning of debts accrued and accounts payable.

Then he recalled something else. A richly appointed office. A letter from the kaiser. A hard-faced woman, her fierce cold hands, the heavy scent of chloroform.

He laughed at the absurdity of it, even though laughing made his head hurt again. He had gotten caught up in someone else's con. He wasn't even the mark. He was a passerby who got knocked over by mistake and wound up being run over by a trolley.

Aggie's hand touched his shoulder. "I know this must be upsetting to you. If it's any consolation, it's upsetting to me, too."

"You'll get over it, I expect." He waited for the room to stop spinning.

"I would have come to see you if I'd known you were here. I thought you were dead and buried." Her voice was gentle, tinged with sadness and regret. She had mourned him, he realized.

Dodger got to his feet, then reached down to help Aggie stand. "You picked the wrong hospital for that."

She smiled at him, but with the dark spectacles covering her eyes, he couldn't tell if she thought he was being funny or frivolous or bitter. Christ, he barely knew himself. "So you don't hate me?" she asked.

"I don't hate you," he assured her. He stood next to Aggie, and for a moment it seemed that he had awoken from a terrible dream and that everything was back to how it had always been. Then he became aware that Lizzie and Victor were arguing.

"...for the same reason we didn't bring the Mesmerator into the lab," Lizzie was saying. "I want some time to understand our results before Moulsdale tries to weaponize it."

"Fair enough," said Victor grudgingly. "But let's start on the lowest setting."

"Midrange is perfectly safe." Lizzie was already unpacking the two copper-paddled wheels from their box and setting them up on the rosewood desk. "Dodger's been using the highest setting for weeks."

"And has the headaches to prove it," added Dodger.

Lizzie waved this away. "A small price for your memories, wouldn't you say? Aggie, come sit over here."

Aggie held up her hands, as if trying to calm a runaway

horse. "Mind telling me what you're going to do to me before you attempt to electrocute me?"

Lizzie stepped around Aggie's hands and clamped an electrical lead onto her right ear. "We know you've both already experienced some sort of unusual feedback from each other's eyes. We're just going to see if we can evoke the response at will."

Aggie touched the small metal clamp on her ear. "Will it hurt?"

Lizzie attached the other lead to the electrode on the side of Dodger's neck. "Not at all."

Aggie looked at Dodger for confirmation. "What do you say?"

"I say no more mucking about with my brain." He removed the clamp from his electrode and pushed it back into Lizzie's hands. "You want my help? I need a stake."

"Are you angling for funds?" Victor chuckled appreciatively. "I guess I can manage a couple of shillings." He rummaged in his waistcoat pocket, then paused, looking at Dodger intently. "In case you have any ideas about running away, I should inform you that without weekly infusions of ichor, your new life is going to be even shorter than your old one."

"Nevertheless, I'll take the infusion of silver," said Dodger, holding out his hand. In his head, he filed away the additional information. In order to escape, he would need to find a supply of ichor.

"After." Lizzie reattached the clamp, and Dodger found himself seated face-to-face with Aggie.

"Aggie? You'll have to take off the spectacles," said Lizzie.

Aggie hesitated, and Dodger gently put his hand out. "May I?"

She nodded, and he pulled off her dark lenses. This close,

CORPSE & CROWN   **203**

he could see the swirl of dark brown and green in her irises, where before there had been only green. He became aware of a tone in his left ear, and then the room tilted and the angle of his vision shifted. With a wave of disorientation, he realized he was looking at a lean, sharp-featured boy with bright, uncanny eyes. There were faint markings visible around the iris, like the lines etched to indicate minutes and hours on a clock face.

Himself. He was looking at himself, from Aggie's eyes.

Oh, Lord. He grabbed for Aggie's hand, and for a moment, he felt a current between them, of attraction, perhaps—or something deeper, stronger and more insidious. Aggie pulled away as though she had been stung.

"That's enough of that," said Aggie, drawing the device from her ear.

Lizzie disconnected Dodger, as well. "What happened? Can you describe it?"

Aggie had restored her dark spectacles and with them, some of her composure. "It felt like I was looking out of Dodger's eyes."

Dodger scratched his head. "This is completely barmy."

Victor jotted down a note in a folder marked Dreadnaught Protocol. "Did you experience anything, Dodger?"

"Yeah." His smile felt lopsided. "What she said. Felt like I was looking out of Aggie's eyes."

Even through the opaque lenses, he could feel her alarm. *That's right*, he thought. *It goes both ways.*

"This is astonishing," said Victor. "Think of the implications for sharing information over long distances. This might be the most valuable discovery since electricity!"

"No," said Aggie, in a tight, clipped voice. "We're not telling anyone about this."

"But Aggie," said Victor, looking almost comically distressed. "This is an important scientific discovery."

"No, Victor." She was hugging herself, absently rubbing one arm with the opposite hand. "This is my life." She looked down at her hands. "You don't understand what it's like to be poor and female. I chose to become a nurse because I wanted to make my own way in the world. If Moulsdale knows that I have some freakish link to Dodger, I'll become little more than a servant—or a slave."

"But Aggie," Victor said, "how can we ignore something so spectacularly important?"

"We're not going to ignore it," said Lizzie. "We can study it privately. But we're not going to rat out my best friend to Moulsdale and ruin her life."

24

IN THE FINAL DAYS LEADING UP TO THE KAISER'S visit, Dodger was kept busy. Exhausted from the previous day's brain-tuning sessions and Grimbald's training exercises, he was shaken awake by Wiggins after what felt like two hours' rest. "Time to do a bit of work," said Wiggins.

"Thought I was supposed to be in top shape for the kaiser," said Dodger, feeling as though he might keel over.

Wiggins was unmoved. "A little light cleaning shouldn't tire you out."

Now, standing in front of the hospital, Dodger pretended to scrub the dirt off the building's facade while expending as little effort as possible. Gazing at the crowd of East Enders waiting for the gates to be opened, he discovered he could read someone's newspaper, even though the fine print was over fifty feet away.

Today's edition of the *London Daily News* boasted a ten-year-old photograph of Queen Victoria and Kaiser Wilhelm under a cumbersome headline:

Her Majesty to Visit the Royal Victoria Hospital and School of Bio-Mechanical Medicine and Science this Monday! A marvel of Bio-Mechanical engineering to be revealed!

Reports of the hospital's increasingly severe financial straits were dismissed by Ambrose Moulsdale, the school's head of medicine and Her Majesty's most trusted personal physician.

"It is entirely untrue that the hospital's financial well-being depends on the success of this visit," stated Moulsdale.

Dodger was reading about the queen's remarkable hardiness when a sudden gust of wind blew the paper out of the man's fingers and up into the freshly budded branches of a plane tree.

The newspaper's owner, who had an abscess on his cheek, was vocal about his displeasure. Even though Dodger couldn't hear the man, he could read his lips. *Bollocks*, he said to his companion, a young woman with a violet in her black hat and a bandage on her left hand. Gossip told a darker tale about the queen. Some said the elderly monarch had to be restrained so she didn't wander about on her own at night. She had been overheard by at least one patient uttering peculiar statements about cabbages and cabals.

This, the aggrieved man said, was what came from clinging to the waxwork facade of monarchy at the dawn of the twentieth century. He was about to share his opinion with the man on his left when something caught his eye. *Cor, blimey*, he said, pointing behind the gate.

Corpse walkers, said the other man, giving a little shiver of distaste as he observed the other Bio-Mechanicals moving like drunks, with awkward, fixed determination.

"Aren't they meant to be dangerous weapons?" asked a

woman with bright red cheeks. "These lot don't look fit
enough to fight off a hausfrau."

"Looks can be deceivin'," said the costermonger.

It's people who are dangerous, thought Dodger as two guards
moved to open the front gates. *The likes of us are just rabbits for
poaching.* He thought of Aggie, staring back at him with his
eyes. That was one expensive kiss they had shared. It had cost
him his freedom. Aggie's throwaway comment still rang in his
ears: *If Moulsdale knows that I have some freakish link to Dodger,
I'll become little more than a servant—or a slave.*

Not that he wanted Aggie's life to be ruined, but it didn't
seem to bother anyone that *his* life was apparently as dispos-
able as a leaky chamber pot. He felt a right mark, remembering Victor's high-flown talk about serving the Crown. What
it all boiled down to was this—folks were betting on him to
win a contest as though he were a dog or a horse. If he failed
to perform as desired, he expected his fate would be the same
as a dog who loses a fight or a racehorse who doesn't place—
the knacker's yard.

That's what falling for a girl did to a bloke. Aggie wasn't
even that pretty, he told himself, feeling sour. She would
probably lose her looks by the time she was thirty. Or sooner.
By the time she was twenty-five. She had probably already
peaked, looks-wise. All downhill from age seventeen.

Not that he would live to see her prettiness fade if they decided to experiment on him some more—or if they shipped
him off to some German battlefield. Besides, none of it mattered. She could be fifty and he would probably still be daft
over her.

"Oi! Stop draggin' your feet and go pump some water!"

Dodger doffed his cap, acknowledging the porter's reprimand. Then he picked up an empty bucket and carried it over to the water pump. When the bucket was almost full, he wrapped a bit of rag around his hand so the handle wouldn't open his blistered palms and hefted it over to the others.

He passed a small boy who kept darting back and forth between the crowd and the Bio-Mechanicals, getting closer and closer, until his mother yelled, *"Villn zi tzu esen eir?"* Dodger translated the Yiddish in his head: *Do you want them to eat you?* The woman grabbed her son's ear and wrenched it to drive her argument home. Sobbing, the boy clung to her skirts.

A girl who had come to the hospital to check on her father's surgery squinted at the Bio-Mechanicals from a safe distance. "What're they up to anyway?"

"Nothing kosher," said the mother of the crying boy. She pointed up at the second story, where a pair of workmen on tall ladders were arguing about the proper way to hang a banner leftover from the queen's Diamond Jubilee, held five years previously. "What's that say?"

"Queen of Earthly Queens," read the girl. "What's it mean?"

"Must mean the queen's after coming for a visit," said a man with a suspicious-looking sore on his cheek. "What's she want with a place like this anyway?"

Dodger, who had paused to rest the bucket on the ground, realized the man was talking to him. *He doesn't realize what I am.* "Dunno," he said, ducking his head so the brim of his cap concealed his eyes. He had tied a red cravat around his throat and pulled his collar up to hide the electrodes, but there was nothing to be done about the eyes.

"Don't you know anything?" The girl, who had rags wrapped around her feet for warmth, was as superior as only a twelve-year-old can be. "Them corpse walkers is meant to be soldiers, in't they?"

"Not all of 'em," said the man with the sore. "I hear they take young girls for other sorts of work."

The girl made a face. "Ugh, disgusting."

The boy, listening now, stepped away from his mother. "Do they really eat children?"

"Mostly they eat rotten meat," said the man. "The rottener, the better. Maggots is like candy to them."

This got everyone's attention.

"They're not like lubberkin," the man explained. "You can pay the fair folk off with a saucer of milk or a place by the fire. These wights, well, they're nasty like redcaps, but no holy water will deter them." Warming to his subject, the man with the sore took on a more sonorous tone. "You see, the disasters wrought by science are a singular curse upon mankind. And there's only one thing that can kill them."

The crowd leaned forward, distracted by this impromptu bit of street theater. Perfect targets. Hoisting the bucket as though it were a little too heavy for him, Dodger took a step, pretended to trip and then splashed a man who was dressed a bit more nattily than the others.

"Garn, how could I be so clumsy!" Under the guise of patting him dry, Dodger lifted a fine linen handkerchief, his pound notes and money clip and a signet ring with a dark black stone. Whistling as he went back to the pump for more water, Dodger felt almost like his old self.

Money was the key. With money, you could acquire whatever else you needed—even if you weren't entirely sure what that was. Victor's admonition kept replaying in his mind: *In case you have any ideas about running away, I should inform you that without weekly infusions of ichor, your new life is going to be even shorter than your old one.*

Whatever ichor was, he was going to figure out where else to get it. Because where there was a demand, there was a market. And where there was a market, there was a black market.

It was then, with money in his pockets and a feeling of lightness despite the heavy bucket in his hands, that he saw her in the crowd.

A blond girl, shockingly gaunt and unsteady on her bare feet. Her red velvet dress was stained and greasy, and when she raised her bleary eyes, she didn't seem to recognize him.

"Spare a thrupenny bit, guv'nor?"

"Nancy." Setting down his bucket, he took a step toward her. "Are you all right?"

"Better than that," she said, snaking an arm around his neck. "For a bob, I'll prove it."

"It's me," he said, gently removing her arm. "Dodger. Don't you know me, Nance?"

"'Course I do," she said, but her eyes remained unfocused and clouded.

"Are you sick? Thought you was getting better." He wondered if she had gotten sick while still recuperating. He had never seen her so thin and wan.

She shrugged. "My side was paining me, but Twist gave me some medicine." She rubbed her face with one filthy sleeve. "I ran out, though, and he says he can't give me no more."

"Oh, Nancy. You want to stay far away from Twist. He's no good."

"Don't tell me how to live my life. Where have you been anyway?"

Dodger kept his gaze averted. "It's a bit hard to explain.

Here." Pulling a bob out of his pocket, he placed it in her hand. "Do not give this to Twist for medicine. Get yourself a decent meal and something new to wear. Have you seen Bill or Faygie?"

"Oi," called Wiggins. "Back to work, you."

"I have to go now," said Dodger. "But tell Faygie I'm going to try to get to the pawnshop."

"Sure," said Nancy, happily spinning the shilling in her fingers. "So good to see you, too." She rewarded him with a flash of her old cheeky grin before rushing off.

Dodger picked up the empty bucket. He had made a mistake in giving Nancy the money, he realized. He could lecture her all day long about clean clothes and nourishing food, and it wouldn't do a lick of good. His old friend was in the grip of a monster, and she would go wherever it took her.

ZS

A GRAY PIGEON TRYING TO NAVIGATE THE LON-
don fog alighted on the window ledge of one of the Royal
Victoria Hospital classrooms, preened itself for a moment and
then peered in at the twenty or so young men and one young
woman all seated at their desks, heads bent to their papers.
At the head of the class, a bored proctor stared out into space
and picked at the pimple under his starched linen collar. Will
looked out the window and caught the bird's orange eye for
a moment. Then, with a rattling coo and a disgruntled flutter of wings, the bird took off again.

Can't say I blame you, thought Will as he watched the pigeon fly out of sight. *I wouldn't stay here with me, either.* As he
sat through the debacle of his chemistry exam, unable to answer fully a third of the questions, he was painfully aware of
Byram, sitting a few feet away on his right. A lock of dark,
curling hair fell over his friend's aquiline profile as he bent
over his paper, scribbling diligently away. Byram must have

been aware of Will's gaze, but his concentration never wavered and he didn't look up once.

Maybe he's worried the proctor will think he's cheating. Will forced his attention back to his own paper, but he knew in his heart of hearts that in the old days, Byram would have given him a smile, a wink, some kind of gesture that said it was going to be all right.

That was, then. This was some new phase, that had begun without warning or explanation, and Will could not find his bearings in it.

After the professor returned to the classroom and ordered them all to put down their pencils, most of the students vacated their seats as quickly as possible. Dispirited, Will remained slumped in his chair as his classmates chattered with one another. Out of sheer habit, he looked around for Byram, then watched in disbelief as he spotted his former best friend with Outhwaite and Mothersole, comparing notes on some of the trickier questions. Those two had been Byram and Will's sworn enemies since first form at Eton, but Will couldn't say he was surprised by the shift in allegiances.

What he didn't understand was why. They hadn't had a fight, unless you counted Byram's barbed comments about Will's drinking. *But I started drinking more when he started pulling away*, thought Will, so that was an effect, not a cause. He gathered his things and stood up, readying himself to join the exodus.

There had to be some kind of chemical equation to express what happened when the bonds between friends break. Something like denaturing, which, he suddenly recalled, was what happened to proteins when exposed to a strong acid or base, and was the answer to one of the questions he had blanked on during the exam.

"Then I realized I'd written down the wrong bloody reaction," said Mothersole, moving slowly toward the door. Byram did not take the bait.

"No point in fretting about it now," he said. Will tried not to stare. A few months back, Byram had made Will double up and cry with laughter as he tried to imagine Mothersole failing in various specialties: dermatology, gynecology, urgent care. Now he was all compassion.

"You headed down for lunch?" Mothersole's question was clearly directed at Byram and Outhwaite—Will might as well have been invisible.

"Actually," Will cut in, surprising himself, "Byram and I need to discuss something first."

"Ooh, sounds serious," said Outhwaite, not bothering to disguise his smirk. The old Byram would have punched him on his arse-shaped chin, or at least made a snide comment.

The new Byram frowned at Will. "Can't it wait? I'm ready for a bite to eat myself."

"No," said Will. "I don't think it can." The other students flowed around them in the narrow corridor, and he felt a funny lurch in his stomach as the last few stragglers made their way out of the classroom. Lizzie, who always remained behind to try to trick the professor into confirming what she had gotten right, was the last person out.

"All right," she said, "I think I might have gotten part of the last section wrong."

"You always say that," said Byram, "and you never get anything wrong."

Lizzie made a face. "I think I may really have messed this one up. How about you, Will?"

"I might have gotten *one* question right," he conceded. "Otherwise, it was pretty much a wash."

"Ouch," said Lizzie, as if she were in the same boat, when he knew as well as she did that she was managing to maintain her 3.8 grade point average while working overtime on some top secret engineering project for the kaiser's visit. "Hey, you two headed for lunch?" Without waiting for a reply, she added, "I was going to bring something up to Justine's room. With everything that's been going on, I haven't really had a chance to spend much time with her."

"How virtuous of you," said Byram. "I'm afraid I find myself a bit unnerved by the whole iron lung contraption. It's like talking to a living zeppelin."

"I think you think that admitting that is somehow charmingly authentic," said Lizzie. "But really, that's the sort of feeling you ought to try to overcome. After all, how would you feel if it were you, trapped in there like that?"

"Desperately bored. But since, blessedly, I am not the one confined to a metal cage, I choose to avoid being confronted by the melancholy constraints of her existence."

"That's absurd," said Will. "And untrue. You know you're just saying that to be shocking."

"Fine. Have it your way. Yet I am afraid that I cannot join you for luncheon with the sweet Justine, as Will here has urgently requested a private conference." Byram pulled his watch out of his waistcoat pocket. "We have about twenty-five minutes remaining until we're expected at rounds, so I suggest you get on with your mission of mercy, Lizzie."

"Good Lord, Byram, what's gotten into you?" Will hadn't

planned on confronting Byram like this, in front of Lizzie, but the words seemed to be bubbling up of their own accord. "Are you trying to alienate all your friends? I thought it was just me, but now I'm thinking you're trying to drive all of us away."

Byram made an impatient sound. "Fine. Have it your way. I'm letting the team down. Selfish, terrible me. You can all band together and discuss how awful I am. Meanwhile, I'm off to lunch." With a mocking sketch of a bow to Lizzie, he set off in the direction of the dining room.

"It's getting worse," said Lizzie.

"I know. I thought at first... It doesn't matter. I don't know why he's acting this way."

"I meant his limp. It's getting worse. He's going to need more than a cane soon. He'll need surgery, and even then, he might still need crutches."

She was right. Watching Byram now, it was clear that he was moving more slowly and deliberately and yet still his limp was more pronounced. *He's in pain*, thought Will, *but he doesn't want me to know. He doesn't want me to care.*

Which means I have to let him go.

The gin palace brought back unpleasant memories of his encounter with the haggard blond fellow and his thuggish companion, so Will decided to try a public house. The Three Vultures, despite its unpleasant name, had a raffish charm. A rather regal brass vulture sat atop a liquor cabinet that boasted a decent assortment of spirits, but most of the customers seemed inclined to purchase beer on tap, which the barman drew by pulling back brass-handled levers.

Unlike the gin joint, there were tables and chairs. At one

table, a group of elderly men were playing a hand of crib-
bage; in another, two workers were debating something over
their pints of beer.

"Not me," a wiry fellow with deep-set eyes was saying. "I
wouldn't touch no corpse walker juice."

"Just think, Martin," said a thickset man with a potbelly
that looked as firm as a cannonball. "If corpse juice brings
corpses back from the dead, what could it do for the likes of
us?"

Martin remained unconvinced. "I don't trust nothin' that
comes out of the Royal Victoria." He spat a wad of something brown on the ground. "Bunch of butchers, they are."

"This bloke's set up his own shingle," said the potbellied
expert. "Says he's bringing this groundbreaking new treatment
to the people, at a fraction of the cost." Glancing around, he
surreptitiously pulled a small glass flask from his coat pocket.
From his vantage point at the bar, Will could see that the
flask was filled with an absinthe-green liquid. "See this? This
here's distilled life force, Martin. I broke me left arm as a tyke
and it never healed right—two weeks of drinking this, I was
golden." He flexed his arm.

Martin gave a suspicious sniff. "How much do it cost,
then?"

Good Lord, thought Will. Either these men where confabulating some story, or some unscrupulous fellow was selling
bootleg ichor to living people. From what Will understood,
ichor was a concentrated fluid—an aqua vitae that, when ac-
tivated by electricity, brought Bio-Mechanicals back to life.
He had never heard of a living person taking it before.

"What'll you have, Percy?"

Will turned to face the grim-faced barman, who looked

as creased and lined as a week-old newspaper and smelled as if he had been cured in tobacco. "Oh! I'm afraid my name's not Percy," said Will.

The barman wiped the counter down with a rag so filthy it probably added dirt to the surface rather than took it away. "You look like a Percy." It didn't sound like the barman thought this was a compliment. "You want something?"

"A stout, if you please," said Will.

The barman, wiping down a tankard with a rag, made no move to serve him. "Which one?"

"Oh, I don't know. Whatever you think is good."

With a brusque nod, the man chose one of the taps and filled the tankard.

"Thanks. What is it?" Will sniffed the rich, yeasty aroma.

"Stout. What you asked for." The man looked irritable. "Five pence."

Will pointed at the chalkboard. "But the sign says three."

"Only if you bring your own tankard."

"Yes, I see, of course. Sorry." Aware of some less than friendly looks from the other patrons, Will put the money on the bar. The barman turned away, leaving Will to his drink and his solitude.

That's fine, thought Will. *I only wanted a drink.* But as he sipped the foamy head off his stout, he suddenly regretted not remaining in his room. He had been alone and feeling dismal there, and now he was alone and dismal here. The only difference was that he was going to be in even worse shape in the morning, when he had to face the results of the chemistry test and his row with Byram.

Maybe he should just finish this one pint and then take

himself back to his bed. Then he saw something out of the corner of his eye that made his stomach tighten.

At the back table, a girl in a red dress was pleading with two men. "Come on, don't be so hard," she said, with a flirtatious toss of her hair. "Is it the money? Look, I've got some." She held out her palm, revealing a shilling.

"You've had enough already, Nancy." The speaker turned so his fair hair caught the light, and Will felt his belly tighten as he recognized the man who had propositioned him outside the gin palace.

"But I don't feel right, Twist." The girl—Nancy—had lost a lot of weight since the night Will had seen her draped over Byram by the bar.

"You just need to wait two days," said the second man. "It's too soon for another dose." From across the room, Will caught a glimpse of a familiar, round face, a receding ginger hairline and protuberant eyes behind wire-rimmed spectacles.

Henry Clerval—Victor's oldest friend and would-be murderer. What was he doing in London? He had left the school last semester, and when he had failed to return, Will had all but forgotten about him.

Whatever he's doing here, it can't be any good. Time to leave. Will stood up and felt a prickle of alarm when the blond girl— Nancy—walked unsteadily over to him.

"All by your lonesome?" she asked.

"Actually, I was just finishing up," said Will, setting down his tankard. "Have to be getting back to get my beauty sleep."

"You're beautiful enough." She reached out to touch his hair, and he flinched.

"I really do need to go."

She frowned. "Wait—don't I know you from somewhere?"

"Leave it, Nance," said Twist, giving Will a nod of recognition. "He's not interested."

Nancy looked from Twist to Will and back again. "Oh, it's like that, is it?"

Will stood up. "I don't know what you're talking about."

"Don't be embarrassed," said Nancy. "We like what we like. There's no need to feel…" She frowned, as if searching for a word, and then her eyes rolled up in her head and she crumpled.

"Aw, Nance," said Twist, as if she had let him down by collapsing.

Feeling like an imposter, Will knelt to take the girl's pulse. He thought he could feel it under his fingers, but it was so faint he wasn't entirely sure. "She needs a doctor," he said.

"I'm a doctor," said Clerval, standing up. Then his eyes met Will's.

"Thank you," said Will, not looking at Henry. "But I think we should take the girl to the Royal Victoria." It galled him beyond belief that Henry had gotten away with trying to murder Victor, but there was no way to acknowledge the crime without exposing Victor as a Bio-Mechanical.

"It's too late," said Twist. "Hospital gates are closed till morning."

Will glared at Henry. "I'll get my brother to help."

Henry licked his lips nervously and backed away. "Of course, of course—please give Victor my best."

Ignoring him, Will turned to Twist. "I'll need help lifting her, and we'll need to get a carriage."

"You can use my delivery wagon," said the barman. "It's around back. But have it back before daybreak."

Twist was just staring down at Nancy as if he were sleep-walking. "It's not my fault," he said. "I told her—just a little bit, to help get you back on your feet."

"We don't have time for this now." Will was surprised by the firmness of his own voice. "Do you know what she's been taking? Laudanum? Opium?"

"Ichor." Twist looked on the verge of tears. "It's supposed to help with the healing."

For the Gods eat not Man's food nor slake their thirst with sable wine, thought Will, suddenly recalling a line from the *Iliad*. He might not know his chemistry as well as he should, but he knew his mythology. According to Homer, the Greek gods had ichor in their veins instead of blood, and this rendered them exempt from death.

"Come on," he told Twist. "Help me lift your friend." He bent and slipped his arms under Nancy's shoulders as Twist lifted her legs. He hoped to God Victor would know what to do to help her, but he had a premonition that this night would not end well.

Mortals always fared badly in myths when they tried to emulate the gods.

26

IT WAS NEARLY MIDNIGHT WHEN LIZZIE AND
Aggie entered Justine's room, waking her up.

"My goodness," said Justine, blinking as Lizzie adjusted the
gas sconce on the wall, turning up the light. "What's going
on? It's a bit late for a chat." Justine was trying not to eaves-
drop on their thoughts, but the tension in their bodies was
impossible to miss.

"Sorry to wake you," said Aggie, offering Justine a cup of
water with a metal straw. "It's a bit of an emergency."

Justine took a sip of water. "I wasn't really asleep." When
you spent most of your life encased in a metal cylinder from
the neck down, sleeping during the day and waking at night
was an occupational hazard. "What's happening? Is there a
letter you want me to read?" She was hardly going to be much
use doing anything else.

"In a way," said Lizzie. "We want your diagnosis." Before
Justine had time to react, she added, "Boys, come on in."

There was the faint squeak of wheels as Victor and Will

wheeled in a young woman on a gurney. Byram followed behind, looking on like a disapproving chaperone and thinking intensely jealous thoughts. The gurney was turned so that
Justine could see its occupant—a bone-slender blonde in a
stained and tattered red velvet dress.

"I don't understand," said Justine.

"This is Dodger's friend, Nancy," said Aggie. "The girl
who was beaten and had the collapsed lung."

"I thought he said she was recovering," said Justine. "This
girl's on death's doorstep, from the looks of her. Is she even
breathing?"

"Barely." Will stepped forward and launched into a long
explanation that involved a public house, Henry Clerval and
bootleg ichor. Apparently, ichor was the newest fad for gin
fiends, absinthe drinkers and opium addicts. The girl, Nancy,
had been taking ichor to promote healing—but either the
ichor Clerval had supplied her was bad, or else it had made
her dependent on the substance.

Will left out part of the story that involved a thin blond
thief named Twist. It seemed that Will and this thief had been
attempting to bring Nancy to Victor for help, but ran out of
steam before reaching Victor's room. Reluctantly, Will had
taken the unconscious girl to the room he shared with Byram
before running up the stairs to fetch his brother. Byram, it
seemed, was not as indifferent to Will's activities as he tried
to appear. He had been openly hostile to Twist, all but shoving him out the door.

Interesting. But not as interesting as the reason that all her
friends had brought the unconscious Nancy to Justine's room
in the first place.

"So why have you brought her to me?" Justine had a suspicion she knew the answer, but she wasn't used to having this many people in her room, and it was difficult to tune out the discordant tumult of so many different thoughts and emotions coming at her at once.

"Because we need to know if Nancy is still in there," said Lizzie. "Victor and Will think she's beyond saving, but they don't want to make a mistake."

"Everyone thought I was dead," said Victor. "But my mind was perfectly fine. We need a test to tell us if Nancy is trapped inside her body—or if the vital spark of her is already gone."

With a sinking feeling, Justine understood. "You told them about me, Lizzie?" She already knew the answer, though. She could hear Will, thinking about what he would give to know what went on in Byram's mind. Byram, on the other hand, was musing over how awful it would be to have a lover who could peer into your thoughts and discover every hidden secret and doubt.

Forget about them. Blocking out their internal voices, Justine focused on Lizzie, who was crossing her arms and lifting her chin. "I'm sorry, Justine, but this is more important than preserving your privacy."

Justine felt a surge of anger. "Shouldn't that be my decision?"

"I beg your pardon," said Aggie, "but what about my privacy? I shared your room for weeks and you never told me that you could read me like a diary."

"Oh, she can't read just anyone's thoughts," said Lizzie. "Just mine. When Professor Makepiece put us both in the galvanic magnetometer, some kind of bond was established."

That was not precisely true, but Justine did not correct her. Lizzie's mind was easier to read, but Justine could hear anyone, provided they were standing less than a few yards away.

"I'm sorry," said Aggie. "I misunderstood."

"Then so did I," said Will. "I thought Lizzie said that Justine could tell if there was anything left of that poor girl's consciousness."

Ah, so that was what they wanted. "You're asking me to probe her mind?" asked Justine.

"I don't know if it's possible," said Lizzie, removing something from the bottom of the gurney. It was a cap of vari-colored wires attached to a battery with a switch. "But it's worth a try. I'm suggesting we use a galvanic charge to augment your brain's natural powers."

"It may be too late to save Nancy," said Victor. "But if she's really gone…"

Then maybe I can have her body. Justine looked into Victor's eyes. She had known him longer than any of the others. Back when he was still her father's favorite Bio-Mechanical project, he had been kind to her. "How do you know I'll tell you the truth?" she asked quietly.

"Because I know you," he replied.

"Let's try it."

Lizzie smiled, then dabbed Justine's brow with a green liquid—ichor? After that, she placed the cap on Justine's head and nodded at Victor, who turned a switch. Justine felt a slight tingle from the electricity as Lizzie placed one hand over Nancy's forehead, then touched Justine's brow in the same place. Of course, all this was entirely unnecessary, but Aggie's reaction told Justine that she was right to keep her abilities a secret. *No one would ever trust me if they knew my mind doesn't need augmenting.*

"Is it working?" asked Lizzie.

Her scalp tingling, Justine closed her eyes and let herself

sink into Nancy's mind. Once, as a very little girl, Justine's mother had taken her for a swim in a pond with some other children. That had been the day before the illness that had weakened her legs and lungs, and she still remembered the feeling of slipping under water and into a different world.

Inside the still waters of Nancy's consciousness, there were tiny ripples of memory—a color, a feeling, a sense of longing for something or someone who was no longer close.

You're drifting apart, thought Justine. She pictured Nancy's mind as a school of silvery fish, being tossed this way and that in a sea storm. *Do you want to stay together?*

Together, thought the tempest-tossed flashes of Nancy's dispersing mind.

I could keep you together. With me.

The pellucid flashes were farther apart now, but there was one last coherent thought: *With you.*

Justine found it harder than she would have expected to swim up to the surface again. She became aware of a liquid, rhythmic sound, as if the ocean had a heartbeat, and realized that the sound was growing fainter. *She's dying*, thought Justine with a flare of panic. *She's dying and I'm going down with her, like a passenger in a sinking ship.*

Justine tried to cry out for help, but couldn't find her voice. For some reason, Victor and Lizzie appeared to be moving in slow motion.

The room darkened into grainy shadow, and now Justine was floating up through the depths of Nancy, but instead of finding herself back in her body she was outside her head, floating up to the ceiling of her room where she hovered at the level of the decorative wooden molding, looking down as Victor bent over her body.

"Something's wrong! Her body's shutting down," said Victor, ripping the cap off Justine's head.

Justine watched with a sense of resignation tinged with sadness as Victor flipped the hatch and pulled her wasted body out of the iron breathing apparatus.

"I can't find a heartbeat," he said, listening with a stethoscope.

"Oh, no," said Lizzie, her hands covering her mouth. "No, it can't be."

Aggie was shaking Justine's limp body gently and massaging her hands in an attempt to wake her up. "Come on back to us, Justine."

Will was crying and Byram was comforting him.

It was only when Victor removed his stethoscope and took Lizzie into his arms that Justine understood. She was dead.

With a final, desperate surge of strength, she dove back down into the lake of Nancy's mind, pushing herself deeper, past the silvery fading memories and the last, lingering desires. *Help me stay*, she begged, and the pieces of Nancy caught at her and pulled her deeper still.

When she opened her eyes again, she saw that Lizzie was crying into Victor's chest. "It's my fault," she was saying. "I should never have taken the chance."

"Don't be sorry," said Justine, in an alto voice that sounded unfamiliar to her own ears. Sitting up on the gurney, she smiled into ten pairs of startled eyes. "It worked."

27

AGGIE PULLED THE COVERS OVER THE GIRL WHO looked like Nancy but spoke like Justine. "You're sure you don't need me to stay with you?"

"I'm sure. I'm feeling amazing, really. Not even sure I'll be able to sleep." Justine smiled. Her new face was freshly scrubbed of grime, her dark blond hair washed and combed, and her slender body dressed in a fresh, lace-trimmed nightgown. "Thanks for letting me stay in your bed, Ags," added Justine, now happily ensconced in the room Aggie shared with Lizzie.

"I'm still not convinced we did the right thing." It had seemed strange and callous to leave Justine's lifeless body in the iron lung. Aggie wondered which of the nurses would discover her.

"I don't see how the doctors can help," said Justine with a shrug. "All they could do would be to study me."

"But do you really want to give up your identity? Your name?" Aggie assumed that Justine Makepiece had savings. As Nancy, she would be poor.

"I'm afraid that giving up my identity happened when I switched bodies," said Justine. "I can't see a judge giving me access to my money while I look like someone else."

On the other side of the room, Lizzie gave an exasperated huff and pulled the covers over her head. "Stop talking. I need to sleep before it's time to treat the queen and Dodger again."

Justine frowned. "What about you, Aggie? Don't you need to close your eyes, even for a little while?"

Aggie considered it. Even before tonight's craziness, it had been one hell of a long week. She glanced at the clock—5:00 a.m., which gave her an hour to rest. The Queen was always at her stroppiest first thing in the morning—she disliked the current night nurse—so Aggie needed every second of rest she could grab before dealing with the feisty and addled monarch.

There was a faint snore from Lizzie's bed. Her roommate had already fallen asleep. That decided her. Sinking down into a chair, Aggie covered herself with a shawl. "I'll just sit for a moment."

"I'll pay you to stop talking," said Lizzie, slurring her words. "Ten dollars to let me sleep."

"How much in pounds and shillings? Besides, you were asleep," said Aggie.

"Twenty."

"Pay me in pastries," said Aggie. "Preferably cinnamon buns."

"I'm not sure whether I like cinnamon buns," said Justine, barely containing her excitement. "But I think I'm starving. I want food!"

Aggie mumbled something, realizing that she would have to sneak some food back for Justine before too long.

Don't worry about that now. Rest. Trying to find a comfortable position, she realized she was still wearing her dark specs. Yawning, she removed then and placed them on a side table. The room was still shadowed, so she wasn't worried about taxing her eyes, but her fatigue was making the furniture appear to tilt and spin.

A familiar pair of slightly bulbous blue eyes gazed back at her from underneath a frilly mobcap.

Oh, no.

Aggie turned on the light. "Lizzie? You have to wake up. The Queen's out of her room and wandering about."

Lizzie rubbed her eyes. "What are you talking about? How do you know?"

Aggie fumbled for her spectacles. "Because I just saw her."

"Oh, thank goodness you decided to come in early," said Shiercliffe the moment Aggie and Lizzie walked into the receiving room. "We're having a bit of a crisis this morning." The matron's tone was even, but she was still in her dressing gown, her graying braid visible under her sleeping cap.

"What happened?" asked Aggie.

"The night nurse discovered poor Miss Makepiece had passed away in the night, and rang the alarm. Unfortunately, the nurse who was supposed to be watching Her Majesty left her side, and now..." Shiercliffe nervously closed the neck of her dressing gown. "We have the night staff searching all the wards, but so far, we haven't located the queen. The kaiser is due to arrive tomorrow! If she isn't found..."

"Leave it to us," said Aggie.

"She does seem to like the pair of you." Shiercliffe looked older and less formidable than Aggie had ever seen her before. "Perhaps try the dining hall? Her Majesty talks about sausages a great deal."

"Great idea," Aggie called over her shoulder as she dragged Lizzie toward the back staircase.

Half an hour later, Lizzie and Aggie were running out of places to look. They had checked Dodger's room, which looked horrifyingly like a prison: no Queen and no Dodger. They had unlocked the supply room that Victor and Lizzie had renamed the Department of Neuroscience: empty. Desperate, Aggie had opened the door to the morgue, where she was greeted by two cadavers that had been used for a student anatomy class.

"Don't suppose either of you have seen the queen? No?" She slammed the door shut, rubbing her arms to drive away the chill.

"You're getting loopy," said Lizzie. "Maybe we need to stop and get something to eat."

"Our malfunctioning Bio-Mechanical monarch might be running around London. I think we need to keep going," said Aggie.

Lizzie grabbed her arm. "Wait. Do you think they've left the building?"

Aggie froze, struck by a sudden mental image of Dodger leading the dotty and vulnerable Queen through the back alleys of London's roughest neighborhoods. Was she imagining it, or seeing it through Dodger's eyes? She felt like tearing her hair out. Here she was, hanging on to her position at the teaching hospital by a thread, and the queen was her sole responsibility. If something happened to her, then Aggie might as well pack her bags tonight.

"If they've gone," she said, "there's no telling what could happen. What if someone they meet realizes they're both Bio-Mechanicals?" She and Lizzie knew firsthand what happened when people formed a mob.

"All right, let's think this through," said Lizzie. "When you saw the queen, did you get any clues as to where she was?"

"I didn't pay attention," said Aggie. "I just assumed they would be down here somewhere."

Lizzie gave her an assessing look. "There is one way for you to find out."

It took Aggie a moment to catch on. "Oh, no," she said, reflexively putting out her hands. "You want to let Dodger into my head?"

"It's the only way, Ags."

Aggie swallowed. "All right. What should I do?"

"What did you do when it happened before to make contact with Dodger?"

Aggie removed her spectacles.

"Do you want to sit down?" asked Lizzie.

"I'm all right." She actually felt giddy with fatigue. Her earlier desire for a cinnamon bun had morphed into a deep-seated craving for an enormous slice of shepherd's pie. Most embarrassingly, she wished that someone would give her a hug. Not that she would ever admit any of this to Lizzie.

"Think about Dodger," said Lizzie. "Try to reestablish the link."

Aggie had been expending effort *not* to think of Dodger. This was much easier. She pictured him tipping his top hat to her and offering to show her the way; pouring water over her hands at Jenny's flat; moving to protect her from Oliver Twist the day her eyes were injured. Feeling a mixture of tenderness and guilt, she thought of Dodger with his head in her lap, gazing up at her with his weirdling eyes.

Then, with a jolt, she felt the dizzying shift of perspective as she found herself looking out of Dodger's eyes: sunrise. Cobblestones. A porter with a walrus moustache.

"Aggie?" Lizzie's voice called her back into her own body. "Did it work? Do you know where they are?"

"I think so," said Aggie, replacing her spectacles. She wasn't exactly sure where she was headed, but even with the visual link broken, she still felt some faint connection that said *warmer, warmer, warmer* as she moved down a corridor and turned a corner until she reached a door.

On the other side of the door, under a blue May sky, six or seven Bio-Mechanicals were standing very still, as though under some sorceress's spell. Three of them were holding large metal pestles over wooden mortars, but they had paused in their pounding. Another had been chopping firewood for the kitchen but was now leaning on his axe, while a hunchbacked fellow had set down his sacks of bone meal and was listening to something with a rapt expression. A heavyset porter with a big walrus moustache was watching, but for some reason, he was not shouting at his charges to return to their jobs.

Aggie and Lizzie stepped around the Bio-Mechanicals and now they could see the queen, still in her mobcap and nightdress, leaning on Dodger as she ran her fingers over one of the Bio-Mechanical's electrodes.

"Behold," she said softly, "the Corpus Victoriam. Subject or object?"

The Bio-Mechanical, who had a thick scar running down his forehead, just looked blankly ahead.

"Object," said the queen, with an air of resignation. She

looked up at Dodger. "What say you, my thieving magpie boy?"

Dodger bowed his head. "Loyal subject, Your Majesty." Then he looked over his shoulder at Aggie and gave her a wink. "Think we've been twigged, ma'am."

The Queen scowled. "Witch doctresses abound."

Aggie dropped into a curtsy. "Come on, Your Majesty. You must be famished from all your walking. Wouldn't you like a cup of tea and a nice bit of buttered toast?"

The Queen brightened. "With sausage?"

Aggie smiled down at the petite monarch. "I think it can be arranged." Then she met Dodger's gaze and even behind her tinted lenses, she could feel the pull of him.

"Seems our beloved Queen's right fond of Bio-Mechanicals," he said, cocking one eyebrow. "Wonder why that is?"

She had no easy answer, not out here in the open, but as Aggie led the queen away, just before the door closed, she heard the Bio-Mechanical with the scar down his face say, "Subject."

Aggie felt a lurch in her chest. Suddenly it all seemed perfectly obvious. The Queen's jumbled speech wasn't a sign of a disordered mind. Quite the opposite, in fact.

Like the Roman emperor who had survived by pretending to be a fool, Victoria was hiding in plain sight.

28

THE QUEEN WAS A BIO-MECHANICAL.

More than twelve hours had passed since he had discovered the shocking secret, but Dodger couldn't get over it. All day long, he had been waiting for someone to talk to him about what had happened, but instead, he appeared to have been forgotten in the final hours before the kaiser's arrival. There had been no brain-tuning session and no hard labor. For the first time, he had been given a piece of meat with dinner.

"We're building up your strength for your showdown with the kaiser's bruiser," the porter explained, setting the mutton down in front of Dodger.

"It's a demonstration," he told Wiggins. "Not a fight."

"That's what they tell you," said Wiggins. "But think about it. Once a man has a new kind of weapon, he immediately looks for an excuse to pull it out and use it. And not in a demonstration—in a fight."

Dodger felt sick. "Bloody hell," he said. "You have a point."

Wiggins had surprised him by giving him some salve for

the seeping blisters on his hands. "Try not to fret," he said before locking the door. "You might want to emulate your cellmates and live in the moment."

Unfortunately, Dodger did not have the luxury of ignorance. Unable to eat more than two bites of the tough mutton, he had fallen asleep thinking of expensive horses and how they were coddled by their trainers, before realizing that he had never actually spoken to a horse. Perhaps they had some complaints, as well.

Then, still bone tired, he had woken up with an abrupt start, unsure what had roused him. Was it the pain in his hands and the ache in his shoulders and back, or the snuffling, snorting noises of his sleeping roommates? Perhaps it was the frantic scrabbling of rats inside the walls—but he should be used to that.

Turning over on the thin, lumpy straw mattress, he had looked up and gasped when he realized that the Queen of England was perched on the edge of his straw pallet, dressed in her nightcap and gown.

"Corpse walker?" she inquired. "Shambler? Abomination?"

He nodded, still groggy from sleep. "Your Majesty?" He'd sat up, reaching for his workman's cap. He was painfully aware he was undressed beneath the threadbare blanket, but there wasn't much he could do about that at the moment.

"Bestir yourself," said the queen, hoisting herself upright. "We shall inspect the corpsemen."

Intrigued, he had managed to get his britches on under the covers. *Well, fancy that*, he thought. *The richest woman in the world is a daft old bat. Suppose it's up to me to keep the old bird safe till someone official comes along to claim her.* It was his duty as a patriotic British citizen, after all.

Besides, there might be some sort of reward involved.

"At your service, Your Majesty," he said, standing up and executing his best court bow. Then he had looked at her properly, and his eyes had focused on the slight ripple in the lace at her throat.

Electrodes. His weirdling eyes homed in on them, showing him a close-up of the telltale metallic rods.

Corpse walker. Shambler. Abomination.

She hadn't been asking him to identify himself as a monster. She had been asking him to confirm that she was like him—reanimated.

Later, after the queen had been rounded up by her keepers, and with nothing in his cell to distract him, Dodger had spent most of the day worrying about how badly he was going to lose to the German corpse walker, and what Moulsdale thought to do with a disappointing Bio-Mechanical. Now, stomach growling with hunger, he lay down on his pallet and wondered if Queen Victoria's secret was the kind of information that could get a fellow sprung from a cage—or get him killed.

He closed his eyes and tried to work out the angles but found himself thinking about Aggie instead.

He had been thinking of her a great deal since he'd discovered how they were connected. Sometimes he could feel her thinking about him, a sensation like the barest brush of mental fingertips. At other times he could slip in as subtle as a thief and ride around in her head, seeing what she was seeing. A patient's nervous smile; a livid red burn on a smooth, pale arm; a teaspoon of sugar being emptied into a cup of black workman's tea.

A sharp jab in his side made him open his eyes. Wiggins was standing over him and prodding him with his stick a few moments later. "Lady wants to see you," he said. "Hold out your hands."

Dodger yawned and gave a big stretch. "But I'm knackered," he complained, stalling as he reached under his straw mattress for the tiny bits of wire and the dented needle he'd stashed there.

"You're breakin' my heart." Another prod, this one harder. "Come on, sit up."

Dodger sat up and extended his hands. "Is this really necessary?"

Wiggins clicked the handcuffs shut. "Don't want to get in trouble if you forget yourself."

This was new. For a moment, he wondered if it was Lizzie, come to visit him without Victor. But no, he knew better. He could feel the connection, opening up. It was Aggie, and she was close by. "Just don't lose the key."

Wiggins patted his pocket reflexively. "No worries on that count." He yanked the chain, hauling Dodger to his feet. "Ready?"

Dodger, pulled off balance, nearly fell on top of the porter. "Sorry."

"Watch it."

"Can you just scratch behind my ear? Whenever I can't use my hands, I feel an itch."

Wiggins cuffed him hard enough to make his ears ring. "That better?"

"Not really." Walking in front of Wiggins, though, Dodger allowed himself a smile. He had the key to his handcuffs up his sleeve, and whatever Wiggins had packed in wax paper for his supper tucked into his trousers. Ahead of him, he could feel Aggie as if she were a magnet, pulling him toward her.

He wasn't sure what he was going to do with all these props and guides, but that was all right. He was an improviser, and his best plans always unfolded in ways that surprised him as much as everyone else.

29

IT HAD BEEN LESS THAN FORTY-EIGHT HOURS since Aggie had discovered that Dodger was alive, but it felt like much longer.

She sat in the supply room Victor and Lizzie had commandeered as their office, nervously adjusting her dark spectacles as she waited for the porter to bring Dodger back. *I shouldn't be here*, she thought. There was a very long list of things she ought to be doing—tending to the queen, checking in on Justine, possibly even eating something or catching up on some sleep. She was expected to start helping the queen an hour earlier than usual, to be ready for the kaiser's arrival tomorrow.

Instead, she was waiting for Dodger, stomach knotted with nerves or anticipation or both. *Remember what you're here for*, she told herself. This wasn't a social visit. She was going to make a clean break and get her life back. She'd thought about him almost continuously since discovering he was alive. They were connected. But if she were to have a life of her own, the one she thought she'd recovered with the return of her vision, she had to resist his pull and listen to her more disciplined self.

The porter pushed him into the room, then turned to Aggie. "You want me to stay, miss?"

"No, that won't be necessary, Wiggins." She had cleared the room a little, so she could sit behind the protection of the desk when Dodger came in. Not that it was any real protection, but it made her feel more in control.

"As you like." With a knowing grin that was more in his eyes than in his mustachioed mouth, he doffed his cap at her. Lord only knew what he thought she liked. She waited till the door was shut, wondering if Wiggins was the sort to wait outside, peering through keyholes.

There would be nothing untoward to see if he did.

"Thank you for meeting me," she said, as though this were a job interview. "We didn't get much of a chance to speak earlier, what with all the to-do about the queen."

"Ah," said Dodger, with a faint look of surprise. "Well, it weren't no trouble to come. Nothing better to do, besides looking forward to the big day when I'm to be paraded in front of the kaiser like a prize pig."

As if to prove his point, he wobbled and knocked into a small medicine cabinet, causing a few vials of chloroform to rattle out onto the floor. With a pang of guilt, she wondered if the other Bio-Mechanicals felt exhaustion, as well, but just didn't have the language to express it. "I won't keep you long, then. But—would you like to sit?" She gestured to a chair, and Dodger peered at it with interest.

"Indeed I would." Yet he continued to stand in front of her, looking relaxed but respectful with his hands clasped together. It took her a moment to realize that his hands had been cuffed in front of him.

Oh, dear Lord. She was going to have to help him—which meant touching him. This had to be some kind of divine punishment. "Do you need assistance?"

He looked abashed, as if admitting it embarrassed him. "If it's not too much bother. My back's so sore. Not used to all the lifting."

"I'm sorry." Pushing her chair back, she pressed her skirts down and maneuvered around the desk to where Dodger was standing. She hesitated a moment before touching him, then gripped his arm and his waist, guiding him down into the chair. He leaned back a little too quickly, bumping into her.

"Sorry! Little light-headed, I suppose."

Funny, but she felt the same. "Have you eaten?"

"No, but there's a sandwich tucked into my trousers, if you can reach it?"

She crossed her arms in front of her. "Come on, now."

He gave her his most earnest face, not an easy thing with these strange new eyes. "Thieves' honor."

"I swear to God, Dodger, if this is a trick…" She reached just under his waistband, no funny business. Located the sandwich with a crinkle of wax paper, brought it out and handed it over with a surprised lift to her eyebrows. "Well…here you go, then."

He raised the sandwich as if he were toasting her. "Ta, lovely."

"I probably shouldn't ask, but is there a reason why you're carrying a sandwich in the waistband of your trousers?"

Dodger grinned at her. "They serve us workhouse rations, but I, er, managed to liberate that from Wiggins."

"That's terrible." She couldn't help answering his grin with one of her own, but as he started to fumble, trying to use his bound hands to unwrap the sandwich, she felt embarrassed for him. "Do you want me to…?"

"Ta, luv."

She took the sandwich from him and peeled back the wax paper.

"Ham and cheddar on rye," he said approvingly. "Go ahead and tell me what's on your mind."

"Right. Of course." She held out the sandwich and instead of taking it in his hands, he took a bite, looking her in the eyes till the last moment.

"Go on," he said, swallowing. "You must have had a reason for this change of heart."

She held out the sandwich again. She often fed patients, but this felt different. Despite his bound hands, he didn't seem helpless at all. If anything, she was the one trembling. "When we first saw each other again, you said I had stolen your eyes."

He chewed and swallowed. "Sorry about that. I realize it's not your fault, now."

"Oh." It was odd—the longer she spent with him, the more comfortable she felt. This close to him, she couldn't help but recall their two forays into the rookeries. He had liked her. More than liked her. And she had liked him.

"There's a serious look," said Dodger. "Am I in trouble?"

"No, of course not." She offered him the sandwich a third time, but he shook his head.

"What is it you want, Aggie?"

Now, that was a loaded question. Suddenly aware of how close to him she was standing, she retreated a step, rewrapping the sandwich and placing it on the desk. *Be bold*, she told herself. No point in observing the niceties, given the way they were linked to each other. "I want to know how we're going to handle this—this connection between us."

"How d'you want to handle it?"

She felt the tug of an invisible string, as though speaking the words out loud strengthened the bond. *He's trying to get into my head*, she realized. And strangely, dangerously, it didn't feel like an intrusion. It felt like joining up with a lost piece of herself, which made no sense at all.

Because it's his feeling, not mine.

Aggie thought of Shiercliffe and steeled herself against the treacherous longing to be closer to him. Moving back to her seat behind the desk, she cleared her throat. "I want you to leave me alone. And I pledge to do the same with you."

Dodger felt the quick kick of his pulse. Leaving Aggie alone was the last thing he wanted, but he knew better than to say that out loud. "Fine, then. Cards on the table?"

"Please."

"Seems to me you're asking for me to give up the only advantage I have in this game."

He watched her as she opened her mouth to defend herself, then looked at his shackled hands and changed her mind. "I can see why you would think that," she allowed. "But in a sense, both of us have been altered in ways we didn't choose for ourselves."

"You've got my eyes, you mean."

She tugged at the cuffs of her sleeves, clearly discomfited by his directness. "And in return, you have implants that give you extraordinary abilities." She was gathering her courage, and Dodger was surprised to find he admired her for it. *Don't be too sympathetic, mate*, he reminded himself. *This is a negotiation.*

"I see where this is headed." Dodger leaned back. "You want to make a trade. I get my old peepers back, you get these little beauties."

"Very funny."

He shrugged. "I try."

Aggie sat up straighter. "All right," she said. "I'm going to be blunt here. I can't function if I know you can just spy on me whenever you please."

Dodger winced. "That's a strong word. It's not like I'm peeping on you when you're getting ready for bed. Although, now that I think about it…"

"It's not funny. How can I relax, knowing you can watch me undress anytime you feel like it?"

"How do you think *I* feel, knowing you can watch me in my birthday suit?" He brought his manacled hands up, as if trying to conceal his nudity.

He could tell from the expression on her face that this thought had not occurred to her before, but she recovered quickly. "Please be serious. I would never spy on you like that, and you know it. I need to know you're going to respect my wishes."

"You could always try trusting me," said Dodger, even though that was absurd, since he was spying on her a bit—although never when she was undressing or indisposed. Still, shouldn't she know there were some lines he would never cross?

She raised her chin. "I will trust you—if you give me your word that you will stay out of my head."

Without planning his response, Dodger leaned forward, putting his handcuffed hands on the desk. "What's in it for me, then?"

Aggie seemed surprised. "What would you like?"

"Make me a cambric shirt."

That surprised her. "Yes," she said, as if this were not an absurd request. "Of course, I know the clothes they've given you leave much to be desired."

"Without any seams or fine needlework."

She blinked. "Beg pardon?"

"Then wash it in yonder dry well, which never sprung water nor rain ever fell."

She gave a soft, sad laugh when she caught the reference. "Parsley, sage, rosemary and thyme?" She had a pleasant singing voice, low and husky.

"That's the tune, all right."

"Scarborough Fair is in Yorkshire, you know. Where I'm from." She looked a little rueful as she added, "The song makes it sound like a goblin market, all magical trinkets and impossible tasks, but the reality is much more mundane."

He did not smile back at her. "Your science is as bad as any goblin magic."

She drew in a breath. "So what are you saying? That you don't trust me? That there's nothing I can offer you?"

"I want my eyes back."

She let her breath go as if deflated. "I can't make that happen."

"I want my life back."

She looked defeated. "Ask me something I can do and I swear to you, I will do it."

He studied her. "Did you really think you could just strike a bargain with me that only benefits you? What did you think— that I'm so smitten that I'd just give up my one advantage?"

She hung her head, clearly embarrassed. "I could put in a

good word with Shiercliffe. Perhaps get you a better room—gentler treatment."

"I'd still be a slave, though." He took a breath. "Aggie, I'm out of time. The kaiser arrives tomorrow. Help me get out of here before I have to face off against his corpse walker." He hadn't known he was going to say it until the words came out of his mouth.

She sucked in a sharp breath. "If I did that, I would lose my position."

"Least you have something to lose."

"That's not fair. Would you sacrifice your life to save mine?"

He shrugged. "Seems like I did just that—not that I was given a choice." He held her gaze, willing her to feel the connection between them.

She looked away, and suddenly Dodger's throat closed up, making it hard to swallow. So that was that. He hadn't known how much he wanted to escape until this opportunity had presented itself. Now her face told him the cage door was slamming shut again. He hated to plead with her, but desperation forced the words out. "Ags, please. I've got a bad feeling the size of a cannonball in my belly."

"Dodger," she said, "I want to help you, I really do." The word *but* was unspoken, yet he heard it loud and clear. Even so, the anguished expression on her face nearly made him do something foolish, like apologize for what he was about to do.

But right now, it was every man—or Bio-Mechanical—for himself.

"I understand perfectly," said Dodger. "You want to help me. You just don't want it badly enough to actually do it." Raising his voice, he called, "Wiggins! The lady is done with me now."

38

WIGGINS OPENED THE DOOR SO QUICKLY IT WAS instantly apparent that he had been standing just outside it the whole time. "Everything all right then, probationer? You got what you wanted?" His tone was perfectly respectful. It was his eyebrows that revealed the thread of mockery.

"Yes, thank you." Aggie stood, flustered and uncertain whether she was disappointed or relieved. She had no answer to her request. But maybe that was her answer. Dodger couldn't or wouldn't break the connection. For some mad reason, she felt a tiny bit relieved.

"Hang on," said Wiggins, checking the chain of keys at his waist. "Where's the bloody key to your cuffs?"

"Maybe you should have given it to me for safekeeping," said Dodger.

"Very funny." Wiggins looked through his jacket pockets. "Blast me, I couldn't have dropped it."

As Wiggins searched, Aggie tried to avoid looking directly at Dodger. She was unsettled by Dodger's suggestion, but underneath it was another feeling that was not so easy to name. She thought of her mother's accusatory tone, warning her how she would wind up if she allowed herself to touch or be touched by a boy. She had a flash of Shiercliffe's thin, disapproving frown.

But it wasn't so easy to dismiss someone when you could see how the world looked through their eyes. She'd felt a connection with Dodger even before she'd received his eyes. With them, she saw as he saw, and sometimes…felt as she imagined he was feeling.

"All right, then," said Wiggins. "I'll find the blasted key later. We'll be on our way."

"I do hope you won't get in trouble for that lost key," said Dodger. "Let's try to think where you might have left it." Dodger's voice was as helpful as a wife's, trying to joggle her husband's memory. "Hmm. Did you have it when you were eating lunch?"

Aggie noticed something that should have occurred to her before—Dodger didn't appear unhappy at being taken back to his cell. In fact, he had been the one to call Wiggins. Why?

"Lunch… Hang on," said the porter as something on the desk caught his eye. "Is that my sandwich?"

"I don't know. Does it look like your sandwich?"

Wiggins's fist shot out, knocking Dodger off his feet. Aggie's startled yelp made him smile, which looked awful—his mouth was filling with blood.

"Surely there's no need for that," she said. "And the professors wouldn't want him damaged. Especially with the kaiser arriving tomorrow."

Dodger's face registered nothing, but she saw a flash of something in his eyes. Had he expected more from her?

"I won't damage him. I know my job," said Wiggins. "And I don't blame him for thieving. Clearly, it's his calling. I blame meself for not paying more attention." He stroked the edges of his moustache. "Won't make that mistake again."

"You think you won't," said Dodger. "But you will. The problem is, you're focusing all your attention on guarding against one kind of theft—" with a quick twist, Dodger had his handcuffs off his wrists, and with another twist, he had Wiggins's right hand cuffed "—and you leave yourself open to a different approach." Yanking Wiggins's hand behind him, Dodger got his second hand cuffed.

Wiggins was sputtering, outraged. "How the bloody hell did you do that?"

Dodger held up the key he had swiped. "You should pay more attention to your belongings, mate."

Aggie found herself giving an unintentional snort of laughter.

"This is the kind of low trickery I should have expected from one of your tribe," said Wiggins. "Sneakiness and cowardice— the hallmarks of your people."

"My people," said Dodger, sounding bemused. "Why, Wiggins, I thought you were a philosopher, not a garden variety anti-Semite. Or did you mean Bio-Mechanicals? Never mind—open wide." Dodger pinched the man's nose until he opened his mouth, and then crammed in the half-eaten sandwich. "That should keep your mouth occupied." He pulled a vial of chloroform out of his pocket as Wiggins stared, bug-eyed, and tried to protest around the sandwich stuffed in his mouth.

For a moment, Aggie was dumbfounded. Then she realized how she had been tricked.

"You hoodwinked me," she said. "When you knocked into the cabinet—you've been planning this all along!"

"I'd say I keep my eyes open for opportunities," he corrected her. Then, with a sudden move, he stripped off his ragged shirt, revealing a leanly muscled chest and the marks of recent beatings on his back.

"You're hurt," she said.

"What do you expect? Bio-Mechanicals aren't meant to have feelings, remember? They're just cannon fodder. So why would the guards care how they treat us?"

"I didn't know." Which was hardly an excuse—she hadn't bothered to think of it, but as a probationer nurse for the hospital that created Bio-Mechanicals, shouldn't she have considered the implications? She looked at the glint of the metal alloy over his heart, and the electrodes at his neck. They did not make him any less human to her, and she could not understand how anyone could see this vital boy as something less than an animal.

Then he used the key to pry the top of the vial of chloroform and she realized what he was about to do. "Dodger, wait," she said. "Chloroform can be dangerous."

"Can't think of another way to borrow our friend's uniform."

Wiggins looked frightened. Like many people in a low position of authority, he had confused himself with his position and had not considered what might happen to him if he lost it. Spitting the sandwich out of his mouth, he said, "I swear, I won't make trouble."

"I shall treat that assurance with the same confidence you would, if our positions were reversed." Tipping the vial onto his wadded-up shirt, Dodger took a step toward Wiggins.

"Wait!" Aggie moved in front of Dodger. "Do you honestly expect me to just sit idly by and let you get away with this?"

"Well, you can help if you like. Otherwise, idle sitting would be acceptable." Dodger pressed the chloroform-soaked shirt to the man's face, and for a moment, Aggie considered screaming for help. But only for a moment. She wasn't sure what made her decide to help him, or if it was weakness or bravery that made her do it. She only knew that she could not summon guards to stop him.

"That's enough," she said, watching as Wiggins finally succumbed to the chloroform, his muscles going lax. "Anymore and you could kill him by accident."

Dodger removed the handcuffs from Wiggins's wrists and fastened them on his waistband. "You sound as though I'm doing this as some kind of lark. If I stay, Ags, they're going to stick me in a ring with some German killing machine. And you know as well as I do that I won't last long, no matter how much they've tried to prepare me."

She shook her head. "That can't be right. They haven't said anything about having you fight the kaiser's Bio-Mechanical."

Even as she said the words, she wasn't sure she believed them. She could well imagine Shiercliffe and Moulsdale lying to achieve their ends, and even though she still wanted to believe that the Bio-Mechanical program was for the common good, she had begun to feel doubt creeping in. The cause still sounded noble—who wouldn't want to stop the senseless killing in war, and to make sure no more young men with bright futures died on the battlefield? Yet Dodger was a young man, too, despite his transformation. Shouldn't he be spared, as well?

Of course, it wasn't all about Dodger. What if the only

way to make a superior Bio-Mechanical soldier was to create
a being that had self-awareness?

"Doesn't matter what they say," said Dodger, cutting into
her thoughts. "What do you think they're going to do with
us? We're two roosters in a cockfight. They're not going to
judge us on how pretty our feathers look."

Aggie felt her left temple beginning to pound. She didn't
want him to leave. Not like this. "But Shiercliffe said it was
just a demonstration." It was more a token protest than a real
argument. She knew what she needed to do now.

Dodger knelt down beside her. "I might not be fond of
Wiggins here, but when he told me I'd wind up fighting the
kaiser's corpse walker, I knew he had the right of it." He began
peeling away Wiggins's navy-and-red porter's uniform with
calm efficiency, revealing a pale, flabby, pear-shaped body
mercifully concealed by long, sweat-stained woolen under-
wear. There was a rip in the seat—clearly, Wiggins was the
kind of man who kept good care of what the world saw but
didn't bother with what he looked like in private.

"What are you doing?"

"What does it look like?" Dodger pulled on Wiggins's
jacket over his ragged shirt. "I've got some mates down in
Brighton. Figure this might solve both our problems. I get
out of here, and you don't have to worry about me spying on
you. I reckon our bond shouldn't stretch beyond city limits."

"It won't work, Dodger. First of all, that jacket is way too
big on you." Aggie checked Wiggins's pulse—still steady.
"Second of all, you do realize that you won't have more than
a few days before you need an infusion of fresh ichor."

"There's a doctor not far from here who's got the goods."

Dodger stuffed his own ragged shirt and trousers down the front and pulled the man's leather belt as tight as he could.

"You mean Henry Clerval? He's not competent to bandage a wound."

Dodger shrugged. "He doesn't need to be the world's greatest surgeon to sell me some bootleg ichor, Aggie."

"What if it's not the right formula? What if it's a fake?" She wondered if he could tell that she was running out of arguments—or that she could feel his yearning for freedom as if it were her own emotion.

"At least I'll have tried something. Now, what do you think?" He tugged Wiggins's cap down low, concealing his eyes.

"I think you're too stubborn to listen to reason."

"You might be right, sweeting, but there's nothing to be done about that, now is there?"

Anyone else would have been fooled by his shrug and his wink, but Aggie could read him. He was terrified. Of course, she was pretty frightened herself. Both for him, and for what she was about to do.

"There is one thing to be done." She removed her dark spectacles and handed them to Dodger. "You can wear these… and I can come with you."

31

SLIPPING OUT A SIDE DOOR THAT OPENED ONTO
a back alley, Aggie worried that someone might spot her pro-
bationary nurse's uniform and question where she was headed.
The moment they walked around the side of the hospital,
she could see that this was not going to be a problem. Even
though the kaiser was not due to arrive until the following
morning, the streets surrounding the Royal Victoria were already teeming with throngs of people.

"Good Lord," she said, taking in the number milling about
outside the hospital gates. "They're not threatening to burn
the place down, are they?" She was only half joking—the
last time she had seen a gathering of townspeople outside a
hospital, they had been waving torches and shouting incendiary words. She no longer trusted crowds, even though many
people in this crowd were laughing and smiling.

"It's in honor of the royal visit," said Dodger. "Here, maybe
you want to stay close. There are a group of sailors that look
like they've started celebrating early." He offered her his

arm, and after a moment's hesitation, Aggie slipped her hand through his elbow.

"Where? I can't see any sailors," she said, looking around.

"You will," he promised.

"Just how well can you see now, Dodger? Especially in this light." The last rays of the sun were just setting, which meant that it was probably close to eight, when the hospital closed its gates for the night. Given everything that had happened already, the day felt both much longer and much shorter.

"Don't know. Haven't yet seen what I'm looking for, though." Dodger guided Aggie around a group of old women putting the finishing touches on a sign that read Rule, Victoria, For the Next 100 Years!

"Incredible," she said. "Who would want to stand around waiting all night, just to catch a glimpse of the queen?"

"It's as good an excuse for a party as any," said Dodger. "Folks need a bit of pageantry now and then."

"So it would seem." Some men and women were wearing little Union Jack ribbons pinned to their wool jackets, while others were waving small flags enthusiastically enough to poke the unwary in the eye. Others, drinking gin to stay warm, were noisily singing "God Save the Queen" and the music hall favorite "We Don't Want to Fight," with its rousing second verse:

But by jingo, if we do
we've got the ships, we've got the men
and the Bio-Mechanicals, too!
We've fought the Bear, we'll fight the Hun, because
we're Britons true.
The kaiser will be on the run
when we show what we can do!

"They certainly seem patriotic," she said as Dodger maneuvered her through a tight knot of young men wearing sailors' distinctive caps and bell-bottoms.

"Seems to me like the same sort of crowd that shows up for public executions. Good pickings, I should say. Care to change careers? We could make a fortune tonight."

"Your new eyes might even be an advantage."

"There's a thought. But this kind of mob can turn unruly. If they caught a bloke stealing, they probably wouldn't bother to wait for the constable or the hangman."

Aggie tried to pull him back. "Then let's turn around. I know you want to believe he can help you, but Clerval is a quack."

"He's my only chance at freedom, Ags."

Aggie knew it was useless, but she tried one last time. "Remember that poor girl we tried to help, the night we first met? She believed in a quick fix, too." The thought of watching Dodger being operated on in some back alley surgery made her shudder.

"But I've got you here, don't I?" He pressed her hand to his side with his elbow. "You're going to watch, to make sure it's all on the up-and-up."

"Oi, Red," said one of the sailors, stepping in front of Aggie. "You're going the wrong way. Don't you want to see the kaiser and the queen?" His breath reeked of rum.

"Just nipping home to get my flag," she said with a smile, and he let her pass.

She tried not to think about what would happen if the kaiser arrived before she got back. Shiercliffe had done so much for her, but this transgression was one that would not, could not be forgiven. *Am I doing what my mother warned me against? Am I throwing my career away for a boy?*

"I'm going to need to get back before it gets late," she reminded Dodger.

"Back by midnight," he promised.

Midnight had to be safe, she reasoned. There was no way Shiercliffe could spare the time to check on her room tonight.

Still, things were not going according to plan. She and Dodger had barely covered more than a few yards when they found their way blocked by a line of wheelbarrows heaped with ready-to-eat meals for sale. The patriotic tunes here were intermingled with the costermonger's chants of "fresh cockles, alive, alive-o" and "pies, pies, savory or sweet, best in town and can't be beat!"

Children, mostly barefoot, darted in and out of clusters of people, playing tag and begging and making up dirty limericks about Victoria's lapdog.

Suddenly, an old woman in a ragged kerchief and shawl pushed herself between them. "Posy of violets, to match yer sweetheart's eyes?" She thrust the little bouquet at Aggie.

"Sorry, Granny, but my eyes aren't violet," she said, but Dodger surprised her by releasing his grip on her arm to grab the old woman and pull her into a fierce hug.

"Faygie, you mad, lovely thing! What are you doing here?"

"I've been looking for Nancy," said the old woman in a surprisingly youthful voice. "The barman at the Three Vultures says Twist and some posh Percy brought her here." It was only then that Aggie put the voice and the name together. Underneath the stage makeup and powder, this old peddler woman was the young girl in the gray dress she had met the night she was blinded.

Oh, Lord, thought Aggie, should she tell Faygie and Dodger about Nancy? She couldn't decide what to do, since Nancy's fate was now bound up with Justine's.

Best to say nothing, she decided.

"Where are you lot off to?" asked Faygie.

"Never you mind," said Dodger. "You find Nancy, and when you do... Here, give her one of these for me." He pulled Faygie into his arms and held her for a moment.

Faygie pulled back and gave Dodger an assessing look. "What's all this? You going soft on me?" Not realizing that she was unlikely to see her friend again, she gave him a little push. "Go on, I'll catch you up at the Three Vultures tomorrow?"

"Sounds like a plan," said Dodger, taking Aggie's arm. As they walked away, she slipped her hand into his, and he squeezed it.

She felt a pang of regret. If everything went according to plan, she would never see him again after tonight. She didn't want to think about how that would feel.

More than that, though, she didn't care to think about how she would feel if it all went badly.

32

THERE WAS AN ENGRAVED BRASS SIGN OUTSIDE Henry Clerval's door that read Surgery, but once the door was opened, it certainly didn't look like a proper doctor's office. The faint, musty odor of dead rodent still lingered on the air, despite the application of carbolic acid, and an old-fashioned paraffin lamp could not quite dispel the gloom—although it did make it possible to make out the peeling remnants of green floral wallpaper, a rusted cast-iron sink and a wooden bed that still bore the stains of previous operations.

There was a tray of surgical implements—scalpels, a retractor, needles of various thickness and length and fine catgut ligatures. There was a glass bottle of ichor and a length of rubber tubing suspended from an adjustable metal stand, all ready for transfusing. At least, Aggie assumed that the substance in the bottle was ichor. It might have been the gold glow from the paraffin lamp—electrical light was cooler in tone—but the contents of the glass bottle appeared a darker, muddier shade of green than the ichor she was used to seeing.

In the far corner of the room, a Tesla coil stood like an enormous metal mushroom beside a contraption that resembled a cobbled-together version of the school's galvanic magnetometer. The metal helmet had clearly started out life as someone's cooking pan, while the crank that turned a handle seemed to have been borrowed from a bicycle. The electrical leads had been wrapped in odd bits of frayed and tattered rags, giving them a slightly raffish look. There were clear glass bulbs containing bits of filament, attached to a wand not unlike Lizzie's etheric magnetometer, but not exactly like it, either.

Someone was trying to recreate instruments they had seen used, she thought. How well they had succeeded was a matter for debate.

Feeling like Shiercliffe, Aggie ran her finger over the table where the surgical tools were displayed. Dust. "Perhaps we should just leave." They had already been waiting for over an hour, and she was starting to worry that she wouldn't get back to the Royal Victoria before midnight.

"We haven't even met the sawbones yet," said Dodger. His voice betrayed nothing, but Aggie could feel the tension in him. She hadn't considered it before, but now she wondered if the connection between them was growing stronger. Over time, Victor's transplanted left arm had begun to influence his thoughts and feelings. At one point, a whole other personality had emerged and taken over. Now, Victor appeared to have integrated with the arm's original owner. Was that what was going to happen to her and Dodger? Suddenly frightened, she turned to him, not sure what she wanted to say.

"Listen," he said, as if reading her mind, and then, in the back of the room, a door opened. A familiar figure emerged, wearing a white coat and a smugly superior expression.

"My apologies for keeping you waiting. I'm Dr. Henry Clerval. Now, what brings you here today?"

He didn't recognize her, but she certainly remembered him. "Hello, Henry," she said. "We're here to ask you a few questions."

Lots of people thought they knew what it was like to be poor, thought Aggie, but unless you knew what it was like to be truly destitute, you didn't know what you might risk for a remedy.

If you were just plain poor, your choices were still fairly straightforward. Meat was spoiled? Chuck it out. Fleas in your mattress? Wash it clean. Someone you trusted with your secrets sells you out and steals your eyes? Turn the tables and screw them over.

But when you were desperately poor, you made compromises. You trimmed the rotten away and kept what still looked palatable, because there was no other food to be had. You couldn't afford to wash out the fleas, so you rubbed oil of camphor all over yourself and hoped it offended the fleas as much as it did you.

You asked a fake doctor to help and prayed the medicine he gave you was real.

"I need your help with a little problem." Dodger removed his spectacles and pushed down his collar, revealing the electrodes on either side of his neck.

"Ah. I see." Henry sounded taken aback. Most Bio-Mechanicals did not introduce themselves or their medical complaints, of course, but Aggie wondered if there was another, less savory reason for his reaction. Even in a place as desperate as this, Henry might not have had many patients—or any complaints he could not palm off with a bit of snake oil and a conjurer's flickering of lights. Perhaps he did not feel up to the task of helping Dodger.

"Don't worry," said Dodger, interpreting Clerval's hesitation as a concern about payment. "I've got the funds." He patted his pocket.

"Of course." Henry straightened his cravat, composing himself. "Not to worry, you've come to the right place, my friend. I have what you need."

Aggie shot him a dark look. "That remains to be seen," she said. "Can you explain precisely where you obtain your ichor?"

"That would be from me," said a familiar voice. Aggie's stomach twisted as Oliver Twist walked through the door. "Stone the crows," he said, removing his stovepipe. "What happened to your eyes, Dodger?"

Looking at Twist's gaunt, high-cheekboned face, Aggie saw the events of that awful day in February unreel in her mind: Twist's clawlike hand, grabbing for her medical bag. Dodger and Twist, grappling and fighting. The glass bottle, shattering against the brick wall. Strangely enough, she could recall that she had been in pain, but not the pain itself. What was clear, though, was that looking directly at Twist made her feel sick to her stomach.

Fighting back a wave of nausea, she turned to Clerval. "What is *he* doing here?"

Clerval frowned. "Oliver Twist? He is my business associate."

Aggie lifted her chin. "I will not remain in the same room with this person. Either he leaves, or we do."

"I am afraid you have me at a disadvantage, miss." Twist

gave Aggie a disarmingly boyish smile. "I seem to have offended you in some way, but I can't recall the occasion."

Dodger took a step forward, his jaw set and his fists clenched. "You must be joking. You don't recall trying to steal Aggie's medicines? You don't recall the fight that bloody wound up blinding her?" He gave a hoarse laugh. "No, of course you don't. And as for what happened to me, well, let's just say I don't seem to have your luck for coming out on top."

Twist flinched as though Dodger had struck him. "I don't recall that night at all, Dodger. But I don't doubt a word of it." He turned to Aggie, and for the first time, she realized that he was not as haggard or ill-seeming as he had been the last time she had seen him. "Miss…Aggie, is it? I cannot express how deeply I regret my actions. I was out of my head. I can't tell you how sorry I am."

"You're always sorry," said Dodger. "Until you do it again."

"I've quit the drugs. Everything except the ichor, and that doesn't addle my judgment. Please, you must believe me. I'm a changed man."

Dodger shook his head. "You must have me confused with a mark, Twist. Remember, I know you. I've heard this song and dance before."

Aggie grabbed Dodger's arm. "Maybe we should leave."

He turned and looked at her. Without the tinted spectacles as a shield, she felt as if she were falling into a well. "I can't go back, Aggie."

Still holding Dodger's arm, Aggie turned to Henry Clerval and Twist. "There are plenty of snake-oil salesmen around Brick Lane who are all too willing to hand out bottles of laudanum and cocaine along with promises they can't keep. Is your ichor the same as we use at the Royal Victoria?"

Twist raised his right hand. "The very same. I take it myself."

Henry nodded, as well. "I can assure you that this ichor is the same high quality and possesses the same efficacy as what they have at the Royal Victoria."

In his head, Dodger could hear Faygie's voice, warning him. *Marks get conned because they want to be conned. They want to believe in the quick profit, the instant attraction, the miracle cure. They assume that they are cleverer than they are, or that they have a plan for beating the odds.*

But Faygie wasn't here, and Dodger had never thought he was slated for a long life anyhow. Just a free one.

"It's up to you, Aggie. I won't make you stay here. If you want to go straight back to the Royal Victoria, I'll take you there."

She looked into his face and knew what he was really saying: *If you want me to, I will trade my chance at freedom for you.* No matter how uneasy she felt about all this, she could not make him do that.

"I can wait an hour. Have your treatment."

For a long moment, he just stood there, looking at her. Then he leaned his forehead into hers so she could feel the tremble that passed through him. When he drew back, his strange new eyes were so close that she felt dizzy. *I could fall into him*, she thought. *We could fall into each other.*

"So," said Clerval, bringing their attention back to him. "Are we decided? Shall we proceed?"

"Yeah," said Dodger, giving Aggie a last, searching look before pulling off his jacket. "We're in."

33

BILL SYKES WASN'T SENTIMENTAL. SENTIMENT was a luxury reserved for the pretty, the charming and the rich, and he was none of those things. In the craps game of life, he'd landed a face that provoked fights and a body that could win them, and no other advantages. No gift for disguise, no talent for misdirection, no ability to charm his way out of impossible scrapes. His dog, Bullseye, liked him for the same reason Nancy did—because he looked like a bit of security in a hostile world. Because he touched her with affection and didn't cause her pain.

Although he hadn't touched Nancy. Not in ages. Funny thing was, he had thought that if he stopped the touching, he would stop her from thinking she was in love with him. She thought he was different from other blokes because, instead of pursuing her, he held her at arm's length.

He wasn't different. He just couldn't bring himself to take what she offered under false pretenses. He'd made that mistake once, and she'd cried afterward and told him he did love her, he just didn't know it.

But now she was gone, and he wondered if maybe she'd been right all along. The thought of her injured or dead was like a knife twisting in his gut. Was that guilt or affection or as much of love as a gargoyle like him was capable of feeling?

Concentrate on the job. He could still do right by his Nancy. Help her, if she was injured. And if she was dead...bring her body back, give her a decent burial. Mourn her. That's what this mission was about. Going to the one place where you were likely to find the sick or the dead. He hoped to find Nancy among the ill, not in with the cadavers. But he was preparing himself for the worst.

"Oi," said Faygie, struggling to walk alongside him in her old woman's getup. "Slow down. I'm meant to be ancient. I can't go racing about like a bloody gazelle."

Bill forced himself to slow his pace, automatically listening for the clatter of Bullseye's claws on the pavement before remembering that he had left her at Faygie's pawnshop. It was strange, going somewhere without Bullseye padding along after him. You would think having a friend who could actually speak would more than make up for it, but Faygie's presence kept reminding him of all the things that could go wrong.

Well, get over it. A dog would be a hindrance in the Royal Victoria.

Besides, he'd come to rely on the comfort of having Bullseye trotting along by his side. And he knew what happened when you got to needing someone or something.

Safer to count on no one but yourself.

Leaving the crowds gathered around the front gates, Bill and Faygie headed toward the side of the building. He took a running jump and caught at the ledge of a window, then hoisted himself up so he could break through the glass. It took moments, and then he had the door open for Faygie. They moved quickly until the sound of someone else's footsteps made Faygie slow down so she was moving with an old woman's heavy, trudging gait.

Then they turned the corner and nearly ran into a tall, hard-faced woman dressed all in black.

"You two. Where do you think you're headed?"

"I'm off to clean the wards," said Faygie, in an old woman's tremulous quaver.

"You're late," the woman told Faygie. "Mind you make this the last time you don't show up when you ought to." She looked at Bill with a sharpness that prickled the hairs on the back of his neck. "I don't know you."

"First week on the job."

"A porter? Where's your uniform?"

He shrugged. "They said I was to get mine today."

She sniffed. "Has no one told you to address me as Matron?" She sighed. "Very well, then. I'll take you to the laundry to get a uniform. We can't have you walking around here like that."

"As you like, Matron." Bill tugged the brim of his cap and followed her toward the laundry.

Justine was going stir-crazy in Lizzie and Aggie's small bedroom.

At first, she had been content to laze around, marveling at her ability to breathe on her own. Lizzie and Aggie had barely spent any time with her, but they had brought her some food before rushing out again to prepare for the kaiser.

After a while, she had decided to risk getting up and moving about the room. The first time she attempted to stand up, she crumpled to the ground. The second time, she managed to grab hold of a chair and haul herself up with her arms and then stood, trembling, almost giddy with pleasure and nerves.

Walking took longer. She wasn't sure whether it was because she hadn't walked since she was a small child, or because Nancy had lost some strength in her muscles, but each small step exhausted her.

Now that she had spent more than forty-eight hours in her new body, Justine thought she was getting the hang of it. Getting dressed in Lizzie's second-best blouse and skirt had taken an hour, but she had managed it. Justine couldn't quite manage the corset, which meant that everything hung wrong, but it was still amazing to see herself in the looking glass, wearing another woman's face and body—looking like a typical, everyday sort of girl. With legs.

She spun around, laughing, and then laughed some more when she toppled to the ground.

She was aching for Lizzie and Aggie to come back so she could show them her progress. She was also getting peckish—and then, around six o'clock, she realized she was actually famished.

Where on earth were the girls? For most of her seventeen years, Justine had cultivated patience. She had thought she had perfected the art of waiting, but perhaps she had used up all her self-control. Or perhaps what she had mistaken for philosophical equanimity had just been a side effect of her body's weakened condition. All of a sudden, she felt strong and eager and restless and hungry enough to eat an entire roast pig. So why not do something about it?

She asked the question silently, then repeated it out loud as she realized that she didn't have to sit around being hungry and impatient. She could get up, go back to the Royal Victoria and find Lizzie and Aggie. Or else she could sneak into the cafeteria on her own and cadge a bit of supper.

She grabbed Aggie's spare shawl and draped it over her head so she looked like a new immigrant and then stood for a moment with her hand on the doorknob. Did she really dare to do this?

She dared.

An hour and a half later, Justine was exhausted and, she had to admit, more than a little lost inside the hospital. She appeared to have wandered into the laundry, but she couldn't recall if the dining hall was on the same floor or not. She was looking for a chair to collapse into so she could catch her breath when the big man in a porter's uniform spotted her and gave a hoarse shout.

"Nancy? Nancy!" He lurched forward and grabbed her around the waist. "Where the hell have you been, girl? We've been worried sick, Faygie and me." He looked down at her, taking in Lizzie's too-large second-best skirt and blouse.

"Who is this?" Shiercliffe looked furiously back and forth from Justine to Bill. "What is this young woman doing here?"

"She's—she's my sister," said Bill.

"I don't know what game you're playing," said Shiercliffe, taking a small whistle out of her pocket. "But I do know that it ends here." She blew on the whistle twice, producing twin, piercing shrieks.

"Come on," said Bill, grabbing Justine's hand and tugging her out of the room. "Let's scarper."

Justine shook her head. "I... I'm not sure..."

"Are you daft, lass? We've got to get out of here."

Justine hesitated. Could she trust this stranger? Dipping into Bill's thoughts, she saw a vivacious, dimpled girl with long, loose, thick hair that gleamed gold in the sun. Nancy. *I hadn't realized how lovely she was.* In his mind, there were dozens of images of Nancy, some of her much younger, grinning at him with a gap in her front teeth. A more recent memory of her crying over him, and one that was startlingly sensual, her long hair gilded by firelight as she looked up at Bill as if he held the secrets to all the riddles in the world.

Someday you'll want me the way I want you, Bill. Only thing, with my luck, by then it'll be too late.

Bill. That was the big man's name. In Nancy's voice, it sounded like music. Justine was surprised to discover that he was only seventeen.

"All right," she said. "I'll go with you."

It was a moment too late. A porter arrived, short and bulky and balding, but carrying a large club. "What's going on here?"

Bill punched the man before he could react, then grabbed Justine's hand and started running down the hall.

Behind them, Shiercliffe's whistle was blowing as she tried to summon more help.

"Here, we'll go out the side door," said Bill, but as they turned a corner, they saw porters racing toward them. Spotting a staircase, Bill moved swiftly. Justine had never seen anyone race up a staircase, let alone felt herself yanked along for the ride. Gasping for breath, she stumbled as they got out on another floor—and ran straight into Dr. Grimbald.

"Watch it!" Dr. Grimbald had spent much of his life in the military, and even though he was wearing surgical whites in place of a uniform, his voice still carried a commanding officer's authority. "What do you mean by racing around? This is a hospital."

Bill looked as though he wanted to spit in Grimbald's face. "The hell you say. This is a bloody horror show."

Suddenly, Justine saw Victor, coming up behind Grimbald. Recognizing Justine, his eyes widened. "Dr. Grimbald," he said, "this man is abducting this girl."

Bill released Justine's hand and bent in a fighter's crouch to confront the two men. "Go on," he growled. "Just you try it."

Grimbald moved in, and the two men started grappling. Grimbald was a trained soldier, used to the rifles and bayonets and the rules of combat. Bill was clearly used to dirty fighting in close quarters. In two moves, he had Grimbald hauled up against him, his arm braced against the surgeon's throat in a chokehold. Eyes trained on Victor, he said, "I'd back off if I was you."

Victor retreated slowly.

"Keep going."

"Listen, if you would just allow me to explain—"

"You keep flapping your lips, I'll snuff him." Bill tightened his grip on Grimbald's throat.

Victor was silent.

"Nancy, come around."

With an apologetic glance at Victor, Justine stepped closer to Bill. She didn't know why she felt this urge to remain with him, but she couldn't just let them arrest him when he had been trying to help her.

Trying to help Nancy, she corrected herself.

"Come on, Victor," Grimbald was saying.

Suddenly Victor stepped forward and pulled something out of his pocket—a hypodermic. With a quick strike, he had injected Bill before the larger man could react. Still holding onto Grimbald, Bill turned to Justine, his eyes wide with surprise.

"Nancy," he said. "I should never have let you go out alone." Grimbald took advantage of the man's momentary distraction to jab his elbow into Bill's side, freeing himself.

Justine watched Bill's knees fold up as the morphine Victor had injected in his bloodstream took effect. He hit the floor hard.

Justine tried to back away, but Grimbald stepped in front of her. "Mind telling me what all that was about, young woman?"

Before she could stop him, Victor said, "That man mistook her for someone he knew."

Grimbald rubbed his neck. "And why was that? Was the man inebriated?"

"I suppose he must have been," said Victor, looking at Justine for a moment before his gaze slid away.

But Justine had already figured out the chessboard, and she knew she needed to make a different move if she wanted to prevent Bill from being inducted into Her Majesty's Bio-Mechanical army.

"No," she said. "He wasn't drunk or crazy. He thought I was someone else because I'm in someone else's body—but I'm Justine Makepiece."

34

"WHY SO GLUM, AGS? IF THIS DOESN'T WORK OUT, you'll be free of me."

Dodger was bare chested, lying on the hard wood of the surgical bed as Henry attached the rubber tubing to the bottle of concentrated ichor. The helmet of the galvanic magnetometer had been placed around Dodger's head, since Henry maintained that the galvanic charge would amplify the effects of the transfusion. She had seen countless operations at this point, yet for the first time, her stomach was knotted with tension, while Dodger looked so cheerful she could have throttled him.

Twist, who had gone morose, was sitting in a corner of the room, drinking a cup of tea that she suspected had been sweetened with something a good deal stronger than honey.

"It's not too late to change your mind," she said.

"Everyone always forgets the last line of the song, you know." She frowned. "What song?"

"Scarborough Fair." He took her hand and she made a face.

"Dodger, you shouldn't touch me. Now I'll need to wash again before the transfusion." She tried to pull away, but he grasped her tight.

"First, the singer sets his old love an impossible task, right? Sew a shirt without seams, wash it in a dry well."

"And she sets him the same. I know the song, Dodger." She tried not to think too much about his hand on hers, his fingers lightly tracing over the lines of her palm. "My mam used to sing it. Two lovers who no longer trust each other— that was her favorite tune."

"Ah, but there's that tricky last line," said Dodger. "And endings change the meaning of everything that goes before."

She was just about to ask him what he meant when Henry said, "Are we ready to proceed?"

"Ready and waiting," said Dodger, giving her fingers a squeeze before releasing them. "We need to get our Aggie back to her room before the witching hour."

Aggie decided not to tell him that it was already past midnight. Clerval, who had never been a particularly efficient student, had taken nearly three hours to prepare all his equipment and go over his notes. *In for a penny, in for a pound*, she thought. *No point in leaving now.*

"Nurse, can you tie off the patient's arm just below the elbow?"

He's promoted me along with himself, thought Aggie. "I just need to rewash my hands," she said, moving toward the sink, but Henry just gave an impatient click of his tongue and said, "Never mind, I'll do it myself."

As she washed her hands, she heard Henry chatting calmly to Dodger as he applied the tourniquet. In the past, she had watched doctors inject the ichor into a muscle in the arm or leg, but this procedure was clearly intended to introduce the concentrated serum directly into the patient's bloodstream. By the time she was finished disinfecting her hands, she discovered that Henry had already attached the needle to the cannula and was about to inject it into the Basilic vein.

"Henry, wait," she said. "According to Shiercliffe, the median cubital vein is a better choice for transfusions."

"Don't distract me." Before she could say anything, Henry had plunged the needle in, causing Dodger to wince. She smiled at him reassuringly, then watched as the green fluid began to flow into his veins.

"How are you feeling?"

"Right as rain," said Dodger. "In fact, it feels quite marvelous."

The transfusion took much longer than Aggie had expected. She forced herself not to check her fob watch, worried that it would make Dodger nervous, and instead tried to distract him by reading from a newspaper she found on a chair. She'd amused Dodger with a lengthy description of how to avoid pickpockets until the bottle of ichor was empty, but then Henry insisted on giving Dodger a second pint, just to be on the safe side.

She eyed the new batch of ichor, which looked to be a different shade than the previous one. "Isn't there a danger of giving him too much?"

"Two units is recommended," said Henry in a condescending tone. "If you're worried, ask the patient how he feels."

"Me?" Dodger grinned. "I'm ready to dance a mazurka, I am."

"What did I tell you?" Henry flipped a switch, turning on the Tesla coil. A fizzing, sizzling sound filled the room as arcs of blue electricity formed above the metal coils. "I'm going to apply the galvanic charge now," said Henry. "You might experience a slight tingle in your extremities, which is absolutely normal."

Dodger gave Aggie a wink. "Nothing that might embarrass me in front of the lady, I hope?"

"Nurse DeLacey is a professional." Henry flipped the switch, and the helmet began to hum.

"Oi, that's what you call a tingle?" Dodger looked a little flushed, and his Bio-Mechanical eyes had begun to glow.

Aggie glanced at the bottle of ichor, which was emptying rapidly. "Doctor," she said, "should we slow the drip rate down a little?"

"No need," Henry assured her. "It's all going swimmingly."

"Doc?" Dodger's voice sounded a little less certain. "I feel as though I could—"

His eyes rolled back in his head.

"What's happening?" She turned to Henry, who had gone white and was backing away.

"I don't— This wasn't— I think it's just a temporary reaction."

Dodger began to shake so violently that the table legs were clattering against the floor. For a terrible moment, Aggie's mind refused to function. It was Twist who jolted her into action by jumping up and yelling, "Untie the tourniquet, woman! We need to get that needle out!"

Her hands started to move of their own accord. "Hold him down," she said, and Twist moved in, his breath reeking of whiskey. Within moments, she had the needle out, but Dodger continued to jerk and writhe, his eyes spinning unnaturally. "Get something between his teeth," she told Twist, "so he doesn't bite his tongue."

They managed to insert a tongue depressor into his clenched mouth, but as Dodger continued to shake and writhe, Aggie realized that every second that passed could be doing permanent damage to his mind.

Henry Clerval was pressed against the wall, staring as though he had seen the devil. "Have you seen this before?" Aggie asked him, tamping down the panic she could feel rising inside her. "Is there an antidote?"

Henry shook his head. "I've been tinkering a little with the formula...trying to improve it."

"Imbecile," said Twist. Grasping Dodger's shoulders, he said, "Come on, man. Shake it off. Come on back."

He loves Dodger, she realized. Or at least, Twist must have loved him once, and the embers of that feeling were flaring up now.

Because Dodger was dying. The realization punched through her, rendering her momentarily stupid with pain. Then she thought of Shiercliffe, staring back at her with contempt, and pushed the feelings down and away. She had to act like a nurse now.

"Mr. Twist?" No response. "Oliver?" He still didn't look at her, his lank blond hair hanging down around his gaunt face as he held Dodger down, but she knew he was listening. "Can you hire us a carriage? We need to take Dodger back to the Royal Victoria."

It took Twist ages to find a coach, and once they were inside, the vehicle moved with maddening slowness through the crowds of East Enders celebrating in the streets. Aggie lost all sense of time as she kept checking Dodger's erratic pulse and encouraging him to breathe. By the time they reached Whitechapel Road, she was startled to see that the sun was rising. Then the bow bells of St. Mary's chimed six times, confirming what she already knew—she'd been out all night.

Aggie knew her career was over. There was no way her absence would not be noted, and no way she would not be penalized for it. She no longer cared. All that mattered was getting Dodger the help he needed, but as the hired carriage stopped moving, she realized that they had a problem.

"The crowds are too thick for us to get right up to the hospital gates," shouted the driver. "You'll have to get out here."

As Twist paid the driver, Aggie tried to think of a way that the two of them would be able to carry Dodger between them. Dodger gave a low moan.

"Dodger!" She placed her hand on his forehead, which was hot. His eyes fluttered but did not open. "Can you hear me?"

He moaned again.

"Easy, mate." Twist opened the carriage door and slung Dodger's hand over his neck.

Dodger squinted at him as if he were drunk. "What happened?" The words came out thick and slushy.

"You had a bad reaction," said Aggie, slipping her arm around Dodger's waist. "We're taking you back to get help."

"Nuh," said Dodger as they maneuvered him out of the carriage. "I'm fine." The moment his feet hit the ground he stiffened, his face going blank as his eyes began to spin.

The dark spectacles. She had forgotten to bring them. If anyone looked too closely, they would see instantly that he was something other than strictly human.

"He's having another fit," she said to Twist.

Twist scowled. "Damnation."

"We need to get through these crowds somehow," said Aggie. "Pardon me," she said to the people directly in front of her. "Medical emergency! We need to get this man into hospital."

"Sod off," said a man with breath that stank of gin. "I've been waiting here for five hours to see the bloody exhibition. Not moving now it's about to begin."

"It's hopeless," said Aggie.

"Not at all," said Twist. "They want entertainment? I'll give them entertainment." Taking a deep breath, he shouted, "The Queen's touch! The Queen's touch! Make way for this poor soldier, injured in service to the Crown! Make way for a miracle!"

When they were in sight of the front gates, the crowd was packed more densely and people grumbled and refused to move. Twist stepped up his sales pitch.

"Who here will bear witness to a miracle? By the divine gift of English monarchs, we beseech the queen to touch this poor, afflicted soldier!"

People began to move but not quickly enough. Desperate, Aggie chimed in. "As in the days of old, we ask for the gift of the royal touch!" Conducting the crowd like a choir, she began to chant, "Royal touch! Royal touch! Save the soldier with the royal touch!"

"Good one," said Twist, readjusting his grip on Dodger, who was stumbling along between them. "You're a natural."

The crowd warmed to the chant, and soon the ringing sounds of thousands of voices could be heard, demanding that the queen perform a miracle laying on of hands.

Supported between them, Dodger's breathing was becoming more labored. *Hang on*, Aggie told him in her mind. *We're so close.*

Twist met her eyes, and she realized that he was coming down from whatever manic bit of hope and drive had been keeping him aloft. They were stuck out here, so close to the medical facilities that could help Dodger but incapable of making it any farther till the crowds dispersed.

Dodger didn't have that long.

Leaning over him, she began to sing. "Are you going to Scarborough Fair? Parsley, sage, rosemary and thyme…"

He seemed to breathe a little easier, and then a huge roar came up from the crowd and she stood up, trying to figure out what was happening.

The gates were opening.

At first, Aggie thought that the school had listened to the crowd's entreaties, but then, as she heard the clatter of hooves, she realized something else was happening.

A royal carriage was making its way through the crowd. Aggie assumed it must belong to the crown prince or some other member of Queen Victoria's immediate family, until she realized that the black heraldic eagle perched on a crown was not Britain's royal coat of arms. "That's not one of ours," she said, with a dizzying sense that events were speeding up out of all control.

Twist frowned. "What do you mean?"

Dodger reared up, his eyes oscillating until his pupils narrowed to pinpricks. "It's the kaiser's monster," he said with startling clarity. *He can see inside the coach*, she realized.

"Dodger!" Aggie moved in front of him so he could focus on her face. "Are you all right? Are you in any pain?"

"Not yet," he said, and then his eyes rolled back in his head.

"Watch it," said Twist, yanking them to the side as the carriage swerved in a wide turn before passing through the open gates of the Royal Victoria. The hooves of the big bay horses clattered on the cobblestones as the crowd parted to let the carriage through.

"This is our chance," said Twist. "Come on." Panting from the effort of supporting Dodger's limp weight, he and Aggie followed the carriage through the gates. One scarlet-coated soldier in a spiked metal helmet stepped in front of them.

"Halt," he said, and then, in English, he added, "No closer."

"We need medical help for this man," said Aggie.

The guard did not budge. "You wait. Now the kaiser is here. Go back," he said.

"Really, your English is remarkable," said Twist, gazing at the poker-faced guard with what appeared to be rapt admiration. "Now, do be a love and let us through. We need the kaiser's divine touch."

The guard looked dubious. "What is this divine touch?"

Aggie's heart was pounding so hard it was difficult to speak. "We were hoping His Imperial Majesty could touch our friend and heal him," she said, her voice surprisingly even. "Look," she said, suddenly knowing what to do. *Give the guard something small he can agree to. One agreement can lead to another.* "I'm going to need to put him down. My arms are turning to jelly. We'll just prop him up over there by the wall, out of your way." She indicated the far wall. "Is that all right?"

The guard nodded impatiently. Underneath his spiked metal helmet, his face was dusted with golden down—he was probably no more than a year or two older than she was.

As Aggie and Twist lowered Dodger gently down by the wall, a footman jumped down from the back of the carriage, opened the door and unfolded a step. Then he stood back and saluted as a figure in a navy blue admiral's uniform emerged. The man, who appeared to be in his early forties, sported a thick moustache that resembled the capital letter *W*, a gaudy gold-and-red sash and a half dozen medals and ribbons on his chest. Most strikingly of all, when he turned, Aggie saw that he was wearing a tall, black-furred hat decorated with a white skull and crossed long bones that made him look like an uneasy mixture of royal guard and pirate.

"Eure Kaiserliche Majestät," said Moulsdale, hurrying to greet his visitor in a black wool coat that was buttoned up, presumably to conceal that he was not properly dressed underneath. "Forgive me for not being here to greet you sooner," he said, speaking in the slow, clear, overly emphatic manner usually reserved for the very young and the infirm and elderly. "We did not expect you for another three hours!"

"I heard that my beloved grandmother had arrived early." Kaiser Wilhelm had an almost perfect upper-class British accent, except for the faintest hint of something Germanic in the roll of the *r*. "Surely you would not want me to keep Her Majesty waiting." His voice dripped with honeyed mistrust.

"Of course not," said Moulsdale, "but we had hoped to see to Her Majesty's needs first so that we could completely concentrate on the honor of your arrival, Your Grace."

"That choice," said the kaiser, "was mine to make, not yours. I was told that I would arrive at the same time as my darling grandmother."

"I am terribly sorry if we have offended you in any way," said Moulsdale. "That was most certainly not our intention."

The kaiser clicked his heels together. "Do not grovel. I dislike groveling. We will move on from this subject."

Moulsdale gave a little bow, which prompted someone in the crowd to shout, "Down with the kaiser!" Another voice chimed in. "Down with the kaiser!" In a moment, the chant caught on, and dozens of voices were now joining in a chorus of "Down with the kaiser!" One lone voice added, "Go home, Willy, you gormless pillock!"

The kaiser did not turn to face the crowd, but Aggie was close enough to see one side of his moustache twitch spasmodically. "You British," he said tightly, "make it very difficult to retain our friendly disposition." Turning to a Prussian guard, he barked, *"Achtung!"*

The guard clicked his heels and saluted, then opened the carriage door.

"My humble apologies," Moulsdale said, clearly fearing that the German emperor intended to climb back into the carriage and return to his lodgings. The kaiser held up a hand, forestalling any further speech.

"I believe your rabble require a little lesson in decorum." Kaiser Wilhelm issued another string of German commands, and a second figure stepped down from the carriage. The soldier was strikingly tall—nearly seven feet, even without the spiked helmet—and strikingly ugly. He was broad shouldered in a Prussian blue uniform trimmed in red, but underneath the helmet, his skin was tinged an unhealthy green, with dark shadows obscuring his deep-set eyes and scars crisscrossing his cheeks and nose.

On closer inspection, Aggie saw that there were electrodes at the soldier's neck, emerging from the collar of his uniform like the spikes of a weapon.

He's a German Bio-Mechanical, she realized with a cold prickle of unease. Dodger's grim prediction came back to her:

If I stay, Ags, they're going to stick me in a ring with some German killing machine. And you know as well as I do that I won't last long.

Perhaps he had been right, but now it seemed he might not last regardless. Checking on him, she was relieved to find that his breathing was no longer labored, but his face was blank. She met Twist's eyes, seeing her own concern mirrored there. Every moment that went by now put him at greater risk, but she could not figure out how to get him past the German emperor and the head of medicine. She looked around the courtyard, trying to figure out a way to get past the guards and through the front doors.

Suddenly, she spotted two familiar faces—Victor and Lizzie, looking shocked as they took in the scene unfolding before them.

She turned to Twist. "Do you think we could try—?" she began, but before she could finish her thought, the kaiser began addressing the crowd.

"My dear British subjects, thank you for your warm welcome." The kaiser's tone was dry, but the crowd fell silent when he spoke. The kaiser gestured grandly toward the German Bio-Mechanical soldier. "The German Empire is pleased to present our newest and most advanced model of Bio-Mechanisch. We call him *Der Totenkopf*—the death's-head."

There was a ripple of sound from the crowd. "Cor," said one childish voice, "how're our troops going to stand up to *that?*"

Slumped against the wall, Dodger shuddered.

"Don't worry," said Aggie. But when she looked down, she realized he wasn't shivering in trepidation; he was having another seizure. His teeth were already clenched, so there was nothing she could do but lay him down and turn him on his side.

She was only dimly aware of the other drama playing out in front of her as the kaiser turned to Moulsdale with a look of triumph. "And now I am most eager to see your newest model, Professor. Where is he? Bring him out!"

Moulsdale cleared his throat and tugged at his coat collar as though it suddenly felt too tight. "If you had come a little later, we would have been entirely prepared and had our Dreadnaught prototype ready to greet you," he said. "As it is, I am afraid you will have to be a little patient."

"I see," said the kaiser, stroking the waxed tips of his moustache. His pale eyes registered everything—the unruly crowd, Moulsdale's discomfort, the fact that the staff of the Royal Victoria were still unprepared just hours before his scheduled arrival.

Moulsdale made a flourishing gesture, like a circus ringmaster directing the audience's attention away from an unexpected mishap. "Perhaps, if Your Majesty would come inside, we can offer you some tea and other refreshments?"

The kaiser was just taking a step toward Moulsdale when Dodger did something entirely unexpected. One moment, he was on the ground beside Aggie, knees drawn up to his chest, every muscle clenched in spasm. In the next, he sprang into a backbend before landing upright on the balls of his feet, as nimble as an acrobat.

The kaiser stopped in his tracks as he spotted the movement. *"Gott im Himmel,"* he exclaimed. "What is this?"

"Dodger?" Aggie took a hesitant step toward him. "Are you all right?"

He turned to her, and although his uncanny eyes were no

longer spinning, there was no hint of recognition in them. Instead, they gleamed with feral intensity, as if lit from within by ichor-light.

"*Unglaublich.*"

Aggie turned. The kaiser was standing just behind her, his guards anxiously hovering at his side. "He is a new kind of Bio-Mechanical, yes?"

Dodger looked directly at the kaiser, his eyes turning with a click.

"Entirely new," said Moulsdale, his momentary look of surprise quickly replaced by a showman's gleam of satisfaction. "I hope Your Imperial Majesty will forgive the, ah, subterfuge, but we wished to surprise you."

This rather rosy version of events was undermined by the guard, who stepped forward and said something in German. Aggie caught the words "royal touch" and *"heilen,"* which she supposed meant *healing*.

"Fascinating." The kaiser stepped in front of Aggie. "So your plan is to emphasize visual acuity and speed over strength and durability, but the Bio-Mechanical has malfunctioned?" The kaiser smiled. "I would not have suspected England's top scientists of being so superstitious, but if you desire a healing emperor's touch, I can oblige." He moved his hand toward Dodger, but before he could make contact, there was a blur of motion.

"Watch out!" Moulsdale unceremoniously pulled the kaiser out of the way as Dodger leaped onto the roof of the carriage with preternatural agility and speed.

Clerval's black market ichor seemed to have some unexpected side effects, thought Aggie. Yet looking up at Dodger as he surveyed the scene below him, she had to wonder. How long would these effects last—and what toll would they take on Dodger's body and mind? She looked for Lizzie and Victor and spotted them making their way toward Dodger.

"*Mein Gott,*" said the kaiser. "His reactions—incredible."

"He is rather special, isn't he?" Moulsdale beamed, as if he were personally responsible for Dodger's reflexes. "Compact, responsive, fearless. We call this model..." he paused for dramatic effect "...the Dreadnaught."

"Ripping! He has recovered," exclaimed the kaiser. "Now we can pit your Dreadnaught against my Totenkopf and see which prevails."

35

"WAKE UP."

Will blinked up at his brother, confused. "Victor? What time is it?" The room was still dark, except for the small lantern in Victor's hand. He didn't think he had overslept, because he hadn't had anything to drink for the past forty-eight hours. After the shock of watching Justine die—and then come back to life—he had desperately wanted a drink. But after he and Byram had made their way back to their room the night before last, he had been sober as a judge. Which made what happened afterward with Byram all the more incredible.

Byram. Oh, good Lord.

This was the second night they had spent together, and the initial giddy uncertainty was just now settling into joy. Or, at least, it had been, but now his brother was standing over his bed, fully dressed and stern-faced.

Bollocks. Will tried to pull the covers up, but Byram was already turning over, throwing an arm lazily over Will without opening his eyes.

"It can't be morning yet," said Byram. "I refuse to believe it's morning."

"It's nearly 7:00 a.m.," said Victor, addressing both of them with an aplomb that suggested he was not entirely surprised to find his younger brother sharing a narrow bed with his best friend. "You've overslept."

Byram opened his eyes, looking thoroughly tousled and disreputable. There was a bruise-shaped mark on his neck, and if that wasn't incriminating enough, neither he nor Will were wearing nightshirts. They had spent much of the night of Justine's death and rebirth talking. Or rather, Byram had done most of the talking. For the first time, Byram had admitted how afraid he had been of needing and trusting someone when his own body was betraying him.

They had spent the second night not doing much talking at all.

And now his brother was standing over them. *Zounds*, thought Will. This was not the way he had wanted Victor to find out.

"What's happened?" Byram swung his legs around, keeping his bad foot turned away from Victor.

"Be quiet and listen," said Victor. "That will give you a clue."

They were all silent. Outside the partially open window, they could hear the sound of a crowd, chanting, "Fight, fight, fight."

"Not again," said Byram, his dry tone contradicting the tense set of his jaw. "Don't tell me the mob outside wants to set this school on fire."

"Not at all," said Victor. "But they do want blood. The kaiser arrived early, and Aggie just told me he wants Dodger to fight his Totenkopf right now, in front of the hospital gates."

"Now?" Will rubbed his eyes, wishing he didn't feel so tired.

"Yes, Will, now. And Moulsdale's stalling while Aggie and Lizzie get the queen ready. Meanwhile, I need you to get out there to support Dodger. He trusts you."

"What?" Will stared at his brother, then quickly turned his back and began pulling on his combinations. "I don't understand."

"Dodger tried some experimental treatment, and it's sent him round the bend." Victor shook his head. "The crazy part is that it might just give him the edge he needs against the German's Bio-Mechanical." Victor raked his hand through his hair. "I told him he wouldn't have to fight the German. I gave him my word. If he dies…"

Will was buttoning his shirt. "But what can I do?"

Victor paused. "Be there for Dodger. He trusts you…and you never betrayed him."

Will gave an involuntary shiver at Victor's tone. "You're being far too hard on yourself. As always. But I'll be down in a moment."

"Thank you, Will."

Victor was halfway out the door, but Will could not let his brother go without saying something. "Victor…about Byram and me. I'm sorry you had to find out like this."

Victor turned. "I'm not judging you, Will. There are many who would call me an unnatural creature—"

"But only in an admiring sort of way," said Byram as he tied his shoe. "Ooh, look at that good-looking unnatural creature." In a different voice, he exclaimed, "What a fine specimen of an unnatural creature! Y'know, Gladys, sometimes, I kind of wishes me 'arold were more of a hunnatural creature."

"—and yet I seem to have granted myself the right to love and be loved," Victor went on, without missing a beat. "I can't see denying anyone else that same freedom. Even if your taste is appalling." His eyes sparkled as he said it.

"He is appalling, isn't he?" Will held his brother's gaze for a moment, but the moment was a bit too fraught with emotion, so he said, "Well, then," and busied himself with attaching his collar. "Let's go witness history."

"Your Majesty, please," said Aggie, following Queen Victoria around with her black silk dress. "We have to get you dressed."

"Yes, yes," said the queen. "But which face to wear to greet my grandson?"

I'd like to rearrange your face, you old bat, thought Aggie. The kaiser had reluctantly agreed to wait half an hour for his grandmother to arrive, but now they had less than ten minutes left before Dodger and the Totenkopf faced off in front of the hospital and an increasingly unruly crowd. But the queen was refusing to cooperate. "How about this," Aggie said, trying to keep the impatience out of her voice. "Let's get the dress on while you figure out the face?"

Victoria stopped pacing her room and allowed Aggie to help her insert one arm into a sleeve. "You don't understand," said the queen, sounding peevish. "The costume is a given. The mask is the ticklish mutable."

Aggie glanced over at Lizzie, who was collapsed in a chair by the queen's bed. "I thought you said she was lucid?"

"She was," said Lizzie, barely managing to cover a yawn with her hand. "I was up with her till nearly ten last night, working on her magnetic fields. She sounded perfectly sane when I went to bed."

"She isn't addled," said an unfamiliar voice. "She's just wired a little differently than she used to be."

For a moment, Aggie didn't recognize the lovely young woman standing in the doorway next to Ursula Shiercliffe. She was dressed like Shiercliffe's younger sister in a severely elegant black dress, her dark blond hair smoothed back into a chignon. Was this some society girl who had decided to become a nurse? Then comprehension dawned. She stopped herself from saying Justine's name out loud just in time.

Aggie glanced over at Lizzie, who was hastily sitting up and trying to repin her bun, which had slipped sideways. Lizzie gave a subtle shrug, apparently as confused as Aggie was.

"It's all right," said Justine. "The matron knows about me, and we've struck a deal. My cooperation, in exchange for Bill Sykes not winding up as a Bio-Mechanical, like your friend." She exchanged a quick look with Shiercliffe. "So here I am, in borrowed finery so I can be trotted out to impress the kaiser." She gave Lizzie a look and Aggie knew that something else had been telepathically communicated between the two.

Shiercliffe, oblivious to these undercurrents, gave an approving nod. "We will explain how British ingenuity restored Miss Makepiece's health."

"I see," said Aggie. But it was more than just the new clothing that had made Justine seem so different. In the short time since Aggie had seen her last, Justine had settled into Nancy's face and body more fully and made them more her own.

Queen Victoria gave a dry cackle. "Why, look at you! You have two faces, young lady," she said, clapping her hands together. "I never considered that."

"There," said Aggie, taking advantage of the queen's momentary distraction to button up the back of her gown. "Now, please, Your Majesty. We need to get you downstairs to greet your grandson before the match begins."

"Always enter a scene as late as possible," said Queen Victoria. "And leave the moment the chocolates are gone."

"We are bound to do the former," said Shiercliffe, pulling out her pocket watch and checking the time. "In fact, if we do not get there in the next few minutes, we may find that we are too late."

Aggie froze. "But I thought—don't they have to wait for the queen to arrive?"

"That is the protocol," admitted Shiercliffe as she maneuvered a wheelchair out of the corner of the room. "I think the kaiser must already suspect that the queen is not his grandmother, or he would not be pushing so hard." Placing the wheelchair parallel to the queen's bed, she paused. "I'm not even sure there's a point in all our rushing about. The kaiser's arsenal is superior to ours, and he will have his confirmation of that when his Bio-Mechanical defeats ours. Lord Salisbury will withdraw all the funding from our hospital and funnel greater resources to the navy."

She glanced at Aggie. "I'm mostly sorry for you, Agatha. I so wanted you to have the career and the life you deserve. I've done things that perhaps I shouldn't have, to try to help you. And as for that boy…" She looked away. "It seemed to me that his life was a fair exchange for yours."

Aggie stared at Shiercliffe, icy cold horror chasing through her veins. *She turned him into a Bio-Mechanical for me.* On the heels of that thought came another, worse one: *I could have figured this out. I just didn't want to know.*

"It wasn't a fair exchange," she said. "He was worth more than you realized. But even if he was the worst person in the world, it wouldn't matter." Aggie's voice trembled but she spoke clearly, willing Shiercliffe to hold her gaze. "The moment you chose to harm him, you stopped being a nurse."

Shiercliffe looked stunned, and for a moment, Aggie thought she saw the glisten of a tear in the woman's eyes. But only for a moment. Then Shiercliffe blinked hard and straightened her shoulders. "Perhaps you're right." She grabbed a hypodermic, some gauze and a small bottle of carbolic acid from a table. "Perhaps I do deserve your scorn," she said, filling her pockets with the first aid items. "In any case, I will retire, no matter what happens today."

"Don't be so quick to plan for defeat." Justine arranged a white lace cap on the queen's head. "We may still be able to save Dodger and this hospital—and keep the kaiser's ambitions at bay." Then she looked directly into the queen's eyes for a long, wordless moment.

"Well stated, corpse jockey," said the queen, straightening. For the first time, she seemed utterly logical as she attempted to pin a jeweled brooch in the shape of the Imperial State Crown on her gown. "It is one thing to defy protocol and quite another to ignore a monarch when she is right in front of you. Especially when she is also your beloved granny." With an exasperated sigh, she held out the brooch to Aggie. "Blast my rheumatism. Come on, you daft wench, what are you waiting for? Help me!"

The harsh command was just what Aggie needed. Shaking off the paralyzing fear and guilt, she pinned the brooch in place. "Ready, Your Majesty?"

"I was created ready," replied the Bio-Mechanical Queen.

36

THE DEATH'S-HEAD BIO-MECHANICAL WAS GOING
to kill Dodger on the cobblestones in front of the Royal Victoria Hospital.

That was Aggie's first thought as she pushed Queen Victoria's
wheelchair into the courtyard. The huge Prussian and Dodger
had both stripped to the waist like boxers and were circling
each other as the crowd shouted out bets. Moulsdale, Grimbald
and the kaiser stood observing like judges at a sporting event.

It did not look like anything resembling a fair match.

Dodger's lean muscled torso had only a thin metal alloy
over his heart, while the massive German's chest had been
fused with scales of armor that were ridged with angry, puck-
ered red scars. Perhaps Dodger might have an advantage as a
sniper in a battle, but not in this kind of close physical contest.

"Shall we make a little wager?" said the kaiser. "If your
Dreadnaught wins, then I shall share all my technology with
you. If my Totenkopf perseveres, then you shall let me have
your creature so I can study his eyes."

"I'm not sure that we want to assume this is a fight to the death," said Grimbald.

"I see you are uncertain about your contender," said the kaiser.

"Of course we are certain," said Moulsdale, his feathers clearly ruffled by the insult to his Bio-Mechanical. "We'll take that bet."

"Men are such idiots," said Shiercliffe, under her breath.

"We need to help him," said Aggie. Flanked by Lizzie and Justine, she maneuvered the queen's wheelchair closer to the combatants.

Moulsdale, Grimbald and the kaiser turned and began to bow at the sight of the elderly British monarch, while Dodger's eyes tracked the source of the crowd's excitement.

The Totenkopf, however, did not take his eyes off Dodger.

Aggie cried out as the German's punch landed with terrifying force and surprising speed, slamming into Dodger's midsection. The Totenkopf's right arm had been reinforced with a metal gauntlet, making the blow even more dangerous, but before Aggie could draw in a breath, Dodger had rallied.

Springing up, he vaulted over two footmen and kicked out, landing a solid blow on the big German's chin.

It hardly seemed to register.

Dodger spun and twisted and kicked out again, moving with astonishing skill and grace. Aggie wondered if this was a skill he had possessed already, but when she looked at the crowd, she caught sight of Oliver Twist's astonished expression. So Dodger's agility was a by-product of Henry Clerval's ichor concentrate.

The Totenkopf moved to slam his fist into Dodger's midsection, but before his blow could land, Dodger was already somewhere else. Darting in and out of the larger man's reach, he targeted the Totenkopf's head with lightning quick strikes.

The crowd roared its approval.

Then the German slammed his blunt, squared-off head back into Dodger's face. Dodger crumpled to the ground, and the Totenkopf lifted one heavily booted leg and stomped on Dodger's chest.

Aggie cried out in horror as the crowd gave out a collective moan, but Dodger's metal chest plate must have protected him from the worst of the impact, because he was already moving, rolling out from under the Totenkopf's boot and springing to his feet again. Thrilled, Aggie gave a cheer and Moulsdale glanced at her with momentary irritation, as if she had committed a social faux pas, before returning his attention to the spectacle of brute force against reckless agility.

Dodger had rallied, and now the two Bio-Mechanicals were fighting again, their bodies twisting and grappling. It wasn't pretty, gentlemanly fighting, but dirty street brawling, with elbow jabs and kidney punches. At one point, Dodger bit the bigger man's ear hard enough to draw blood.

"He's a bloody cannibal," shouted one of the spectators.

He's not himself, she realized. *He has no sense of self-preservation. He has no sense of self.*

Then she looked back at the kaiser and Moulsdale. They were watching with the avidity of spectators at a sporting match. To them, the combatants weren't men—they were creatures. They would watch Dodger die with less emotion than they would feel if a cat took down a mouse.

And he *was* going to die, right here in front of her eyes.

Unless I can wake him up.

She had never tried to reach out to Dodger before, and she

had no idea whether she could do it—particularly now, when he was in this altered state of fighting frenzy. Her whole life had taught her to keep her distance from men who had lost control over themselves. *When men are drunk or angry, they'll lash out at anything that gets too close.* Oh, for a slug of gin or a glass of beer or anything that would make it easier to cross the gap between them.

Thunk! Wham! Two fast punches in quick succession battered Dodger back. He was slowing down. The manic green light in his eyes began to flicker on and off. How much fight did he have left in him?

She needed to be in an altered state herself. Tired or drunk or...

She closed her eyes and conjured the memory of his kiss. She thought about that first night, reaching out, pulling him in, closing the distance between them.

She remembered the wild, clamoring hunger to touch him, and his answering touch.

The blow knocked her back, making her stagger. Stunned, she opened her eyes and saw the big German coming at her again.

I did it, she thought. *I'm seeing out of Dodger's eyes!*

Then the Totenkopf drew back his metal gauntleted fist and pain exploded in her jaw.

From what seemed like a long way away, she heard the kaiser's lazy, aristocratic drawl. "Why is your Dreadnaught no longer fighting?" The German emperor sounded distantly curious.

Aggie turned to him and then realized, with a wave of disorientation, what had happened. Somehow, she hadn't just managed to see out of Dodger's eyes. She had managed to shift her awareness into his body. Dancing back away from the German Bio-Mechanical, she glanced at her own body, which appeared to be in a kind of trance.

Dodger, she thought. *Help me. If you don't help me—*

The blow seemed to come out of nowhere. The bright sunny day trembled and dimmed as if a storm were descending.

I'm losing consciousness, she thought. Everything was strangely quiet. *Shiercliffe and my mother were right. A boy has been the death of me.*

No, Aggie, said Justine, speaking directly into her mind. *You're going to be all right. I've called in reinforcements.*

Stars exploded in her head. *This would be a good time to switch back to my own body,* Aggie thought.

These rookeries are a right maze if you don't know them.

She was back in the winding, narrow streets of the East End, lost in the dark and the fog. She could feel Dodger's arm under hers. He was leading her back. *Never mind the coin, lovely. Pay me when you're safely home.*

This time, she knew, home would not be a boardinghouse room, and Lizzie would not be there. At least she and Dodger would go there together, though.

Then, just when she wanted it least, her vision returned and she saw the Totenkopf drawing back his gauntleted fist. The crowd was roaring with fury, and she could make out Twist's voice telling Dodger to snap out of it.

But Dodger's muscles would not obey her. Then she met the Totenkopf's gaze and was shocked to see something un-expected in their depths: regret. He hesitated, but just for a second.

Looking out of Dodger's Bio-Mechanical eyes, though, a second was long enough. With his enhanced perception, it seemed to Aggie as if time had slowed into a series of still images: Shiercliffe watching intently, her hands gripped tightly into fists. The hypodermic needle in Shiercliffe's skirt pocket, revealed as clearly as if the fabric had become transparent. A buxom redhead slipping her hand into Shiercliffe's pocket, then stepping forward.

It took Aggie a moment to understand what she was seeing. It was like catching sight of yourself in an unfamiliar mirror—for a moment, she just saw a stranger. Then recognition dawned. She was looking at herself from Dodger's perspective.

She blinked, and time sped up again. The Totenkopf's gauntleted fist descended toward her head.

Then, unexpectedly, his eyes widened in shock. His arm stopped in its path and dropped to his side. He wavered for a moment before toppling to his knees and collapsing face-down on the ground, a hypodermic sticking out of the side of his massive neck.

Aggie felt a dizzying lurch, and then she was back in her own body, looking down at the Totenkopf. She searched out Dodger and found him looking back at her.

Inside her chest, she felt a wild flutter, as if a flock of doves were launching themselves out of her chest. Maybe it was relief. Or gratitude. Or else it might be something sweeter and scarier than either of those emotions. All she knew was that somehow, she and Dodger had managed to trade bodies, and he had used their connection and his pickpocket's skills to take the hypodermic from Shiercliffe and plunge it into the Totenkopf's neck.

There was a bellow of almost animal rage and Aggie was shocked to see the kaiser rounding on her in fury. "What have you done? You, you pig-dog! I shall have you court-martialed and imprisoned for destroying the property of the German Crown!"

"It's my fault," said Shiercliffe, moving deftly between Aggie and the enraged kaiser. Aggie felt a complicated pang, her initial quick relief dampened by the knowledge of what the matron's past protection had wrought.

"She didn't destroy him." Professor Grimbald was tending to the unconscious Totenkopf. "He looks dead, but he's not."

This news mollified the kaiser somewhat. "Still," he said, "you have displayed poor sportsmanship. There must be a rematch!"

The fickle mob, which had been cheering for Dodger before, was now furious at the abrupt and bloodless end of the fight. Booing and hissing, the crowd surged forward, shouting "foul" and "unfair" and "rematch!" The kaiser's guards and the hospital porters were looking increasingly uncomfortable as they attempted to hold back the human tide. While Grimbald continued to pacify the kaiser, the Prussian guards had pulled out their curved sabers. A group of porters, armed only with billy clubs, swung their truncheons threateningly.

"Elizabeth!" Victor's anguished voice was audible over the din of the crowd as he struggled to get through the mob. Aggie spotted Will and Byram in the mass of human bodies, as well.

Abruptly, an imperious voice called out, "Cease these thanatic theatrics at once!" Queen Victoria, short and stout and peevish, heaved herself out of her wheelchair and stalked into the courtyard in her stiff black dress.

The crowd, chastened, fell silent.

"Your Majesty," said Moulsdale, belatedly remembering to bow.

The kaiser clicked his heels and inclined his head. "I was distressed to hear you were unwell, Your Majesty." His tone did not match his words, and Aggie realized that the kaiser must have heard some of the rumors about Queen Victoria's strange behavior of late.

"As you see, I am in fine health," said the queen, visibly bristling. Then, offering her cheek, she added, "Quite safe for you to give a kiss, my dear Willy."

The kaiser hesitated.

Then the queen added something in German that startled a boyish laugh out of the middle-aged German emperor. "Grandmamma," he said, eagerly holding out his right arm and gathering the diminutive Queen into his embrace. His left arm, Aggie realized, remained immobile at his side.

"My dearest grandson," said the queen, "I do hope we can arrange for our two Bio-Mechanicals to display their unique talents in some other, more sportsmanlike fashion. I dislike these pugilistic matches."

"But, Grandmamma," objected the kaiser. "They are meant to be soldiers."

"Soldiers—and *allies*," said the queen. "After all, we are family, and family does not send soldiers against its own. I propose a new treaty between our two nations, so that we can share our technological breakthroughs and unite against our common enemies."

"Do you mean the French?" asked the kaiser.

"Such an aggravating nation," agreed the queen. "Although their pastries are rather delicious. Now that we have settled that..." She beckoned Justine over with an imperious wave. "I have another, rather more remarkable breakthrough to show you. This is Miss Makepiece, the daughter of the late head of engineering. Until two days ago, both her legs and lungs were paralyzed. Now, as you can see, she has no physical impediments whatsoever."

The Queen made a little gesture with her hands, and Justine descended into a graceful curtsy. "Your Majesties," she said.

"Is this true?" The kaiser reflexively grasped his atrophied left arm with his right.

Justine inclined her head. "Indeed it is, Your Majesty." She raised her chin, and Aggie didn't need to be a mind reader to know that Justine had no intention of telling the volatile emperor that there was no way he could duplicate her cure.

"*Unglaublich,*" said the emperor. "You must tell me all about it, Miss Makepiece."

Justine curtsied again.

The Queen turned to face the crowd. "My good citizens of the East End," she said. "We are pleased to announce that the Royal Victoria Hospital shall be receiving a generous endowment to support its continued efforts on your behalf."

There was a ripple of excited chatter, followed by a series of enthusiastic cheers. When the noise finally died down, one woman began to sing "God Save the Queen." Within moments, the rest of the crowd had begun to sing along, as the kaiser and the slightly shell-shocked members of the hospital staff looked on. Beside them, Moulsdale looked puffed up with the conceit that he had managed this victory.

"There," said the queen, heaving herself back into her wheelchair as Aggie stepped forward to hold it steady. "That's quite enough work for one day, I should think. Time for some tea and scones."

Aggie shook her head in amazement. "Your Majesty," she

said, taking hold of the wheelchair's handles. "I don't know how I can ever thank you."

"That goes for me, as well," said Dodger, kneeling beside the queen's chair. He was still bare chested, and there were dark bruises beginning to form along his ribs and underneath his left eye. But when he raised his chin, Aggie could see that he was thoroughly himself. She felt that flutter in her chest again.

How could she protect herself against a boy who could get inside her head? She had no idea, but for the first time, the idea of taking a risk didn't seem quite so awful.

"Oh, don't you fret about thinking up ways to thank me," said the queen with a wink. "I have ideas enough for all of us."

37

DODGER HAD NEVER IMAGINED THAT HE WAS destined for a particularly long life. Some scheme of his would go wrong, he had assumed, and he would come to a sticky end. The best he had hoped for was that Nancy and the others would eat some berries off his grave and talk fondly of him afterward.

In a way, he supposed he had been right. He'd gambled and lost and carked it—twice, if anyone was counting. What was unexpected was the way he kept coming back.

This new life was going to take some getting used to, because it kept going in the most unexpected directions.

"Do I look all right?" He peered up at Aggie, who had been putting some salve on the swollen and split skin around his left eye. According to the doctors, he would most likely have lost a regular eye in the pounding he had gotten. Luckily for him, the Bio-Mechanical contraptions were far tougher than their flesh-and-blood counterparts.

"You look as though someone mistook you for a batch of dough. Want a mirror?"

"Don't need one," he said, reaching for her hand.

"If you're thinking of hopping into my head..."

He squeezed her fingers. "Never without permission."

"Never again without permission, you mean. Here." She held up a hand mirror so he could see himself, but he didn't really care to see how battered his face was. He had a feeling that his nose was never going to be quite the same, which was a bit of a shame. He'd never really appreciated it before, but it had been a nice nose.

Instead of looking at himself directly, he admired the crisp white linen shirt he was wearing, a gift from Byram. Perhaps he had been wrong about that one. "I do look rather smart, don't I?"

"Indeed you do." She smiled at him for a moment, and he tried to recall why he had thought briefly that she was not pretty. She was more than pretty. She was like some glorious, rosy-skinned nymph who had decided to clamber out of a painting, looked him over and said, yeah, all right, why don't you and I give this a go?

Whatever *this* was. Whatever *having a go* meant.

There were two sharp raps on the door, and Aggie stood so quickly she nearly dropped the mirror on the floor.

Luckily, he still had quick reflexes and caught it.

"Hello, you two," said Lizzie. "There is someone here who has asked most particularly to speak with you."

"If it's Twist..." Dodger began and then stopped.

The short, stout elderly woman that some called the Widow of Windsor walked stiffly into the hospital room, looking around her with patent disapproval. She wore an old-fashioned black bonnet and smelled of camphor and violets, and she looked thoroughly disgruntled, as though her corset was pinching.

Aggie sank into a deep curtsy. "Your Majesty!" Dodger bowed his head.

"Yes, yes," said the queen impatiently. "Obsequiousness observed. Now, where is the strapping specimen of masculinity? We distinctly heard you say that he would also be in attendance."

Lizzie smiled apologetically. "If you mean Victor Frankenstein, I'm terribly sorry. He was meant to be here but was called into an emergency surgery this morning."

"No, no, not him. The other. The German fellow."

Lizzie, Aggie and Dodger all stared at the queen, equally dumbfounded. Lizzie spoke first. "The kaiser?"

"No, no."

Clearly, thought Dodger, the queen was malfunctioning again. "Not the Totenkopf that nearly rang my bell?"

"Yes, yes. Tottie." The Queen smiled. *"Was für ein schöner Mechanischer,* eh? Well, never mind, we shall speak with him anon. Fetch me a stool, girl."

Lizzie hurried to bring a chair over for the queen, and Aggie brought a cushion and helped the elderly monarch arrange herself. "Now, listen to me, my predicates. Do you know who I am?"

Oh, Lord, thought Dodger. If the old lady had been this addled in front of the kaiser, the jig was most definitely up.

"You're the Queen of England, mum," he said, only belatedly recalling that this was not the correct address.

"Fallaciousness. I am called the Queen of Great Britain and Ireland, and also the Empress of India," she corrected him. "But that is not who I am." Reaching out, she touched the electrodes on the right side of his neck. "Are you a loyal British subject?"

"Of course," said Dodger.

"Of corpse," she said approvingly. "Precisely. As you have died and been reborn as a Bio-Mechanical, you are no longer a British subject. Some would say this makes you the property of the Crown. They would send you to fight other Bio-Mechanicals for their own purposes. But you see, my dear, you are not a British subject, anymore than Tottie is a German one." She pulled off the thick velvet bow that had concealed her own electrodes. "Now, speak before you think—who am I?"

"Oh, crud," said Lizzie. "I must have messed something up when I was trying to recalibrate her electromagnetic fields."

"On the contrary, my Yankee Doodler," said the queen, and now her clouded blue eyes suddenly flared bright green, as if the ichor were a gas lamp that had just been ignited. "You did something very right. You and Miss Makepiece both helped wake me. But Miss DeLacey..." Here she turned and gave Aggie a nod of recognition. "You listened to me when everyone else dismissed me."

Dodger felt a flicker of excitement, the way he used to when he was about to wade into a crowd and start picking pockets.

"Your eyes," said Aggie, sounding concerned. "They're turning that weird color again."

"Look at me again," said Victoria, stretching out one gnarled and heavily beringed finger and touching Dodger's forehead, just above the spot between his eyes. "Look with the true eye, and tell me—who am I?"

His eyes shifted focus and he saw the glowing, vital machine inside the sagging flesh. With a swell of excitement, Dodger said, "You're Victoria. First Queen of the Bio-Mechanicals."

Victoria smiled and gave his cheek a pinch. "Very good. And what are you?"

Dodger grinned and spread his hands out, as if presenting himself for inspection. "Why, I'm your eyes, mum."

EPILOGUE

BACK HOME, THE APPLE BLOSSOMS WERE IN FULL bloom by now, dropping their perfumed sweetness all over the boys and girls rolling around under their branches, shedding winter clothes and inhibitions. Here in London, the trees were sad and stunted things, with tight, hard buds that never seemed to flower.

Which was why, Dodger said, he was taking her out for a surprise. Aggie stumbled over something—an exposed root? A stone?

"Can I take this off now?" She tugged at the blindfold over her eyes, but Dodger took her hand in his.

"Just a few steps more."

Of course, she could have just reached out and seen where they were going through his eyes, but she restrained herself. So much of intimacy involved knowing when to maintain your own perspective and when to shift your point of view. She was better at the former, and Dodger was more adept at the latter.

In time, she supposed, they would find their balance.

"All right," said Dodger. "You can look now."

She pulled off the blindfold and gasped. They were in a graveyard, but one with no headstones, only simple wooden crosses or small cairns of piled stones. There were dogwood trees and wild cherries in blossom, and white flowering hawthorn bushes that scented the air. A breeze blew blossoms into her face, drenching her in their sweetness.

"Oh," she said, unable to find any words. She looked at him and even through the dark spectacles he wore, she could sense the smile in his eyes.

Dodger pulled her hand. "There's more."

They rounded a corner and there they were, all her friends, old and new, seated around a picnic blanket. Faygie was unpacking sandwiches from a hamper, while Bill was trying to keep his dog from sticking her blunt nose into the opening. Justine was laughing, her hair covered by a bonnet. Byram and Will were arguing about something, but Aggie could see right off that it was a good argument, the kind that Byram needed from time to time so he could be funny at someone else's expense.

Victor and Lizzie were discussing their preferred type of amputation saws. "You're only saying that because you're so physically strong," Lizzie said. "But in emergency situations, you need the kind of blade that doesn't require the surgeon to muscle through the cut." Looking up, Lizzie squinted and then smiled as she recognized Aggie. Really, that girl needed to start wearing her spectacles more.

"About time you got here," said Lizzie. "We're all starving, and Justine keeps trying to talk about politics."

"This is the perfect opportunity for us to discuss what's going on in Europe," said Justine.

"Never make plans on an empty stomach," said Faygie. "Now, who wanted the mutton and who wanted the cheese?"

It turned out there were only cheese and watercress sandwiches.

"Budge over, then." Dodger helped Aggie settle herself on the blanket.

As they enjoyed lemonade and sandwiches, a black-and-white magpie landed on the grass in front of them, attracted by the promise of food. It gave its distinctive chattering call and suddenly a small flock of the birds descended. Aggie tried to count them, recalling the old nursery rhyme: one for sorrow, two for joy, three for a girl, four for a boy.

"There's seven of them," said Dodger. "What's that?"

"Five for silver, six for gold," said Justine. "Seven for a secret never to be told."

An eighth bird landed, and then Bullseye exploded after them, barking with joy, and the whole flock scattered. Bill whistled for his dog, but these days, Bullseye seemed selectively deaf to some of her master's commands. "I don't know what's got into her," he said, getting to his feet and following her. "Oi! Bullseye!"

Justine stood up. "I suppose I might as well help him." Aggie watched her leave, wondering whether either of them knew exactly how much of Nancy was involved in the tangle of their emotions.

"Oh, dear Lord, eight magpies is totally beyond the scope of nursery magic," said Byram. "We're clearly going to need to consult a fortune teller for that one."

"In the old days, they used to read birds' entrails," said Victor.

Will made a face. "Some of us are trying to eat, you know."

"How are you ever going to become a doctor if you can't bear the thought of entrails?"

Dodger leaned back, gazing up at the canopy of trees overhead. Aggie wondered what he could see up there with his extraordinary vision. "So? Good surprise?" he asked.

"The best," said Aggie, meaning it.

"Just wait till autumn, when the blackberries are ripe. Folks say the thieves' cemetery produces the sweetest pickings in London."

There were a great many unknowns between now and then, Aggie thought, but perhaps you couldn't be completely happy without the feeling that you were moving toward something new and wonderful.

And for the first time in her life, Aggie was completely happy.

"Oh, I have it," she said, startling Dodger into sitting up again. "Eight magpies for chasing!"

"I suppose that will do until someone thinks of something better," he said, dodging her blow before it landed.

Threading his fingers through hers, he brought her hand to his lips. Looking directly into her eyes, he smiled at her with such fierce affection that she felt unmoored.

"Aggie," he said.

She swallowed, fighting the urge to make a joke of this moment. "Yes?"

"When do you think Bill will notice that I pinched his sandwich?"

She burst out laughing while Dodger grinned at her, both half-drunk on the promise of spring and reckless with magpie joy.

★ ★ ★ ★ ★

ACKNOWLEDGMENTS

SOMETIMES, IN THE TIME IT TAKES TO GET A book from brain to printers, a lot happens behind the scenes as people take on new challenges. This was one of those books, and I am very grateful to everyone who contributed their eyes to this project: My agent, Jennifer Laughran; her assistant, Maggie; and my Harlequin TEEN/Inkyard Press Team—Michael Strother, Lauren Smulski, Gabrielle Vicedomini, Libby Sternberg, Chris Wolfgang and Natashya Wilson.

I'm also grateful to my friends. Anne Elizabeth cheered me on and sent me care packages. Carol Goodman read and re-read and encouraged me and was essentially a writing Fitbit.

And then, there is Holly Harrison. Holly, who has been my friend since she was my resident advisor at Wesleyan, was my story guide. During moments when I thought I had lost my way, she found the path forward—pointing out opportunities, warning me when I nearly stepped into a crevasse and asking the questions that helped me find better story solutions. She also took me in and fed me while I worked on the book, and then took me swimming in Walden Pond as a reward. Thank you, my R.A. for life.